THE DISA

DONOR

A Suspense Novel of Fundraising Best Practices

Dear Amre!

I hope you enjoy this look into nonprofit fundraising.

Best

Susan

Susan Madon, CFRE

Category (Adult)

Genre (Non-Profit, Fundraising, Fiction)

Table of Contents

Author's Note

Why a suspense novel about fundraising? I've loved the mystery genre since the 5th grade when I first discovered *Encyclopedia Brown* and *Nancy Drew*. I have spent my career working for nonprofit organizations, and enjoy teaching others from my experience. In this novel, you will find what I hope will be useful nuggets of information and tips for the fundraising professional, board members, and other organizational champions. I hope you will also have fun along the way, playing detective and solving this light mystery!

Susan Madon, CFRE

Cast of Characters

As you know, it takes a community to run a nonprofit. While this list is not comprehensive, here are some of the people you will meet.

Museum Staff

Lupe	Reinowski	Director of Development and Amateur Detective
Stephanie	James-Howard	Executive Director
Ariel	Pensky	Events Manager
Sissy	Truman-Ngao	Head Curator
Felicity	Blacksmith	Gift Shop Manager
Andrew	Tyson	Director of Educational Outreach
Tessa	Hunt	Development Assistant
Moe	Schultz	One of the Museum's founders and Security chief
Krisha	Rao	Database Manager
Paul	Hawley	Prospect Researcher and Grants Writer
Marcus	Ferguson	Marketing Associate
Charlotte	van Clausen	Stephanie's Assistant and Mary Montgomery's daughter
Tom	Unger	Facilities and Operations Director.

Pierre	Renaud	Chief Financial Officer
Ian	Macdonald	Intern and Grandson of a Major Donor
Audry	Dickerson	Head of Programming
Andreas	Konsetavides	Security Guard and Art Student

Key Board Members
Mary

Montgomery	van Clausen	Board Chair
Firoze	Shah	Head of the Finance Committee
Allan	Fisker	One of the museum founders and now Emeritus Chair
Mimi	Johns	Gala Committee Chair
Camilo	Aggio	Famous Chef

Donors and Prospects

Ingrid	San Sebastian	Socialite and Friend of Mary Montgomery
Pietro	San Sebastian	Ingrid's husband and celebrity artist
Marla	Howes	One of the Museum's longest donors and Chair of the Legacy Society

Stacy	Leibman	Entrepreneur
Ralph	Stacy	Her husband and museum volunteer
Kaba	Tadashi	Children's cartoon/Actor and Celebrity

Others

Helene	Descard	Visiting Curator
Hans	Lubdell	Visiting Curator
Abby	Winters	Reporter, Global Art Review
Judit	VonKolbe	Notorious Hanger-on
Jane	Mehra	Consultant
Theresa	Hamilton	Development Legend and Lupe's Mentor
Ben	Terrance	Photographer

Lupe's Friends and Family

Lucia	Reinowski	Lupe's mother and Realtor
Pavel	Reinowski	Lupe's father and Contractor
Henry	Tsai	Actor/Director and head of a small theatre company and Lupe's roommate
Alice	Mayhew	Development Director for a Healthcare Advocacy organization and Lupe's roommate

Law Enforcement

Detective	Allen	NYPD Detective
Lt. Josh	Reyes	Arts Crimes Unit of the FBI

And of course, Borgia, Ingrid's prized Toy Poodle.

Chapter 1
In Fundraising as in Life, Expect the Unexpected!

Thursday, 5 pm

Lupe Reinowski looked over the Museum of Vegetable Culture's Fisker Gallery as her team and the catering crew scurried about setting up for that evening's reception. Tonight, would mark the most ambitious exhibition the small East Village museum had mounted. As director of development, she was justifiably proud of the critical role she played in ensuring the exhibition's success. Not only had she secured the exhibition's underwriting, but she had also found funding for a security upgrade for the valuable impressionist paintings on loan for the show.

Lupe was happy to call herself a *fundraiser*. Her work in acquiring the necessary income contributions and resources for the museum was multifaceted and varied. She enjoyed every aspect, from working with individual donors to overseeing events, seeking grants, and spending time with the members and patrons. She managed a team of six other professionals and, for the time being, also covered the Museum's marketing while the search took place for a new marketing director. Occasionally she felt her head would explode while shifting gears rapidly from one aspect of her job to another, but she loved the variety.

Ariel Pensky, Lupe's membership and special events manager, stepped over to her, iPad in hand.

"All well?" Lupe asked the older woman. At thirty-two, Lupe was a bit young to head the department, but she had worked in development for over ten years. "Mature beyond your years," her mother had always said. Lupe cultivated a sophisticated appearance by wearing simple cut business dresses augmented with vivid silk scarves. This evening, she dressed in a short-sleeved navy dress complemented with a Fuchsia scarf she found on her favorite resale site, The Real Real. Dressing well on a nonprofit salary did present some challenges, but Lupe was always resourceful. She let her shoulder-length caramel highlighted brown wavy hair hang loose and added a pair of artistic gold earrings for a festive touch. She would later put on her roommate's Louboutin pumps to finish the ensemble.

"We're set. Henry and the other bartenders are bringing up the liquor and wine from the basement, and Esmeralda's team has the canapes all ready. They look delicious."

"Good. Have you seen Ben Terrance yet?" Lupe asked. Ben was the photographer hired for the occasion.

"He texted me that he's on the way. He'll take some setup photos, and then I've asked him to get lots of pictures of the sponsors. Everyone is so excited. The advance press has been great."

"I really like the glass vases with the colorful bell peppers." The caterers had provided long rectangular glass vases, which now contained red, yellow, and green bell peppers alternating with pillar candles to be lit when the reception began later. "Thanks for your hard work. I know this is a lot with the gala just around the corner."

"Not a problem. When I was running the restaurant, we had back-to-back events all the time." Ariel explained.

Lupe spotted Morris 'Moe' Schwartz, the chief of security, and went to speak to him.

"Hi, Moe. Any hiccups?"

Moe looked a bit concerned. "We have the extra guards posted, and the new cameras are working fine, but I'm worried the Wi-Fi keeps cutting out in the gallery. The pressure sensors are run by Wi-Fi, and the room is a dead zone."

"I thought you got a router extender to take care of that?"

"We did, but it's not consistent. I really needed more time to rewire the whole gallery for an ethernet connection, but Stephanie insisted we move forward. The fog machine is on ethernet at the other end of the room and is connected to the panic button at the front desk, so at least we have that."

Museum security was a sophisticated blend of technology and physical deterrents such as visible and capable guards and special artwork mountings. Thanks to the special grant Lupe had secured, the Museum had recently upgraded all of the systems. However, since the building was over one hundred years old, retrofitting it was a constant challenge.

An hour later, after the guests had enjoyed cocktails and conversation, Stephanie James-Howard, the Museum's executive director stepped to the podium.

"Thank you all for joining us as we preview the Museum of Vegetable Culture's newest exhibition, *de Legumes: Vegetables in Impressionist Paintings.* We are very grateful to the Wallraf-Richartz Museum and the Musee D'Orsay, who lent us the cornerstone pieces to this marvelous exhibition. Allow me to publicly acknowledge their curators, Helene Descard and Hans Lubdell, who were instrumental in making *Legumes* possible," crooned the glossy and petite Stephanie James-Howard, through a cloud of Bulgari scent. Shielded behind the rather Junoesque frames of two Park Avenue philanthropists, Lupe shifted out of one of the borrowed Louboutin pumps. Her roommate Alice had warned her that the prized shoes ran narrow, and as Lupe's size 9 feet were half a size larger than Alice's, they were bound to be uncomfortable. Seasoned fundraisers Lupe and Alice both knew the cardinal rule of running a successful event. Besides reaching one's financial goals, a top caterer, and a full bar -- was comfortable footwear.

Vanity overruled tonight, however, and Lupe was paying the price. Her discomfort grew as Stephanie droned on as was her custom. Lupe had provided the necessary talking points and reminded the director to keep her comments brief, but Stephanie loved an audience and milked every opportunity in the limelight.

Sissy Truman-Ngao, the Museum's head curator, hissed into Lupe's ear, "Watch. She'll thank Ted in Maintenance before she acknowledges my work." It was a sore point for Sissy that the executive director preferred to pretend the Museum's award-winning exhibitions sprang solely from Stephanie's genius, negating the brilliance of the acclaimed senior curator.

"As some of you may know, and it bears repeating, Edward Manet's *Bunch of Asparagus* and its companion piece *Sprig of Asparagus,*" continued Stephanie, "were painted by Manet for the noted art collector, Charles Ephrussi. Ephrussi was so impressed by the work that he gave the artist 1,000 francs, about $5,000 in today's dollars. In appreciation, Manet painted a smaller work consisting of just one stalk of this elegant vegetable. He sent a note to Ephussi which read, 'There was one sprig missing in your bundle.' She paused for the polite laughter. "Inspired by all the paintings in the exhibition, we have created lovely table settings, which I know you will appreciate. Some of my favorites include..."

"Oh mercy, Stephanie," thought Lupe, "please thank the underwriters!" But Stephanie was on a tangent talking about Bernaudaud eggplant platters.

Lupe felt around with her left foot and carefully retrieved the hot pink Louboutin. Easing out her miserable right foot, she scanned the room for the various donors she hoped to catch up with during the event. Standing erect and alert was Mary Montgomery van Clausen, the chair of the board of trustees. Mary, who was serving her third six-year term on the board, had outlasted five executive directors. Slow to change, but once committed, she was a force to be reckoned with. Mary was definitely an *iron fist in a velvet glove* kind of leader, much to the chagrin of her adversaries.

Mary was standing next to her old friend, Ingrid San Sebastian. Ingrid was battling aging with a fierce determination, even going so far as to marry the young artist Pietro San Sebastian, 35 years her junior. It looked to Lupe like the only thing she ate was the asparagus from the table setting accompanying the Manet pieces. Perhaps there was a little of the green-eyed monster in Lupe who had a voluptuous figure that could easily turn to plumpness thanks to both the Polish and Mexican sides of her family. Ingrid was one of the Museum's top donors, and Lupe knew she would be in good hands with Mary.

Chair of the Finance and Endowment Committee and respected investment banker Firoze Shah huddled in a corner with the Museum's CFO, Pierre Renard. Lupe knew time with Firoze was always at a premium, and Pierre would make the most of having his ear. Seated at a cocktail table near Firoze and Pierre were two of the Museum's oldest donors and supporters, Allan Fisker and Marla Howes. Allan was actually one of the Museum founders and now emeritus chair. Marla, twice widowed, chaired the docent committee and the Legacy society. They were among Lupe's favorite people.

She saw two of her top prospects standing on the other side of the room—Stacy Leibman and her husband, Ralph. Stacy had recently had a successful Initial Public Offering on her tea company and was rumored to want to establish herself as one of the city's top philanthropists. Lupe considered it a personal coup that she wooed the Leibmans to the evening's vernissage and the prior week's salon. Lupe had been courting the Leibmans for several years through Ralph, a youthful retiree who volunteered at the roof garden. A quiet, bookish man, Ralph was the complete opposite of Stacy. She always had many irons in the fire and a talent for cultivating ambitious projects as successful as Ralph's knack for cultivating zucchini and tomatoes.

And, of course, Abby Winters was present. The writer from *Global Art Review* never missed an opening. She took particular pleasure in gloating over the Museum's theme and some of the lesser exhibitions. While Sissy strove for artistic excellence, she sometimes had to bow to the whims of Stephanie and her favorite donors. She wouldn't soon forget having to curate a particularly vile collection of cabbage bowls, created by the son of an industrialist Stephanie was soliciting for a leadership gift. While the gift materialized, it was certainly not at the expected level, and Sissy took the brunt of Abby's print insults and the damage to her reputation.

Ten minutes after she should have wrapped up her remarks, Stephanie at last reached for the velvet cord to pull aside the curtain to reveal the Manet works. "And now, it gives me great pleasure to officially open *de Legumes*!" With a swift tug, the black curtain gave away to reveal an elegant table set with Limoges china and antique sterling on a provincial tablecloth. But the wall behind it was empty.

Pandemonium raged as the guests whipped out their cellphones to take pictures of the empty wall. The guards all ran to Moe, and Lupe's team started rushing to her. Stephanie attempted to regain control of the scene.

"Ladies and Gentlemen. We are the victim of an egregious theft, and I am sorry, but I must ask everyone to remain while we call the police. Lupe! Morris!" She called out to the development director and the head of security.

Lupe immediately stepped up to the microphone. "Honored guests, the bar is open in the lobby. Kindly follow me." But as she did so, the room filled with dense fog, and an alarm blared.

A pre-recorded voice repeated above the fray. "The police are on their way! Stop where you are!"

The admonition had the opposite effect, and chaos reigned. People pushed and shoved in the smoke-filled room, choking and shouting to get out. The chic and refined clientele transformed in a moment to a mad group of soccer hooligans.

Pushing her way out of the room, Lupe completely forgot about her aching feet and made her way out to the lobby, where the guards were struggling to keep people from leaving.

Her other roommate Henry Tsai was standing at the bar, horrified at the scene. Henry was an actor/director and head of a small theatre company for differently-abled performers. As a side hustle, he often filled in as bartender for Lupe and Alice's functions.

"Henry, the Manets' are gone, and I need you and the other bartenders to take care of everyone while we're waiting for the police.

"Cra...! On it!" Henry energetically responded.

Lupe next raced to Esmerelda of *Green Events*, the best vegetarian caterer in town. Quickly she explained the situation and begged the caterer to keep the canapes flowing well past the agreed-upon time.

At that moment, her team landed on her – Ariel, Krisha, Paul, Marcus, Tessa, and her current intern Ian. Anticipating their questions, she briefly gave marching orders. "Ariel and Paul circulate, make sure the wait staff is ok but keep an eye and ear out for the donors and prospects. Marcus and Ian, get more chairs out from storage. See if anyone from maintenance is around to help. Tessa and Krisha, you have the hardest job. Handle the door and don't let anyone leave. Security will help you.

Grabbing a quick sip of water for her mouth had gone quite dry, Lupe found Felicity Blacksmith, the gift shop manager, and Andrew Tyson, the Director of Educational Outreach, helping pass out drinks by the bar.

Mouthing a silent thank you, Andrew winked, "And I thought this would be a dull job!"

Andrew had retired early from teaching middle-school science and relished the general quiet of museum life. Felicity was a dear, always willing to pitch in no matter what happened. Unflappable, the only thing that ever upset her was when Lupe "borrowed" too many tchotchkes from the gift shop for donor gifts without properly allocating them.

Leaning over the bar to Henry, Lupe whispered in his ear, "Be sure they don't get plastered! The police will want to interview everyone."

"Fret not. We're pouring light except for Judit VonKolbe, who noticed." Judit was a notorious hanger-on who somehow managed to cage invitations to all manner of charity functions without actually supporting the institutions.

Lupe looked over to where Moe, Stephanie, and Mary Montgomery van Clausen, were huddled. Stephanie caught her eye and waved her over.

"Lupe, the police and FBI are on their way, but I need you to keep Abby Winter away until we get a handle on this. Did you see anything while they were setting up?"

Lupe thought back to earlier in the afternoon when her team and the caterers were preparing. "Nothing out of the ordinary. The curtain was arranged, and the gallery was closed to the public. It was just the usual event organizing. Tables, chairs, stations, the bar. The gallery was closed to the public, and the only people I remember seeing were our staff and the catering team, but I was in and out a lot."

As usual, there was a last-minute flurry of calls and emails from people who had forgotten to RSVP. Tessa Hunt, her development assistant, was adept at dealing with that aspect of events. And over the years, Lupe had learned that about the same number of people who failed to turn up came at the last minute, so she didn't fret much about catering. She was more concerned that there were enough board and leadership around to spend time with the guests.

Seeing Abby making her way boldly to Stephanie, Lupe raced over to intercept her. "Abby! How about a drink?"

"Are you kidding, Lupe? Don't try to keep me away from this story." She attempted to elbow her way past, but Lupe tackled her with a society squeeze. The move, taught to her by her fundraising mentor Theresa Hamilton was a half hug/half revolution that Theresa had often used to keep demanding guests away from their quarry, usually an event's celebrity speaker. Lupe adroitly employed the move and partially dragged Abby out of the gallery.

"Afraid the gallery is closed until the police have time to investigate. Surely you want to have the full facts before you post your story? How about chatting with Sissy? She can give you more background." Lupe had walked the reporter right up to Sissy gracefully by-passing the two visiting curators. Explaining and signaling an apology with her eyes, she left Abby and returned to the guests who were visibly and audibly upset.

At that moment, two uniformed police officers entered accompanied by two other people whom Lupe assumed were senior officers. The first was a tall, good-looking man in his mid-thirties who had a friendly open face and tightly curled black hair. At his side stood

11

a statuesque blond of about the same age. She was attractive, but her dark eyes were shrewd. *A no-nonsense type*, thought Lupe.

She stepped forward to introduce herself. "I'm Lupe Reinowski, the Director of Development. Let me show you to the gallery."

"I'm Agent Reyes of the FBI Art Crimes Division and this is Detective Allen with NYPD's Major Crimes Unit. Lupe nodded and hustled them through the crowded lobby to the gallery beyond.

The board members and visiting curators were talking loudly to Stephanie, who was using her quiet voice. This was the gentle, soothing, well-modulated voice she was trained to use in difficult social situations. It was part of her curriculum at an exclusive upper-east side day school, along with deportment and calligraphy. After introducing the FBI agents to her boss, Lupe couldn't help but linger in hopes of learning more. She was worried her job was on the line because the *de Legume* exhibition was her brainchild. She could already hear the voices of angry donors and sponsors.

Agent Reyes looked down at the Museum's Executive Director. "Please explain exactly what happened."

"Isn't it obvious?" Stephanie pointed to the empty wall. ''Someone has burgled our Manets!" Her voice rose to a shrill pitch more in tune with her normal voice. From experience, Lupe could tell Stephanie was about to lose her temper.

"Calm down. We need to establish the facts, "said Detective Allen in a steely voice. Lupe cringed. She knew what Stephanie's response would be.

"Calm down! Don't you tell me to calm down! This is a disaster! Those paintings are priceless. My...I mean, our museum's reputation is on the line. You find whoever is responsible and put them behind bars. Get those paintings back, now!" She looked as if she was about to grind her size five stilettos through the terrazzo tiles. Lupe felt an unintentional giggle rising. When Stephanie lost her cool, Lupe had a recurring vision of Rumpelstiltskin driving his foot into the ground when the queen discovered his name.

"Perhaps I should start with your head of security," said Reyes in a placatory voice. His work in the Art Crimes division obviously put him in touch with many similarly entitled people.

Moe stepped forward. "Moe Schultz," he said crisply, offering his hand. Moe was also one of the Museum's founders and had been its security chief for the past 20 years. In his late 60's and sporting a grey ponytail, he was still powerfully built and looked like he could knock out men half his age. He attributed his good health to a strict vegetarian diet, regular exercise, and his wife Josephine's hash brownies.

"We'll need to fingerprint your staff for elimination and confirm the names and addresses of all the guests before they will be allowed to leave," stated Reyes. A fingerprint team had arrived and was working at the empty gallery wall. "Walk us through the day. When was the last time you remember seeing the paintings?"

"We covered the paintings with the curtain at about 4:00, and they were fine then. The only people here at the time were our staff and the caterers and bartenders setting up for the event, which started at 6:00."

"I see you have cameras in the gallery. What other deterrents are in place?" Allen asked.

"We have cameras at all access points, a smoke machine, and extra guards 24/7."

"What about pressure sensors on the paintings?"

Moe looked embarrassed. "I'm afraid they may not have been working. They are controlled by Wi-Fi, and it had been giving us trouble."

Reyes nodded. This wasn't the first time he had heard this story. Many thefts occurred because of a snafu in the precautions. "Ok, Mr. Schultz. Are there just the exits through the main doors and the fire exit?

"Yes. The fire exit leads to 10th Street and 1st Avenue."

"We'll have that area fingerprinted as well," said Allen as she strode over to the technical team.

"I assume the gallery was closed to the public during the installation. Did you notice anyone trying to sneak in to get an early look?"

"I don't think so, but you can ask the other guards and the volunteers at the front desk. Also, Sissy Truman-Ngao, the senior curator, and her team would have noticed if anyone came in."

"Ok. For now, get your guards to help us with gathering the names of the guests. Is there a guest list we can use to check off names? Reyes asked.

"Yes, Lupe Reinowski will have it." Lupe was trying to soothe Mimi Johns, the gala committee chair, and was standing by one of the cocktail tables at the far end of the large gallery.

Moe and Reyes walked over to Lupe. Mimi, who had been sitting, rose majestically and asked in her honey-dripping Southern accent, "Why officer. Just how much longer will we have to wait? It's obvious that the thief isn't amongst us. I suggest you start looking for fences and such and leave us to minimize the fallout of this most unfortunate incident." Mimi craved the mantle of leadership and used the same syrupy tenacity to cajole unwitting businesspeople into buying Platinum tables at the annual gala or insisting on discounts from vendors. She was tough but effective, and Lupe was glad to trust many of the gala's details to her.

"We'll be as quick as possible. An officer will be around to take your names and addresses," said Reyes informing all the assembled board members and their spouses.

Drawing Lupe aside, he asked for the guest list, and Lupe handed over her iPad. "The list is all here, and we can get you the addresses of all the guests. There were a few walk-ins, but Tessa Hunt will have those names at the front desk." Lupe led the two out of the gallery and into the crowded lobby. Fortunately, the attendees seemed to be calming down, the excellent food, drinks, and drama going a long way in soothing tensions. Lupe reminded herself to tip even more generously that evening.

***

It was after midnight when Lupe and Henry reached the apartment they shared with Alice Mayhew, development director for the Healthcare Advocacy organization, Family Matters. Alice and Lupe had been roommates in college and had followed similar career paths, although Lupe's passion was arts and culture and Alice's health and science. After years of living in a ramshackle "junior-two" apartment, the two landed a charming three-bedroom in Brooklyn's Cobble Hill. To make the economics work, they advertised in a nonprofit list-serve and met Henry. A few years younger, Henry was the despair of his Taiwanese immigrant parents. While he earned a BS in Economics from Columbia University, he refused their expected path. He became an actor taking classes at the Actors' Studio and giving private tutoring to make ends meet. Alice and Lupe gave him a break on the rent since the third bedroom in the 4th-floor walk-up was tiny.

Alice came out of her bedroom when they arrived, eager to hear the news. "It's all over the internet and news! This is awful. Do you know anything about who's behind this? Alice was a peppery redhead with enormous energy. Despite the late hour, she was ready to hear all the details.

Lupe and Henry quickly filled her in with what little they knew.

"I'm so worried I'll lose my job over this. I'm the one who came up with the idea." Exhibition planning was definitely not part of a development director's job, but Lupe had a passion for Impressionist art, and having seen an image of the *Bunch of Asparagus* persuaded Sisi to investigate to see if there was enough art from the period to create the exhibition. Along with Stephanie and the rest of the leadership team, they had worked a whole year to secure the funding and manage the logistics of creating the major exhibition. Instead of elevating the Museum of Vegetable Culture's prestige, *de Legumes* would glaringly point out the small institution's limitations.

"No one is going to blame you. It was a great idea, and it's an exceptional exhibition."

"Stephanie will blame me. Heads will roll. I've worked so hard to get this job. She always looks for a fall guy when things go wrong. And this is a disaster." Lupe felt the fatigue and stress catching up and wanted to cry into her pillow.

17

Her old friend hugged her tightly.

"Lupe, the Feds are very talented and will be on the thieves quickly. You can minimize the damage. People forget quickly. But I think it's an inside job," said Alice. "What else could it be?"

"That's what I think too," breathed Henry. "Has to be. Who do you think did the deed?"

Lupe, who had gratefully shed the Louboutin's back in her office for a sensible pair of Keds, put her feet up on the converted steamer trunk coffee table in the living room.

"The mind boggles. Too many suspects. It could be outsiders, any of the staff, one of the waiters, even a member of the board. Some of them showed up early to catch up with Stephanie. But where did they stash the paintings? The police didn't find them in the building."

"We should start a list and assign a grade like we do for prospect rating," said Alice. Lupe could feel herself losing energy as the evening's adrenal surge started to diminish. She felt her eyes closing. Henry, also feeling tired, looked up at Alice with puppy eyes and put on a childlike voice.

"Please, mummy, read me a story. Hen-Hen is so sweepy."

Alice laughed. "OK, we'll tackle it in the morning. Get some rest."

Throwing herself on her bed and placing a pillow under her still sore feet, Lupe's mind continued to race. She thought of the next day and the crisis communications – donors and staff to calm, and her regular assignments. She dreamt uneasily of Stephanie shouting at her and blaming her for the whole fiasco. In her dream, a giant stalk of asparagus came to life and began thumping her on the head.

Chapter 2
A Good Fundraiser Marshalls All Available Resources

Friday, 6 am

The trio gathered around the oval mid-century modern dining table, which Lupe and Alice had discovered when the old convent at St. Polycarp's converted to a pre-k. Henry had contributed six mixed-matched chairs of the same period, which he had re-covered in a cotton batik fabric in varying hues of blue and green. Over a large pot of coffee, yogurt, and muesli, the three considered the suspects.

Lupe explained, "So, the curatorial staff were there early checking the exhibit labels and other graphics. Security did one final sweep and there were extra guards on duty. Three of my development team were working with the caterers and bartenders on the reception set up. And maintenance was also around lending a hand."

"And what about the early birds? Some donors always come early to events," asked Alice.

Yes, Mimi St. Johns and Allan Fisker were there, and Firoze Shah came in to speak to Pierre. Pietro San Sebastian was waiting in the gallery for Ingrid to finish her meeting with Mary Montgomery and Stephanie. And I had given a quick tour to Stacy and Ralph Leibman and they were also in the gallery after. Ben Terrance, the photographer, was also running around."

"Phew," said Henry. "This is a big list. There were four waiters, two other bartenders, two prep-cooks, and Esmeralda managing the service."

"I'm sure the police will be investigating them," stated Alice. "When did Ben arrive? I wonder if he caught anything on camera."

"I'll ask. But I overheard Moe admitting to the FBI that pressure sensors weren't working."

"Oh Jeez," said Henry. "He'll get scorched for that."

"It's not his fault, but I'm sure he'll get blamed. Stephanie pressured him to do the security upgrade quickly. He wanted to rewire the Fisker Gallery," said Lupe. "If the budget wasn't so tight, we could have pushed back the opening to when we were originally planning."

"Don't blame yourself," said Alice. 'There are always more projects and needs than money."

"I'll talk to the bartenders and see if they saw anyone suspicious," suggested Henry.

"And I'll go through the day with my team, but honestly, you'd think we'd have noticed someone walking off with two paintings tucked under their arms?"

"How big are they?" Asked Alice.

"Small. No more than the size of a laptop, but the frame adds a bit."

"Could someone stuff them into a satchel or briefcase?" Henry asked.

"Possibly. And whoever took the pictures had to get them out of the Museum or really hide them well because the police didn't find them in the search," Lupe noted.

"This evening, we should prioritize this list somehow. Why would someone steal the paintings? It's not as if they could sell them on the open market?" Alice observed.

Lupe nodded thanks and rushed off to get ready for work and catch the F train for the 40-minute commute to the East Village.

***

Ordinarily, she enjoyed her daily journey because it gave her time to reflect on the day ahead and all the moving parts of her job. Today, however, she felt all her plans would be upended with the police and FBI presence and the excitement. She was proud of her team, who were very hard working and generally efficient. But as her mentor Theresa Hamilton had often repeated, people's best qualities are also their greatest weakness, and her team was gregarious to a fault. They would no doubt be running around the building gossiping.

She scrolled through hundreds of emails and texts regarding the theft before seeing Stephanie scheduled an all-staff meeting, obviously to address the crisis. Also, Leslie Palmieri from the Meyers Foundation had written that $75,000 in program funding had become available because one of their recipients could not carry out their project in the agreed-upon time. If Lupe could get a proposal in by the end of the day, she would present it to the board at their Monday morning meeting. Thrilled and admittedly surprised that the Meyers Foundation still trusted MVC after such a significant theft, Lupe forwarded the message to Audry Dickerson, the head of programming, and Paul Hawley, her prospect researcher and grant writer. Somehow, she would carve out the time to get something presentable in. She suggested the Community Green Market, a pop-up fresh fruit and vegetable food pantry serving the neighborhood, or underwriting part of the school visits, including the interactive stage production *Vegetable Soup*.

Just then, she saw Stephanie had copied her on an email thread. Stephanie had reached out to Jane Mehra, their advancement and communications consultant, for help with messaging the situation. Lupe felt some relief as Jane was a polished and seasoned professional who always kept her cool regardless of the crisis. She would be at the all-staff meeting and then work with Lupe and Marcus Ferguson, the communications associate, in preparing a strategy.

***

Stepping into the Development department, an airy space on the third floor, Lupe thought back to the old offices in the basement next to the maintenance team and the boiler room. Freezing in the winter, broiling in the summer, and lightless, it took years of politicking, cajoling, and hard fundraising to get the attic converted to an open loft space for Development, Marketing, and Programming to share. Only

Paul complained about the move because he liked the quiet of the basement space. Lupe was only too glad to let him go back to *the Dungeons* whenever he needed peace.

Krisha and Ariel leapt from their desks as soon as they saw her, with Marcus and Tessa quickly following. Ian was late as usual. Perpetually hungry, he had no doubt stopped at the corner coffee stand for a hard roll or bagel to supplement his first breakfast of the day.

"Any news?" asked Ariel, the special events and membership manager.

"Nothing so far. I'm sure the police asked if you saw anything yesterday afternoon while you were all setting up for the event?" asked Lupe.

"Nothing I can remember, and we've all talked about it," Tessa said.

"It was quiet because the school groups had finished by 2 pm. We came into the lobby and gallery around 4 o'clock, and maintenance had already put the buffet tables out for the bar and goodie bags. Tessa and I set up registration at the front desk, and the Green Events people arrived soon after," said Ariel.

"I came down with the final list at 5 pm," said Krisha Rao, who handled the database and online giving and was to Lupe's mind one of the team's most important members. Lupe remembered an early development job for a small arts association, where all the donor information was kept in an Excel spreadsheet. One of the interns

24

inadvertently sorted the file, incorrectly mixing up names and addresses. The problem had not been discovered for a week when Lupe started to send out the annual fund campaign. *Ugh*, she remembered. *The amount of time and effort wasted.*

Ian Macdonald ambled in at last polishing off a bacon, egg, and cheese roll oblivious as usual to Vegetable Culture's plant-forward mission. Not only tardy, but Ian was also a sight to behold. The Museum had a relaxed dress code, but Lupe tried valiantly to keep the development team looking reasonably groomed and presentable in case donors, prospects, or the press should appear. She had given up on Ian, who, besides being the grandson of one of their top donors, was also oblivious to her entreaties. His response was always a smile and an incredulous laugh. "Oh, Lupe, you must let creatives be creative," he would say with a shake of his head, although his dress sense seemed to be the only sign of the *brilliant* creativity he claimed to possess.

This week his announced dress theme was *retro-grunge*. Today he was sporting a grey trench coat, black pencil cut-off jean shorts that skimmed his lean hips, scuffed ankle boots painted a variety of acid rock colors, and a tie-dyed t-shirt that looked like it needed a good wash. Lupe knew appearances were deceiving, and the outfit probably cost more than she made in a month. She glanced over to Ariel, who supervised Ian and gave her a *please try to do something about him* look.

Realizing the time, the group made their way to the Haversbrook Auditorium, where the all-staff meeting was to be held. People streamed in, talking loudly about the evening's drama, not quieting until Stephanie made her way up to the microphone. Lupe saw that Agent Reyes and Detective Allen were also present.

Stephanie adjusted the microphone and briefly recapped the evening's events. "I can tell you we are all horrified, horrified," she repeated, "by the loss of these important works of art. I want you all to think back to yesterday afternoon when the pieces were last seen. That was about 4 pm. Think, think! Did you notice anything or anyone out of place?"

Lupe looked around the auditorium and saw that everyone was shaking their heads and looking blankly.

Stephanie continued, "And if I find out you are shielding anyone, you will be prosecuted just as though you had taken the works yourselves!" Stephanie turned to Agent Reyes, who stepped forward. Lupe at just that moment noticed his appearance; apparently, she reflected, she had been too distracted to notice much about him the previous night. The officer was tall and well-proportioned, neither too slim nor muscle-bound, which appealed to Lupe. She had dated both a runner and a former boxer. Somehow with each, she felt out of shape and unable to compete since her favorite sports were leisurely walks and gentle yoga. Reyes had brown hair and skin, which showed his Latino heritage, but his eyes were green. His lips were full, and his manner relaxed.

Reyes spoke, "We don't want to alarm anyone, but your assistance will be beneficial. Any leads may help us catch the perpetrator and recover the lost paintings. Whatever you may have seen or heard out of the ordinary may help, so please give it your deep consideration. If you prefer to leave an anonymous tip, you can call our hotline at 212-555-1630."

Stephanie returned to the microphone. "And let me remind you that this matter is not to be discussed or posted outside of these walls. We need to control the fallout, and Jane Mehra of Mehra and Jaffrey will be working with us on a communication plan, including frequently asked questions and talking points. You are *not* to speak to the media or post on your social media accounts." Lupe sighed inwardly, knowing the glad tidings were already widely shared on social media.

With the meeting ended, Lupe and Marcus walked to Stephanie's office, where Jane was seated. "Good to see you again, Lupe, although I wish it were over ice-cold martinis." Lupe had worked with Jane on a strategic development plan earlier in the year and admired the older women's wisdom and sense of humor.

Jane Mehra was a tall, blond with an hourglass figure of which she joked some of the sand had fallen to the bottom. She sported a chin-length curly bob through which she often ran her fingers, especially when considering a problem. At the moment, her hairdo was completely disarrayed, sticking out at all sides of her face. As if realizing this, she took off her eyeglasses and used them as a makeshift headband.

"Right. I know it's tempting to get out in front of the story, but in my experience, it is important to take time from the beginning to really consider the message. We have to be honest and transparent about the pressure sensors but not linger over the situation. It would be a good idea to talk about the fast response of the police and the fact that the FBI Art Crimes division is already working on the matter," said Jane.

"But it will make us look bad if they find out about the Wi-Fi not working," whined Stephanie.

"It will make you look far worse if it comes out later," replied the consultant.

"Well, shouldn't we place the blame on someone?" Stephanie jammed her pen into her journal.

Lupe kept her eyes down, knowing Stephanie wanted to make a scapegoat of her or Moe, the security chief. As one of the Museum's founders, Moe had more than a little proprietary interest in the Museum's running, a fact which irked Stephanie. It upset her hard-won balance of power that the other founders often sided with Moe against her and would take their frustrations to Mary Montgomery van Clausen or other board members.

Marcus, the most junior of the four, was giving an impression of a potted Ficus.

Jane took a deep breath. "At this point, we want to limit damage to the Museum and keep the focus on the hoped-for positive outcome. A simple statement like 'We will convene a committee of the board, staff and independent experts to determine what improvements to Museum security are needed' should suffice."

Stephanie looked somewhat appeased, and Jane continued. "I will work with Lupe and Marcus on the press release to send to counsel and the board under embargo. Hopefully, we can get the full statement out by 2 pm and also announce a joint press conference with the FBI and NYPD to take place at 5 pm."

Lupe raced back to her office with Marcus and Jane. Jane issued directives as they walked, "I'll draft the release, and you can work on the FAQ, Lupe? Marcus, please get the press distribution list for me to review."

Lupe's fingers flew as she wrote out a brief list of frequently asked questions for the press, including the background of the paintings and the two museums which had lent them. She added detail of the *de Legumes* exhibition and a short history of the Museum, which had been founded in 1976 by a group of college friends who had been sharing a converted tenement on Avenue A and 6th Street. They all shared an interest in vegetarianism and discovered there was no other museum in the world that focused on the contributions of vegetables to society. The group convinced the local city councilor of the importance of their mission and were given use of a derelict factory, the site of the current Museum. At first, the offerings were modest and focused on urban gardening and apartment composting, with sales of earthworms and mulch providing much of the first year's revenue.

It wasn't until board member Allan Fisker developed a successful vegetable spiralizer and donated the patent to the Museum of Vegetable Culture with the proviso that half the residuals start an endowment that the Museum flourished. With the funding, the Museum was able to hire staff, renovate the building over time and develop educational and cultural programs and outreach efforts. The Museum now included a 300-seat auditorium, galleries, a cafe, the roof garden, a gift shop, and even a demonstration kitchen currently named for a national kitchenware brand.

Lupe emailed the list to Jane and then ran to find Paul and Audry to discuss the grant proposal due later that day. Lupe loved the efficiency of short, stand-up meetings, so she was pleased to see Audry in the break room. The program director was making a fresh pot of coffee, carefully preserving the grounds in the compost bin.

"I was thinking of a proposal for the Community Green Market or *Vegetable Soup*, but we could put in half the money for each?" asked Lupe.

"That would be fine given the time constraints, but I do want to bring a few celebrity chefs to the test kitchen, so it would be good to put our heads together on funding candidates for that. I know we charge a ticket price for those types of programs, but I would like to keep the prices low and offer a few nights of 'give what you can pricing," Audrey said. Audrey was in her late 60s and had been with the Museum for over 20 years. She loved the mission and wanted to engage as many people as possible yet understood the importance of managing revenue and expenses.

"I'll take a look at our past funders and see if there are a couple of candidates for underwriting that program," said Paul, whose lugubrious face masked a ridiculous sense of humor. Paul loved good-natured pranks, once changing the handle of the break room refrigerator door from the right to the left side and sending out weekly vegetable celebration day updates and bad jokes. Who knew that August 17 was National Eggplant Day? *Q. Why do people dance to the vegetable band? A. Because it has a good beet!*

"Paul, use the boilerplate from the Ferguson-Thomas Grant proposal and add in a paragraph each about the two programs. I'll put together the budgets and run them by you, Audry. I'll also use the cover letter from that same proposal and just make edits." Lupe said.

"Sure, I should have it ready within an hour," said Paul as Lupe poured herself a cup of coffee into an MVC cup with the Museum's mascot, 'Mr. Stripey', a ripe heirloom tomato. Inhaling the rich aroma, she felt herself reviving for the tasks to come.

"Would you like some fresh photos? My intern, Tray, took some great ones at the Green Market last Saturday," asked Audry.

"That would be great, thanks!"

Thanking them both, she and Paul rushed back to their end of the office. Tessa pounced. "The main line is ringing off the hook. What do we say?"

"We cannot comment on an ongoing investigation. Please be assured that the police have the matter in hand. Thank the individual for calling and hang up. If they give you a hard time, please take a message and tell them I will call back."

Just that moment, Krisha raced up. Someone had hacked the online giving site.

Chapter 3
Don't Hide the Bad News.

Lupe followed Krisha to her desk, questioning her on the way. "How bad is the damage?" She asked.

"Don't know for sure yet," replied Krisha. "I got a call from Givenow." Givenow was their donation, membership, and ticketing cloud-based platform. "Hackers got into their site and we're one of the organizations affected. I've blocked online sales-and-giving for the time being."

Lupe thought for a moment. Online giving represented 12% of their donations and almost 60% of their membership renewals. They had just finished a membership drive. "OK, run a list of online donors, members who signed up or renewed online, and people who bought tickets through the portal. We should probably go back a couple of years to be safe. Did Givenow give you more information?"

"They are still running tests, but they think they should be able to get more information to us within a couple of hours. They've given us the language we can use to inform the impacted donors and will also pay for one year of credit monitoring," said Krisha.

Lupe sat at the edge of Krisha's desk, which was always organized and tidy. "I'll let Stephanie and Pierre know what's happening. Keep me up to date on Givenow's response. Paul and Marcus are busy with writing projects, so grab Ariel to help draft the email regarding the hack.

Mentally wiping her brow and blessing her team, Stephanie went off searching for Pierre, the CFO. The compact Frenchman was at his desk and visibly brightened when Lupe barreled in with her usual high energy.

"Ca va Lupe! Quelle est notre derniere crise?" Pierre had lived in the United States for 20 years but often reverted to French, especially to tease Lupe. She had studied French in college and periodically took classes but lived in dread that Pierre might want to have a conversation with her in his native tongue.

"Somebody hacked Givenow's storage. We don't know how many of our records are impacted, but I think we should preemptively email our online givers going back two years to minimize the damage," Lupe pointed out.

"Pfft!" Pierre made a uniquely gallic sound. "On top of the theft, Stephanie will not be happy."

"You're telling me," sighed Lupe. "Shall we rip off the Band-aid?"

Pierre smiled with the charm that set the ladies of the Legacy Society's hearts aflutter, much to his chagrin. "Allons y!"

Stephanie's office perched on the side of the roof garden. It was a long glass-encased, high-ceilinged room that mirrored the greenhouse on the other side of the roof garden. Stephanie had decorated it with Empire-style furniture updated with Jim Thompson bright-colored silk and cotton throw pillows and covers. The walls were hung with vibrant-hued numbered prints of cabbages, cucumbers, red peppers, and gourds created specifically for the Museum of Vegetable Culture by David Hockney. Stephanie's current assistant, Charlotte van Clausen, Mary Montgomery's daughter, looked up from her desk. She looked close to tears, but Lupe knew that was her usual expression.

"Hi, Charlotte! Is Stephanie around?"

Charlotte let out a ragged sigh. "No, she's with Moe and the authorities down in the gallery. This is terrible. The board wants to hold an emergency meeting at 3:00, and Stephanie wants to meet with the senior team after, and we have this press conference at 5:00, and I'm just so tired."

Charlotte had recently graduated from Vassar with a degree in Art History and envisioned working in the Museum would give her solid experience before she furthered her studies. Lupe mused that she was probably finding the reality of working for a cultural institution to be much different from the rosy fantasy of long tea breaks, chatting with learned colleagues, and associating with creative types. Much more nose to the grindstone than pinky in the air, thought Lupe, thinking back to her early days in the industry.

"Courage," said Pierre, and he and Lupe made their way to the gallery. Charlotte went back to studying the papers on her desk as if translating hieroglyphics.

Moe was just leaving the gallery as they entered, walking with Tom Unger, the Facilities and Operations Director. The two men spoke quietly, but Lupe could tell they were both griping about the event. Tom didn't share Moe's affection for the mission and was a confirmed carnivore who swore the only vegetable he liked was a baked potato covered in cheese, sour cream, and Bacos. He was, however, a competent facilities manager and always found ways to cut running costs, which made him a beloved of Stephanie.

"How goes the war?" Pierre asked.

"Hmm. Not good. What fingerprints they couldn't identify were blurred. The police are searching the building more thoroughly," said Tom.

Moe's face looked upset, but his body language retained its languid poise. "I'm sure we'll get to the bottom of this. Have the police talked to you again?"

Pierre shook his head, replying, "I'm to meet Agent Reyes at 2:00. What about you, Lupe?"

"I've been a moving target all morning. I'm sure they'll catch up to me. Is Stephanie still in the gallery?"

"Yes," said Moe. "Trust me, today, she only wants good news."

Lupe smiled and sighed, "Oh well, it's been nice working with you guys."

Pierre and Lupe entered the gallery and heard Stephanie before they saw her.

"I want this wrapped up by Monday. This is a dreadful situation and can't be allowed to go unresolved. My board and donors are livid and consider it an outrage that more isn't being done to capture the culprit, " the Executive Director barked.

Agent Reyes nodded. "We are pursuing all credible lines of inquiry and reviewing the backgrounds of all the staff and guests. Please reassure your board and donors that we are working diligently to find the person or persons responsible." He turned to leave and saw Pierre and Lupe. Was it Lupe's imagination, or did his eyes light up a bit at seeing her? *Down, girl*, she remonstrated herself, "You have enough to deal with."

"Mr. Renard, I look forward to talking with you at 2:00. Ms. Reinowski, may I see you at 2:30?" asked the Special Agent.

"Yes, that will be fine," replied Lupe.

"Great. You'll find me in the library," said the officer, who then strode purposely out of the room.

Stephanie turned to Pierre and Lupe. "Had to light a fire under him. If I don't, somebody will put this case on the back burner like the Warhols stolen last year from the Hitchcock Gallery on Madison. Lupe, is Jane ready with the release and other materials?"

Lupe squared her shoulders. "Yes, she should be finishing up by now. But we need to talk to you about another matter. Givenow, our online donation platform has been hacked. We don't know how many of our donor records have been impacted, but I think we should get an email out right away to let people know that their data might be exposed. We've stopped accepting online gifts for the time being. Hopefully, we can get it sorted out soon.

"What?! Is this a conspiracy? Is everyone after *me*?!" Stephanie wailed. Lupe waited for the inevitable foot stamp. But surprisingly, it didn't come.

Stephanie sighed heavily. "Yes, you're right. Get to it. Keep me posted. I'm going to my office and have some herbal tea. Some days, I wonder why I do this job." She turned and walked off.

Pierre excused himself to meet Agent Reyes, and Lupe went back to her office to check on her team. Stopping by Paul's desk first, she OK'd his proposal draft and the photos he had selected from the green market food pantry event and recent school visits. She next stepped over to Krisha's desk, where Ariel was working with her. There Lupe asked for an update on the hacking incident.

Krisha smiled broadly. "Good news, Boss! The hacking only impacted 300 records or so. We won't be able to get the online platform up until Monday or Tuesday, but at least all the data wasn't compromised."

Lupe sighed with relief. She mentally calculated the loss of online gifts for one weekend but realized that this was modest compared to the possible damage. And fortunately, they wouldn't have to reach out to all their members, donors, and ticket buyers.

"Any major givers on the list? I should call them myself," she asked.

"Yes, there are about 20. Most are regular recurring monthly donors, about 40 new members, and some ticket purchases. I'll get you the list of the major gifts in just a minute," said Krisha.

Ariel handed her the draft email regarding the hacking. Lupe read it over and made a few minor changes, then approved it.

Ariel smiled knowingly. She had come to the Museum as an intern five years before as a non-traditional student. Ariel had worked in the Food and Beverage industry for over 20 years and decided at 40 to go to school full time to earn her degree. "I'll bet you skipped lunch again. You've got that low-blood sugar look on your face."

Krisha chimed in, "Let's fix you up something. I can't leave it to Ian. He'll just get you a ptomain hot dog from the corner." Lupe loved being pampered from time to time, especially when she was the recipient of Ariel and Krisha's treats. South Indian by heritage, Krisha nearly always brought in a savory array of dals – protein-rich bean dishes, steamed Iddlies – fluffy mini-pancakes made of rice and lentil flour, and substantial vegetable dishes. No less a gourmet was Ariel, who had taken a course at the Natural Gourmet Cooking Institute and impressed everyone with her vegan quiches, salads, and cocoa rum balls.

"You read my mind. I have to go see the FBI agent at 2:30, but I should have time to wolf something down."

In the break room, Ariel and Krisha warmed a plate of various tasty and nutritious dishes for Lupe. Between mouthfuls, Lupe asked for any other updates.

"We both saw Detective Collins," said Krisha. "I wasn't downstairs during set up, so she only spoke with me for a few minutes, but she kept Ariel longer."

Lupe remembered when Ariel had started working at the Museum. She had been nervous about competing with younger candidates. Lupe recalled many chats with Ariel, reminding her that her work and life experience were valuable tools in her career arsenal. Ariel wowed her with her dedication and eagerness to learn and apply the skills she mastered. Now she was a confident and supportive member of the team tasked with mentoring the intern cohort.

Just then, Ian slumped in on his way to the copier. Lupe internally shook her head and sighed. Ariel had her work cut out for her.

***

Lupe arrived at the library just as the Grandfather Clock in the lobby chimed the half-hour. The whimsical clock was a replica of Giuseppe Arcimboldo's painting of Rodolf II, a 16th Century Holy Roman Emperor as Vertumnus, the Roman god of the seasons. Arcimboldo, his court painter, liked to paint his subjects with fruits and vegetables in faces, hair, and clothes. A nose might be a pear, neck a zucchini, and grapes for hair. The school children loved the clock, a gift from Japanese American actor, Kaba Tadashi who had made a fortune voicing *Tachibana, the Wonder Deer* for the internationally famous children's cartoon, *Creature Comforts*.

Tadashi had struggled for years as an actor and had shared a 5th-floor walkup two blocks from the Museum with a rotating collection of other actors. He happened upon the Museum of Vegetable Culture one Saturday when the Green Market was operating. He said later that being able to feed his body, he could feed his soul and thus win the *Creature Comforts* audition. Not only did Tadashi gift the enchanting clock, but he also emceed the annual gala favoring guests with a wide array of hysterical voice characters as he promoted the live and silent auctions.

Agent Reyes was seated at one of the long tables in the center of the room. Lupe sat down, eager to learn of any news on the theft. Reyes's eyes twinkled.

"I think you have something on your nose?"

Lupe reached up to touch her nose and wiped away a dollop of the vegan chocolate mousse Ariel had given her for dessert. *Whatever*, thought Lupe. So much for making a good impression. Since the box of tissues on the table was empty, she went to the librarian's desk and found some hand sanitizer. She used it to clean off her hand and nose. *Now I smell like rubbing alcohol. Even better.*

"I know we already asked you about yesterday's activities, but I want to know if you remembered anything else. Did any of the staff behave oddly yesterday afternoon?"

Lupe thought, *in a creative enterprise, what is odd?* She reflected on Ian, who yesterday wore a pair of in-line skates, swearing it would make him more efficient. And Felicity's gift shop assistant Silke Borge, who dreamt of being a cabaret singer and often stopped shoppers to give her rendition of such American Songbook classic songs as *You Go to My Head, Sunny Side of the Street,* and *Fascination.* Felicity tried to curb Silke's muse, but Lupe was pretty sure that the tall Nordic beauty was unaware that not everyone appreciated the genre. And who could forget Ed Meyers, the front desk volunteer who believed vegetables were sentient and had their own language. His magnum opus was a treatise on the common language of the Nightshade family, including eggplants, tomatoes, peppers, and potatoes. Ed sucked many unsuspecting people into a discussion of the tonal qualities of goji berries and tomatillos.

"It was a pretty routine day. We have many events in the lobby and galleries, so we're rather systematic about the various elements. My special events and membership manager, Ariel Pensky, and development assistant, Tessa Hunt, handled the setup as usual with assistance from maintenance. The catering and bartending staff would have arrived around 4:00, and I think the curtain covering the paintings was in place before they got there.

I greeted Ingrid San Sebastian to take her up to Stephanie's office. Ingrid met with Stephanie and Mary Montgomery van Clausen, our board chair. They were pitching our winter exhibition on the work of Gregor Mendel. Funny, I just realized I didn't ask Stephanie how it went. Her husband, the artist Pietro San Sebastian, dropped her off."

Agent Reyes nodded, "Then what happened?"

"I came back downstairs, and Mrs. San Sebastian's toy poodle, Borgia, was running about nipping on everyone's heels. She gets easily excited. Ian Macdonald, our intern, finally managed to catch her." Lupe didn't mention Ian's roller skates. "We then returned Borgia to Pietro, who had been chatting with one of the security guards.

"Which guard was that?" Asked Reyes.

"Andreas Konstavides," Lupe replied. "He is in art school and mainly works here as a night guard. He came in to help with the event. Pietro has built quite a reputation for his work, and I'm sure Andreas wanted to sit at the feet of a master, so to speak."

"Did Mr. San Sebastian stay in the gallery?"

"I believe so. The meeting with Ingrid -- Mrs. San Sebastian didn't last more than an hour, and I don't remember him leaving during that time. Stephanie, Mary Montgomery, and Ingrid came downstairs when they finished meeting and went out to the Guinevere Bar at the Hotel Manfred, the new boutique hotel on 2nd and St. Mark's. That's the old Button Factory converted to an upscale hotel. I saw Pietro leave with them. They all returned by 6:00 for the opening."

"Tell me more about Andreas Konstavides," Reyes inquired.

"He's in his early 20s and is fond of what he calls neo-industrial, post-modern expressionism. He's really good at repurposing things people throw away. He believes – and I heartily agree with him – that there is too much waste in our society. He thinks it is the responsibility of artists, especially, to reuse, reduce, and recycle. I've heard him complain about his program sometimes, especially when his professors want him to work in a medium that he's not as fluent in."

"How did he feel about the new exhibition, *de Legumes*?" asked the agent.

"You'll have to ask him, but if it's anything like his reaction to the Pierre-Joseph Redoute exhibition of plant sketches, it would not be positive. Andreas is a brash young man who believes the rules don't apply to him. He doesn't feel the masters have much to teach him," Lupe replied.

"OK. Now I have to ask you about some of your staff. You mentioned that Ariel Pensky and Tessa Hunt routinely handled the setup. I imagine your intern Ian MacDonald assisted as needed. Is that correct?" Asked Reyes.

"Yes. Ian is good with the fetch and carry kind of work that needs to happen. Tessa would have been taking care of last-minute RSVPs and cancellations and setting up the name tags. Ariel used to manage a restaurant and would have been working with Esmerelda Escadia from Green Events, our caterer. We keep a supply of wine, alcohol, and glassware on-site, so she would also coordinate with the bartenders to get that arranged.

"One of the bartenders is your roommate, Henry Tsai?"

"Yes," Lupe felt herself becoming tense. Surely Henry wouldn't have taken the paintings?

"Henry Tsai is the director of the Hepaestus Theatre Corps?" Reyes asked.

"Yes, and he's also an actor. You may have seen him in last year's Aqua Velva campaign? He was one of the group of dancers in a Broadway show."

Reyes shook his head. This didn't surprise Lupe because there were about twenty fit young men in the commercial, and it was only by playing back the commercial frame by frame that the roommates were able to catch sight of Henry -- the third tap dancer to the right on the back row.

"Henry was working with two other bartenders. Usually, we set up the main bar in the lobby and a secondary bar in the corner of the gallery." Lupe felt her cheeks become red. "In case you are wondering, I just don't know how he could possibly have taken the paintings. For one thing, Henry doesn't drive, so where would he have hidden the works? In fact, most of the staff would not be driving because of the construction work outside the Museum. We've lost almost all the parking places we used to have, and it's like a blood sport to get any of the remaining spots. Most of our people and indeed the guests would have taken public transportation or car service."

"Let's put that aside for the moment," said the agent calmly. "You mentioned that Ariel Pensky once managed a restaurant."

"Yes. The Wet-Paint Café in the West Village. It was a really cool space. Guests were given art materials and painted murals, sketches, and graffiti on the walls throughout the place. Ariel was actually part owner, but her partner raided the till and left Ariel to clean up the mess. Ariel had to declare bankruptcy. It took her a long time to climb out from under, but eventually, she managed to put herself through college and came to work here."

"Would you say she is trustworthy?" Asked the detective.

"Of course. Ariel is one of the hardest working people I know, and I prize her integrity. Her partner gave her a raw deal, but she's always made the best of things." Lupe tried taking a few deep breaths to keep herself calm. "I don't for a moment believe Ariel would steal the paintings. I don't know why anyone would, except to keep it in their private collection. It's not as though you can sell them on the open market," Lupe added.

"Did you know that Tessa Hunt's brother did time in Ossining for counterfeiting fifty-dollar bills?"

Lupe felt her eyes widen to the size of Stephanie's Limoges china saucers. This was news.

Chapter 4
Back your Team and Do Look Gift Horses in the Mouth

"No. I had no idea. But that shouldn't matter. Tessa has always been a hard-working member of the team. She applied for the post of development assistant last year, shortly after she graduated from NYU. Her parents have been members of the Museum for years, and she came with great references. To be honest, I'm surprised that I didn't know this. My department is a mini-detective bureau. We spend a lot of time researching donors and usually ferret out the good, bad, and ugly," Lupe said.

"It may be because Germain Harris is Tessa's half-brother," said the agent. "His mother married Tessa's father after she had been widowed while in her twenties. Germain didn't get along with his stepfather and became the proverbial black sheep. He did prove to be a talented artist, and his parents sent him to Paris to study at the Ecole des Beaux-Arts. He decided the life of the impoverished artist was not for him and became a skilled counterfeiter instead."

Lupe tried to maintain a poker face, but as her father would jest, she could only manage her pierogi face puffing out her cheeks and exhaling slowly.

"But I still don't understand what her brother's illegal activities have to do with Tessa," Lupe replied.

"We have several theories. She could have been trying to help her brother and stole the paintings for him to copy. Or he could have sneaked into the gallery and taken the paintings himself. Tessa may have mentioned the event, and he saw the opportunity. We are questioning Harris."

Lupe rushed to defend her subordinate. "I can't believe Tessa had anything to do with the theft. You learn a lot about character in my work, just as I'm sure you have in yours. You'd be surprised at how many people come to nonprofits wanting to make a splash with a major gift who are really grifters. I've had people claiming to be billionaires who are only scam artists and have had to really learn to be a strong BS detector. I think I would know if Tessa was planning a theft of that magnitude. Why just the other day, she went around the office apologizing because she ate an oat milk yogurt left in the refrigerator one night when she was working late. It turned out to be Felicity's, and Tessa insisted on replacing it."

"We'll leave it there for now. There is one other person I want to ask you about." Lupe felt the panic rising again. *Which one of her staff would he suspect? Paul because of his prospect research skills? Marcus, who had grown up in a tough Bronx neighborhood? Or Ian, just because he was...well, Ian?*

"One of the guests, Judit VonKolbe, seems a bit out of place. In fact, her name didn't appear on any guest list." The agent sat back in his chair.

"That's Judit for you. She's harmless but is definitely a 'hanger-on.' I don't know how she does it, but she manages to get into all kinds of social events. Sometimes she comes as the legitimate guest of one of our VIP members, but she has no problem walking in like she owns the place if she can't cage an invitation. It is easier just to ignore her than to make a big scene. She's well connected, and it would be bad publicity to blackball her. Unfortunately, every organization has at least one Judit VonKolbe."

"Nevertheless, we will question her again." *Good,* thought Lupe. *Maybe that will scare her into becoming a member.*

"And what about me? Are you interested in my background?" Lupe probed.

"Fortunately, you left a social media trail that made it easy to document your background—undergraduate Seton Hall and Master's in Arts Administration from NYU. You worked at several arts nonprofits before coming here as development director five years ago. Single, you share an apartment in Cobble Hill with Henry Tsai and Alice Mayhew. You live within your means but are paying off student loans. You have many hobbies but don't commit to any one." Lupe shifted in her seat. She knew what was coming. "This past year, you've tried Thai cooking, running with the Road Runners, pottery, improv, songwriting, tango lessons, and Eastern Philosophy. You are fluent in Spanish and Polish and studied French in college. Your mother is of Mexican heritage from Texas and is a realtor. Your father is a Polish émigré and runs a contracting firm with his brother, who studied painting. You have three siblings…"

Lupe cut him off. "And my eyes are hazel. I highlight my hair. My blood type is A Positive, I'm an organ donor, and my social security number is 288-90-5314. I guess I need to do a social media purge."

"We do want to ask about your Uncle Gustave. What type of painting did he study and where?"

"Uncle Gus studied in Poland and won a scholarship to study art at a small liberal arts college in North Carolina. Unfortunately, his English was poor, and he couldn't keep up with his other classes and dropped out. My father was already here and was able to sponsor Uncle Gus so that the family could stay together.

He still paints for fun but mainly watercolors. I don't even think he has an oil set. And no, I didn't steal the paintings for Uncle Gus."

"Thank you, Ms. Reinowski. As I've asked everyone, please let us know if you remember anything at all that could be of use to us in this investigation."

"I will." Lupe jumped up from her chair and practically raced from the room, eager to escape. Uncle Gus indeed!

Lupe joined the other senior leadership and Jane Mehra in the conference room attached to Stephanie's office. Stephanie smiled when she saw her enter the room.

***

"You'll never believe it?!" Stephanie crowed. "Ingrid San Sebastian wants to make a seven-figure gift!"

The directors applauded. Tom Unger high-fived Audry, and Pierre and Sissy grinned.

"What?! That's wonderful but a bit surprising. Her cumulative giving in is the low six-figures. That's amazing!"

"Yes, she decided she wants to have a naming opportunity. What can we give her?"

Lupe mused. "Well, the galleries, lobby, test kitchen, greenhouse, and the auditorium are all named. We can give her a classroom or a conference room or even a stairwell in a pinch."

"How much were we asking for those?" Stephanie asked.

"$500K for each classroom and $350K for the main conference room. We hadn't worked out a price for the stairwell. And we agreed we wouldn't name the bathrooms!"

"Yes, yes," Stephanie sighed in disappointment. "Ok. How about giving her two adjacent classrooms and put a large acknowledgement sign between the two?"

"Sure. That will work. I'll get the gift agreement ready ASAP."

Stephanie then turned to the other directors. "Jane has polished the press release and talking points which you've all seen. The Board has approved all communications, so we'll distribute them to the staff right away. The press conference is scheduled to take place at 5:00. Does anyone have any questions?"

Audry nodded. "I assume there are no updates on the whereabouts of the paintings or the thief?"

"Nothing. The police are pursuing leads, as they say, but they have no real information. I did learn that Tessa Hunt's brother is a convicted forger with an art background. I think we should fire her."

Lupe felt her anger rising and was about to reply when Jane smoothly interceded. "Firing Tessa for her brother's actions is illegal. It could open the Museum to a lawsuit, and the additional scrutiny would not be helpful. Also, her parents have been patron members for years. I think it sets a better tone to express support for the family unless Tessa is arrested and convicted."

Sissy interjected. "Yes. Tessa hasn't even been accused of anything. Lupe is probably the best person to assess her integrity."

"I stake my own reputation on Tessa's character. Tessa has always impressed me with her talents and resourcefulness. I can't believe she is involved in this incident in any way, and it would be wrong to damage her reputation."

Stephanie was wise enough not to argue the point, but Lupe was certain the matter of Tessa's employment would come up again. She vowed to have a quiet chat with Tessa to let her know she would support her but to watch her back.

Stephanie continued. "The police will let us use the Fisker Gallery beginning tomorrow, and extra security will be stationed. Although that's a bit like locking the barn door after the cow gets loose."

Tom interjected. "The police seem to think the culprit will return to the scene of the crime."

"For what purpose?" Audry asked.

"Evidently, criminals sometimes get a feeling of exultation replaying the incident. Moe's team will be watching individual visitors and looking for anyone who spends a lot of time near the Manet table setting," Tom added.

"The insurance investigator will be here tomorrow to visit the site, so Tom and I will be here to answer questions," Pierre said.

Was it Lupe's imagination, or did Stephanie look nervous? She could feel a slight tremor as the Executive Director tapped her foot under the conference table.

"Also, Felicity brought to my attention an uptick in thefts in the Gift Shop." Added Tom in his role as operations and facility director.

Audry chimed in, "We have had a larger number of school visits than usual, and sometimes the students are given to five-finger discounts, unfortunately."

Tom replied. "It's not the usual trinket-type thefts. Felicity is used to that kind of shrinkage and accounts for it. No, these thefts are some of the bespoke items. Small, portable things but more expensive. A pair of sterling silver chopstick rests, a hand-painted antique salad plate, and a silk scarf, things like that. Felicity estimates the recent loss to be over $5,000, and she's very upset. I want to invest in new cameras for the shop as well."

"But that will cost more than the losses," Stephanie blustered. "I promised the Board we wouldn't dip into the reserve more than we already need to. The market hasn't been great, and we're not going to be getting our usual 6% draw for this year."

Pierre interjected. "The camera installation is a necessary capital expenditure, and I can amortize it over ten years. I think if you have to ask the Board for money, this is the time to do it."

"Yes," added the consultant. "The Board can hardly rule against such a basic expenditure. And I'm sure the incremental cost will be modest."

Tom spoke, "Pierre and I will get the necessary bids for your consideration. Then we'll know where we are. I also want to get the gallery wired properly for ethernet so we don't have to rely on the Wi-Fi for the pressure sensors."

Stephanie shrugged. "Alright, and as long as the connection work can take place after hours. I don't want any galleries closed to the public. The one positive thing about this theft is that we are the center of attention, and I want to capitalize on the turnout. And lastly, before we head to the press conference, I have selected the top three candidates for the marketing director position, so I'll have Charlotte work with you to get meetings set. She'll also send along the candidates' resumes and cover letters. Thank you, Pierre, for managing the initial screening and Lupe for stepping in to cover since Alexi left."

***

The leadership traveled downstairs to the auditorium where the Press Conference was to take place. Reporters from multiple media sources were already gathering along with some members of the Board. Lupe was surprised to see Camillo Aggio, the Italian celebrity chef who had joined the Board the prior year. *Aggi,* as he was known, owned restaurants in New York and Los Angeles and hosted a television show – *Aggi Al Dente*. He had just published a cookbook of vegetable-forward Italian dishes, and the Museum was hosting the launch in conjunction with the gala in two weeks.

Lupe was impressed and a little jealous that Aggi managed to be slim and fit, with food playing such a central role in his life. Lupe had an advance copy of *Aggi Al Fresco* and had tried a few recipes, but in her case, she toned down the olive oil, butter, and cheese, even the vegan types. No matter how vegetable-forward the dishes may be, the calories seemed to find their way to her.

Aggi smiled at her and waved. Lupe curbed a mad vision of her dancing in the Trevi Fountain and walked over to the chef.

"Tempi triste, Cara," said Aggi, although he didn't look particularly concerned.

"I'm sure the police will find out who took the paintings very soon," said Lupe.

"Si. And all is set for my books coming for the gala?" Aggi asked.

"Oh, yes. We're having them shipped directly to Cipriani's on the day of the event. It's a lovely gift for the attendees. And thank you again for creating the menu. Everyone is so excited to taste your creations," Lupe enthused.

"It adds a special flavor to the evening, no?" Aggi chuckled at his pun. Lupe groaned inwardly but laughed. He may be a bad joke teller, but he was a charming man and it was easy to see why Camillo Aggio was so popular.

Stephanie stepped onto the stage, followed by Mary Montgomery van Clausen, Agent Reyes and another man Lupe didn't recognize. Stephanie spoke first.

"Thank you for joining us here today under these extraordinary circumstances. My name is Stephanie James-Howard, and I am the executive director of the Museum of Vegetable Culture. To my right is Mary Montgomery van Clausen, the chair of our board of trustees. To my left is Captain Harry Meyers of the 9th Precinct and Special Agent Josh Reyes of the Arts Crimes Unit of the FBI. They will give us an update on last evening's heinous act of theft.

Make no mistake, we at the Museum of Vegetable Culture take this matter very seriously, and we will prosecute the offender or offenders to the fullest extent of the law. We must set a clear example that art is to be respected. The theft of Edward Manet's *Bunch of Asparagus* and its companion piece is a despicable crime. We owe it to the Wallraf-Richartz, and the Musee D'Orsay, and all art appreciators find and return these pieces quickly. Now I will turn the podium over to Captain Meyers and Agent Reyes."

Captain Meyers stepped forward with Josh Reyes. Meyers was a stocky man of medium height with tousled, grey hair. While he had tied his tie, his suit was rumpled, which added to his unkempt appearance.

"Thank you, Ms. James-Howard. To bring you up to date, we ascertained the following facts. Between 4:00 pm and 7:00 pm yesterday evening, the two Manet paintings were stolen from the Museum of Vegetable Culture. These were part of a larger exhibition of vegetables in Impressionist art entitled *de Legumes*." The captain pronounced the exhibition's title carefully, but it still came out as "Lay gums." He labored on. "At about 7:00 pm, the curtain which had been covering the paintings was removed to reveal their absence. The police were immediately notified, and my colleague from the FBI Arts Crime Unit was called in. An extensive search of the facilities did not recover the pieces, which led us to believe that the art was somehow spirited out of the building between 4:00 pm when they were last seen and 7:00 pm when the loss was discovered. We fingerprinted the loss site but only found blurred prints and a few prints matching staff who have been eliminated from our inquiry. We have uncovered a few leads and are currently discussing the matter with persons of interest but have nothing more definite to share with you at this moment.

At this time, we will take your questions," the captain ended.

The scrum of reporters raised their hands and began to shout out questions. Captain Meyers recognized Abby Winters.

"Thank you, Captain Meyers. Agent Reyes, is it true that there is a staff connection to a convicted forger?" the art reporter asked.

Reyes replied patiently. "I cannot discuss individual leads, but several people are helping us with our inquiries."

"But surely you can confirm that one of the junior staff is the sister of an art forger?"

Lupe saw Stephanie's face redden. Rumplestilskin time was approaching. Lupe herself felt miserable for poor Tessa.

Meyers responded. "In the interest of the individual's privacy, we cannot comment on that allegation."

The other reporters took the lead.

"Sam Talbot, NY Times." A lanky man with a trim goatee stood. "Doesn't the public have the right to know if a member of the staff is implicated in this theft?"

Reyes's face remained impassive. "As we said, we are following various leads; when we have more to share with you, we will, of course, keep you notified."

A strong-boned woman in the rear of the auditorium shouted out. "We're given to understand that the pressure sensors were not working in the gallery. Are the lending museums going to sue because the site was not secure?"

Lupe looked to the front of the auditorium where the representatives of the Wallraf-Richartz and the Musee D'Orsay sat. The two seemed to be closely scrutinizing their shoe wear. Stephanie looked furious, but Mary Montgomery maintained her usual aplomb. It amazed Lupe how the board chair could retain her poise no matter what the situation. She remembered a gala two years prior when the honoree showed up drunk, gave his keynote speech twice, and then sank down between two seats on the dais, dumping a full dinner plate onto Mary Montgomery's Caroline Herrera gown. Mary Montgomery smiled as though the business leader had gifted her with roses instead of a lap full of Chanterelle gnocchi.

Reyes spoke. "We have no information on any action that may be taken against the Museum. While it is true the pressure sensors were not activated, there were always many people in the gallery during the times in question. Among security and maintenance, catering, and the development staff, we are confident someone will come forward to let us know they saw the perpetrator. They may not have recognized the activity at the time, but they may on reflection understand what exactly transpired."

Reyes's answer did not dissuade the reporter. "Ms. James-Howard, in the press release, you are quoted that there will be a review of all security measures. Will you also be firing your head of security?"

Mary Montgomery gave Stephanie her "stick to the party line" look, and Stephanie went to the microphone. "We are conducting an internal review of all of our security procedures and will allocate the appropriate resources as determined. We have not made any staffing decisions, but I can assure you that Morris Schwartz is a trusted and valued member of staff who, as you know, was also one of the Museum's founders. The pressure sensor malfunction was unfortunate, but as Agent Reyes noted, there were many people around the gallery at all times during the reception setup. I am confident someone will recall seeing the culprit in the act. I am recommending that my staff all meditate on the events, and I'm sure when they have reached a Zen state of mind, the truth will be revealed."

Fantastic, thought Lupe. Next, *we'll get some crystals and a shaman.*

Chapter 5
The Effective Fundraiser Knows When to Take Breaks

Lupe returned to her apartment, exhausted in mind and body. Upon opening the door, she smelled the aroma of mushroom Bourguignon and rolled her eyes in delight. Alice was an excellent home cook, and it was her night at the stove.

"You read my mind," Lupe smiled. "I really wanted comfort food tonight."

"Pour a glass of wine while I get the potatoes mashed. Your day was lousy?"

"Comme si, comme ca. We got a seven-figure naming gift which was fabulous, but hackers got to our donor platform, and I found out that one of my staffers is connected to a convicted forger."

"So basically a usual day at the office, eh?"

Henry entered the kitchen carrying a case of wine. "My theater company is having a pre-show reception on our opening night, so I bought some wine at a discount at Trader Joe's. I hope you two can make it. It's the 19th."

"Of course, Henry. My gala is on the 17th, National Eat your Vegetables Day and I'll be ready to be a guest instead of a worker bee," Lupe replied.

"And my golf outing isn't until the 21ᵗʰ so count me in," Alice grinned as she stirred the stew and added wine to the pot and her glass in equal proportions."

Lupe kicked off her shoes, "Do I have time for a quick shower?" Alice nodded. Lupe stepped into her bath and ran the tap until the water flowed hot. She usually preferred a cooling shower after work, but her shoulders felt tense, and she thought the heat would help her relax.

Changing into yoga pants and a t-shirt, Lupe went back to the dining room where Henry was setting the table. Since lunch was usually at a rush, the trio preferred to sit and have a leisurely dinner when their schedules permitted.

Lupe quickly made a salad, and Alice brought the Dutch oven to the table. Henry followed with the wine and a bowl of dilled mashed potatoes. Lupe felt herself relax as she sat at the table to enjoy her friends' company.

The three savored their meal before turning the conversation to the Museum.

Henry regaled them with stories about the performances his actors were preparing. Many of the pieces were autobiographical and ranged from grimly serious to hilariously funny. Henry was justifiably proud of his group, who found ways to express their creativity and build their skills as actors despite physical and emotional challenges. Through much cajoling, Henry had secured RSVPs from a number of talent agents. He hoped some of his students would turn professional while understanding the battle all performers faced.

Alice also had a big week at her organization, successfully recruiting a new board member who understood the need to make his annual board gift. The board of Family Matters had adopted a "give-or-get" policy, but most of the current board had not made either a personal gift or influenced an equivalent amount. Her challenge was a common one, and Alice had researched best practices for getting the board "on board," so to speak, with the importance of giving. Her board members were a mix of medical practitioners, social workers, businesspeople, and philanthropists, and their giving capacity varied. Fortunately, her new executive director was completely comfortable with fundraising and supported her in her efforts to change the giving culture. She made her case by noting that most foundations and corporations even asked what percentage of board members contributed annually in their applications. The board had agreed to a $5,000 annual give-or get-policy.

"And so far, the board members with the most modest means are the ones who are bringing in the gifts. They are hosting small gatherings for friends, soliciting them, and getting people to buy tickets for the golf outing. It's the ones I expected would have no trouble giving that I have to hunt down," Alice said.

"I send invoices to my board. It seems to work. I know it may seem overly business-like, but since they agreed to give financially as part of their board service, I haven't had much push back. Also,

Stephanie lets them know the invoices are coming out, so there are no surprises."

"I could learn from you two. My board members are all in the same boat I am," said Henry.

"Let's make a date for some prospect research for you, Henry. You know we're happy to help," said Alice.

"Yes, as long as you stick to the rules," said Lupe.

Together she and Alice chimed, "No poaching our donors!"

Henry crossed his fingers, "promise!"

After dinner, the conversation turned to the thefts.

Lupe told her roommates about her meeting with Agent Reyes and gave the latest updates.

"So far, there is no real information," Lupe said. "The fingerprints were all blurry, and as far as I know, they have accounted for all the staff. Although Special Agent Reyes did ask me a lot about Andreas Konstavedes, who had spent a lot of time talking to Pietro San Sebastian."

"Yeah, I saw them talking," said Henry. "It looked like they were trying to figure out all the world's problems in one hour. I forgot to tell you I was talking to one of the other bartenders, and Felipe found this." Henry reached into his pocket and pulled out a silver cufflink engraved with a small mother of pearl duck.

Taking it from him, Lupe scrutinized it closely. Who was wearing cufflinks last night? She tried to think.

"Where was this found? Did Felipe say?"

Yes, Felipe picked it up around 5:00 o'clock in the corner of the gallery where he set up the secondary bar. He put it in his pocket and forgot about it. We caught up for a coffee today because he and I are auditioning next week for Costello Rosenthal's new play. We were practicing our scenes. I know he should have given it to the police, and we should make sure they have it, but I wanted to see it first."

Alice mused, "Well, I'm sure they won't be able to get fingerprints from it since it's been handled so much."

"Yeah, that's unfortunate," said Lupe. "But it's interesting. Thinking back now, Firoze Shah was wearing a shirt with French cuffs. It could be his. I know that Aggi came early, but he wore a linen shirt with the cuffs rolled up. It might have been Pietro's. He's usually well-dressed."

Alice added, "Or it might have been dropped there anytime earlier in the day."

"And the police have done their homework. They certainly know a lot about our backgrounds and even asked me about poor Uncle Gus."

"Uncle Gus?!" queried Alice.

"Yeah, they wanted to know about his *art* background. Reyes seemed to think I would steal the paintings for Uncle Gus to copy. Just like Tessa and her brother."

Alice relaxed, "They have to follow all leads, and even though Uncle Gus owns a contracting company with your dad, he did study art once. Stranger things."

"I suppose," Lupe replied. "Oh, and this is odd. We've had some thefts in the gift shop of some valuable tchotchkes. Small portable items but more valuable than the usual notecards and seed packets."

"So, could the two be connected?" Henry asked.

"Not sure. It's a big leap from a silk scarf to impressionist masterpieces."

***

Most Sundays, the Reinowski family gathered for a traditional midday meal together. This weekend, however, Pavel and Gus would be tied up on Sunday with a new client who was flying in from Paris to go over the renovations to his historic home. So it was decided that the family would gather on Saturday for their regular barbecue. Lupe's mother, Lucia, was a proud Texan of Mexican heritage and believed no gathering was complete without her slow-smoked brisket and homemade chicken enchiladas with mole. On the other hand, Pavel insisted on traditional Polish dishes such as Kapustka, Golumpki, and Kielbasa. While Lupe looked forward to seeing her family, she knew she would spend much of the day pushing away the heavy offerings.

The one thing Lupe would not turn down was her Abuelita's famous rice pudding with Mexican cinnamon. Her grandmother on her mother's side would plump raisins in dark rum before mixing these into the creamy pudding. It was decadent and well worth the calories. Traveling to visit her parents took close to two hours because Lupe had to take the New Jersey Transit and wait for her brother Gael to pick her up at the station. It wasn't the ride that was so long it was that Gael was very forgetful. He was an aspiring musician who would often get lost in song, forgetting the time.

Arriving at the midday meal late, as usual, Lupe was not surprised to see a strange man waiting. Lucia quickly introduced him as Tom Howard, a colleague of hers at the real estate firm. Lupe knew it was just another one of her mother's usual setups. No matter how modern Lucia was as a capable business owner, in her mind, Lupe was wasting her life away by not marrying and settling down. After all, her father Pavel had bought her a plot of land next to their house to go along with the other parcels given to her siblings, Jose Luis, Gael, and Rosario. The expectation was that, like her siblings, Lupe would build a house and live with the family.

So far, Lupe had resisted her mother's efforts, and she had no intention of moving back to Parsippany, no matter who she married – if she married. And she felt that her siblings had done more than enough to carry on the family line.

Oh well, thought Lupe, *this one doesn't look too bad. Maybe he'll be interesting.*

Tom smiled at her. "Your mother is a hard woman to turn down," he whispered conspiratorially.

Lupe laughed. "Pretty sneaky is my mother. Missed her calling with the FBI."

"Did you know you are brilliant and the most beautiful woman in greater New York?"

Lupe almost snorted with glee. "Oh dear, you got the full-court press. Did she have me finding the lost city of Atlantis and winning a Nobel?"

"She's got a way with words. It's probably why she's such a good realtor."

"Great. Do I come with ash flooring and Miele appliances?"

Now Tom burst into laughter. Lucia looked over from a distance and smiled.

"Well, at least you'll get a good meal. Mama and Abuela are excellent cooks, and if you like Tex-Mex with Polish side dishes, you're in for a treat."

"Lucia told me to bring an appetite. My last boyfriend told me I ate for two."

"Oh, Mom," thought Lupe.

Sated with fat, protein, and carbohydrates, the family lounged in the backyard of Lupe's parents' home. Lucia brought the conversation around to the recent theft.

"I'm sure it's someone connected to the Museum, Querida," she told Lupe. Lupe decided it best not to mention Agent Reyes's questions about Uncle Gus. Pavel and his brother had gone next door to Rosario's house, where the two were planning an addition for Rosario and her husband Michael's growing family.

"You know I don't trust that Mimi St. John's," she added.

"Mamita, you shouldn't say such things without evidence," Lupe chided.

"Evidence. I have evidence. I was representing two buyers for a house in Rumson. The house was owned by a corporation that turned out to be a shell company. The head of that company was Mimi St. Johns."

"Mom, that doesn't mean she did anything wrong. It's just a good way of doing business."

"I know that. It's just that the company was incorporated in the Channel Islands. Usually, you don't set up your company in a place like that unless you're trying to avoid taxes. In my mind, it doesn't pass the smell test."

Tom looked amused. "Well, your mother does know a thing or two about business."

"Even so, what would that have to do about stealing two Manets?"

"I'm not sure," said Lucia. "Unless she wanted them just for herself or if she knew a buyer in someplace like Dubai or Shanghai."

Lupe thought that highly unlikely but kept it in the back of her mind.

Tom went off to kick a soccer ball with Gael, Jose Luis, and the children. Lupe counted. She now had two nieces and three nephews, and one baby on the way. She loved being an aunt to all of them and enjoyed watching them grow.

"Well, what do you think of him? Tom's a nice man. And he's so good with the children." Lucia noted.

"Yes, mom. But I should introduce him to Henry."

"Oh."

"Do you have any other great theories?" Lupe jested.

"Don't chide me. I also think you should look at the chair of your Finance Committee, Firoze Shah."

"What?!" Lupe almost spat out her iced tea. "Firoze is a man of great integrity and is a solid businessman."

"I was talking to Margo Menhoff, and she told me the Shah's marriage was on the rocks. The Mrs. has been stepping out."

"Oh great," said Lupe. "But that doesn't have anything to do with the paintings."

"Well, this would be a costly divorce. According to Margo, there was no prenup," said Lucia. "He may be looking for some way to make up his losses."

"For heaven's sake, Firoze Shah is a top investor. I'm sure there are easier ways for him to make money than to try to spirit two Manets from a museum in broad daylight."

Lucia shrugged her shoulders. "Just saying."

"Ok, Mom. I think we're getting away from the realm of possibility or even probability. But I admire how you keep up to date with everything. It's truly amazing."

Lucia's father, uncle Gus, and Michael returned.

"Lucia, my dove," said Pavel, a burly stooped man in his late 50s. Pavel always had a glint in his eye to show his sense of humor and fondness for his family, but he and Uncle Gus had built their business from scratch and were shrewd businessmen. Pavel placed a hand on Lupe's shoulder and looked her in the eye.

"Darling, you look tired. Your mother told me the news. You shouldn't let it worry you too much. I'm sure the police will find out who did this terrible thing. The press will soon leave it be, and all will quiet down."

"I hope so, Papa. It's hard on everyone. Not only is it bad for the Museum's reputation, but we're worried the insurance won't pay the claims to the lending museums."

Pavel stroked Lupe's hair and hugged her close. "Ssh, ssh maly ptak, little bird. All will be well."

Lupe looked over at Uncle Gus and prayed it was so.

***

On the long train ride back to her Brooklyn apartment, Lupe reflected on all of Lucia's remarks.

What if she was right? What if Mimi St. Johns somehow wanted or needed the paintings for private sale? In Firoze Shah, could there be some truth that he would like to shore up his financial position because of a divorce? That seemed to Lupe to be unlikely except for the cufflink. Firoze did favor French cuffs. What if he dropped the article while taking the paintings? If so, how did he get them out of the Museum or hide them to retrieve them later? And how could he do this in front of so many people?

Lupe thought about Firoze. He was a tall, slim, attractive man in his early 50s. Always well attired, Firoze was a commanding presence and hardly inconspicuous.

Still full from the massive lunch Lupe nodded off, dreaming of board members chasing her through the galleries. She woke with a start realizing she missed her subway stop and had landed in Coney Island.

The fun never stops, she thought.

Chapter 6
Development is a Jig-Saw Puzzle

Lupe put all thoughts of the thefts from her mind as she concentrated on the various projects that comprised her advancement efforts. She liked to take a few minutes at the end of each day to review her work plan and again edit her priority list first thing in the morning. This week she and her team would prepare for the next appeal, edit the annual report, and work with the gala committee to sell all the tables and get names for the guests. While Lupe appreciated companies buying tables, it was also crucial for actual guests to appear in the evening to provide a good audience for the honoree and participate in the auctions. She recalled a particularly grim event where three tables stood empty. Much of the last-minute work would be to follow up and ensure that people were indeed planning to come to the function at Cipriani's in midtown.

Fortunately, Ariel and Tessa would politely but resolutely birddog the various donors. In addition, they did a great job tracking the many auction items that were arriving daily. Some were small, like gift certificates for stays at donors' vacation homes or reservations to almost impossible to get into restaurants. Others presented more of a logistical challenge. A butter-colored Chippendale leather chaise lounge and two art deco floor lamps were taking up a corner of Lupe's minute office along with designer handbags and the ubiquitous sports memorabilia that always seemed to find its way to auctions. Lupe coveted the spa day at the Four Seasons and the tickets for the hottest Broadway play. She made a mental note to try to bid for these items on the night of the auction.

With Marcus and Krisha, Lupe once again reviewed the list of donors from the prior fiscal year to ensure all names and attributions were correct for the annual report. Marcus had created a clever layout both for online and limited print use. Visually rich, the report featured marvelous photos of events and programs along with illustrative infographics that showcased the Museum's reach. She also double-checked that all financial data was accurate, and no digits were added or subtracted in error.

By the end of the session, Lupe felt comfortable progressing the layout for her Executive Director's approval. Stretching, the team broke for a coffee. Lupe stepped out of her office and into Ian, dressed in a carrot costume for his role as Captain Carrot in the "Vegetable Soup" show. It fell to the interns to play the various characters for the signature school program. Lupe was a bit surprised because they didn't usually host school visits on Mondays.

Ariel caught her eye, smiled, and waved her over.

"Like Ian's outfit?" She asked.

"I didn't realize we had a show today," Lupe replied.

"We don't, but I told him that when he doesn't dress appropriately, his alternative is to wear the carrot costume."

Lupe laughed. "How did he take it?"

"It's Ian. He's fine with it. In fact, I have a feeling Captain Carrot will be our new mascot."

"As long as he keeps the costume clean."

"Yes, Ma'am," Ariel twinkled.

Lupe leaned against the shelf of office supplies in the break room while waiting for a fresh pot of Fair Exchange coffee to brew. Felicity came in; her face was somber. Lupe guessed the reason.

"I heard about the thefts. Moe and Tom will get to the bottom of it. You shouldn't worry so much."

"I know. But I was so proud of my department. I've always been able to meet my projections. This is the first time I won't," mourned the shop manager.

"No one is going to blame you. Everyone knows what a great job you do. You and Silke and the rest of your team. You are a natural, and we're lucky to have you!" Lupe tried to cheer up her colleague.

"You're sweet. And I know we'll make up the loss somehow. I think I'll hold an extra sale to get rid of some of the old stock and then get in some extra quantities of the better-quality items but have them displayed under glass. I also found a bespoke bridal registry that we can be part of. We have some exciting items that newlyweds might like. I found a vendor for vegetable patterned silverware that is very trendy and stylish."

"You always come up with interesting ideas, Felicity. How do you do it? Have you always been in retail?" Lupe asked.

"I was in merchandising out of college for Takashimaya, where I learned how to showcase beautifully crafted items. The Japanese have such a gorgeous aesthetic. From the sublime I went to the ridiculous and headed up retail sales at a toy store on 50th and Lex. It was crazy. Christmas came earlier every year. I was able to stop work for a while to raise my kids, and that was when I got involved here as a volunteer. I started working as assistant manager and later manager."

"And turned the shop from a tired loss to a great source of revenue. You also have won three major awards for shop design."

"Thank you. I know we'll get to the bottom of this mystery. And soon. I have extra people working in the shop and have secured the more valuable items. By the way, have you heard anything new about the other mystery?"

"Nothing. I'm sure we'll get an update soon from Stephanie or the police. I've heard a lot of rumors but nothing substantial."

"Thanks for perking me up, Lupe. It helps to keep perspective."

Lupe laughed. "Perspective? In my experience, something good always seems to come out of most situations. Did I tell you we're being considered for a $75,000 grant because the organization that was supposed to get the funding couldn't do the project they applied for?"

"That's fabulous for us. Not so good for the other organization."

"Yep. I feel sorry for them. It's always tempting to bite off more than you can handle. But my point is that everything usually works out in the end."

"From your lips…"

Lupe stopped by Krisha's desk to talk about the planned appeal. Krisha loved data and enjoyed researching the various donor groups.

"Lupe, I've pulled a list of LYBUNTS and SYBUNTS that we can target and sorted the groups by giving levels." LYBUNT meant donors who had given *Last Year but Unfortunately Not This Year*, and SYBUNTS represented *Some Year but Unfortunately Not This Year*. Lupe knew it was at least five times harder to gain a new donor than to keep an existing one, so she and her team worked very hard to stay in touch with the donors whether they were being solicited or not. The LYBUNT and SYBUNT groups still received regular communications of programs and events taking place at the Museum and letters from Stephanie about future plans.

The summer appeal was for general operating support, which was the most challenging source of revenue to attract. Her department had made a conscious decision to go green and limit the number of physical mail campaigns, so this would be an online campaign for the great majority of donors. Lupe knew from her research that a particular demographic responded well to actual newsletters and mailings, and so she kept that group appeased whenever possible.

Another challenge was to ensure that donors were householded, meaning spouses and significant others were not spammed with numerous requests to every email in their record. Whenever possible, Lupe ensured couples were cc'd and not sent a mass email from their electronic direct mail platform.

Lupe smiled. "The case of the disappearing donor, eh?"

Krisha laughed. "Yes, sometimes we have notes that the individual has moved away from the area or that the initial gift was 'in honor of' or 'in memory of,' but often we don't have any idea what happened to these people.

"Do you know what the average click-through rate was for the last campaign?"

"We've been lucky. The open rate was about 14% which is better than the national average. Remember, we personalized the emails? The click-through was around 2.5%," Krisha replied.

"And the average online gift was $120 or $10 per month. Not bad. How were the unsubscribes?"

"It's low. And it seems mostly to be those people who moved or passed away. I don't remember exactly, but I think the last campaign was something like .18%."

"Great. I'll get to work with Marcus on the content. It's actually been great covering for the marketing director these past few months.

I haven't had to go to battle to get our fundraising emails out. Between marketing and education emails, our members hear from us a lot!"

Before chatting with Marcus, Lupe felt the need to take a short walk. Sometimes, before creative projects like crafting compelling case studies, she relaxed her mind by taking a quick walk around the neighborhood.

It was a lovely June day, and the sky shimmered blue. Lupe felt it was the kind of day when the East Village looked its best, full of history and hope. Looking around, she saw students making their way to the ever-expanding NYU campus. The New York Street scene provided lively entertainment. The tenements of this part of the city might be home to elderly immigrants or tech millionaires. Young families ambled along to the park side-by-side with edgy fashionistas. Lupe loved all the small shops and ethnic restaurants -- some long-established icons and others that just popped up.

Rounding the corner, she saw Ian, still wearing his carrot costume. He was coming out of a small middle eastern café stuffing a huge gyro pita into his mouth, morsels of tender marinated lamb flying to the ground.

"Ian!" She reprimanded. "Would you at least try to eat green when you are representing the Museum?"

"Yeah, Lupe," he responded after wiping garlic-scented sauce from his face with the back of his paw. "But you gotta understand, I'm a growing boy!"

Lupe suppressed a laugh. It was impossible not to like this irrepressible young man.

"I forgot to tell you. That FBI guy called. Agent Reyes. He wants you to call him back. I put a note on your desk with his number."

"Ok, thanks, and can you maybe try falafel next time? It's really filling too."

***

Lupe closed the door to her office, found the note with Agent Reyes's number on it, and called the detective. He answered on the second ring.

"Reyes."

"Hi, it's Lupe Reinowski, returning your call."

'Yes. Thanks for calling. I wanted to let you know that we located Tessa Hunt's brother and confirmed he has an alibi for the time of the crime."

"That's a relief. I knew Tessa couldn't have anything to do with this incident."

"She could still be involved, but we don't happen to think it's likely. We are pursuing some other leads." Lupe wondered if these included Mimi St. John and Firoze Shah but didn't want to ask.

"And what about me?" She asked with what she hoped sounded like a bit of jest in her voice. "Do you think I took the paintings for my Uncle Gus to give him some inspiration?"

"We never really put much credence to that theory, but we have to explore every option no matter how incredible it might seem."

"I'm glad to hear it. I don't look good in orange."

Reyes laughed. "I wish more people thought like you. There would probably be fewer crimes."

"I'm not so sure about that. But thank you for letting me know about Tessa. She's such a good friend and an important member of my team."

"We finished our meeting with her a few minutes ago, and she should be back from the precinct shortly. One more thing, not related to the inquiry?"

"Yes, Special Agent?"

"I don't know how you would feel about it. But once this is all over, I wonder if you would like to have dinner?"

Lupe's spirits soared. She would indeed like to have dinner with the handsome investigator. She started mentally assessing her wardrobe. She and Alice had found a treasure trove of vintage chic dresses at 10 Foot Single in Williamsburg. The pink Pucci style maxi dress, or maybe the geometric mini that made her legs look long. Lupe lost herself in images of an alfresco dinner in a charming little Italian restaurant. *Yes, I do like Montepulciano. You choose a nice bottle.* She envisioned herself gazing into the detective's green eyes. Their hands would touch. Perhaps they would share a strand of spaghetti ala "Lady and the Tramp." It wouldn't matter that they had garlic because they both would have it on their breath.

Reyes cleared his throat. "Um. I'm sorry. I don't want you to get the idea that I'm…."

"Oh, no!" Lupe came back to Earth. "That would be lovely," she replied. "I would like that."

"Great! Thanks. Hopefully, we'll get this wrapped up soon."

Ending the call, Lupe spun around in her chair, humming. At that moment, there was a knock at her door.

"Come in!" Lupe sang out.

Tessa entered, looking despondent.

"May I talk to you in private?" Tessa asked as she closed the door behind her. Lupe groaned inwardly. When a staffer asked her that question, it usually meant they wanted to resign. Lupe had just gotten her team trained up and working well together. She didn't want to have another job search.

"Sit down, Tessa. I know things have been tough for you lately. Is that what you want to talk about?"

"Yes. You heard about my brother, Germain? It's all over the building, and I'm so embarrassed. The police say he's got an alibi for the time of the theft, but now everyone knows all about my background. It isn't easy having a brother like mine. That's why I never talk about it. But now everyone will think that somehow, I'm involved. I think I need to resign and go somewhere else where I can get a fresh start. Maybe even leave New York City." Tessa started to cry softly.

Lupe grabbed the box of tissues on her desk and handed them to the young assistant.

"Tessa, this will pass over. Soon nobody will think about it at all. I know it's hard. But we all support you. I will have your back, and so will the rest of the team. If you want, we can even have a team meeting to talk about it."

Tessa wiped her eyes, leaving a streak of black mascara on either side of her face. She looked up and smiled tearfully.

"I like it here and want to stay. Do you think people will forget? Or will they always think of me as the sister of an ex-con?"

"I know how I feel about it, Tessa, and I've told the police this and the senior leadership. You are an essential member of our organization. You're hard-working, you know your job, and you're learning fast. I think that if you leave, you're going to come across this problem again, and it's better to face it down. My mother always said, 'that which doesn't kill you makes you stronger.'"

"Do you really think that's true? Thank you, Lupe." Tessa started sniffling again, now wiping her lipstick on her cheek.

Lupe hugged her and said, "We'll have a quick team meeting but let's take care of your face first."

Tessa looked surprised and then saw the blackened wet tissue in her hand. "Oh, I must look like a clown!" She exclaimed.

"No worries, look in my emergency drawer. We can fix you right up." Lupe's emergency drawer was legendary. Extra pairs of hose, ramen noodles, snack bars, candy, feminine products, stain remover, spare change, safety pins, a sewing kit, homeopathic cold medication, hair products, makeup, a small flask of brandy, and even a hot glue gun. Lupe felt prepared for almost any daily emergency. Tessa quickly refreshed her makeup, and she and Lupe left the office to gather the team.

As they were leaving, Krisha entered. "Remember how you were joking about the case of the disappearing donor?"

"Yeah," said Lupe

"Well, you'll never believe it, but Marla Howes is missing. I just got a Tweet. It's on all the news channels.

Chair of the Docents committee and the Legacy Society, Marla was a longtime donor and member. In her 80s, she was beloved by all. Why and how would she go missing?

Chapter 7
Even in a Crisis, Plan your Work and Work your Plan

"Marla?" Lupe asked incredulously. "What happened?"

"No one knows for sure, but her housekeeper came into her apartment this morning after her day off and found the place ransacked and Marla missing. They think it's a kidnapping."

"Poor Marla. This is dreadful." Tessa said, forgetting her problems in her concern for the older woman.

"Mary, protect her." Lupe turned her eyes skyward in a quick prayer. "This is scary. I wonder if there is any connection to the theft." Lupe also wondered why Agent Reyes hadn't mentioned Marla's kidnapping.

Lupe thought about Marla Howes's brownstone on the Upper Eastside. Marla elegantly decorated it with a lifetime's collection of antique bric-a-brac, china, sculpture, and textiles. Her first husband had been in the diplomatic corps, and his work took them worldwide. Marla had a keen eye, and her apartment reflected her discerning taste. Balinese coffee tables, vegetable-dyed silk Persian carpets, and breezy curtains made from colorful sarees came together in an eclectic, visually stunning environment. Perhaps the most exciting pairing was the 17th-century rustic trestle table from a monastery in the Pyrenees that Marla had matched with a set of Francois and Sido

Thevenin contemporary dining chairs. It was no surprise that Marla's home was regularly featured in design magazines.

Lupe also remembered a conversation with Marla on the evening of the theft. Marla had hosted a select group of donors for a salon. These events were the brainchild of Jane Mehra to cultivate and steward major gift donors. The evening had been a success with a visiting curator from the Musee Quai Branly-Jacques Chirac. Roselle Clotier gave an engaging talk on the use of calabashes and dried gourds in indigenous African art. A number of the prospects expressed an interest in supporting the Museum of Vegetable Culture's education programs and expanding the permanent collection. Stephanie and Lupe made plans to follow up with each other after the event. Among the group were Ingrid and Pietro San Sebastian, Stacy and Ralph Leibman, Allan Fisker, and Firoze Shah.

Marla had been almost shamefaced when she took Lupe to the side of the room. Lupe remembered how the silver-haired woman quietly told Lupe that two 18th Century snuff boxes had gone missing.

"I can't imagine it was one of the guests, but I have asked my housekeeper, and I trust her implicitly."

"Oh dear," said Lupe. "I can't think who would do such a thing. The guests were all carefully vetted. No one would need to steal. How would you like to proceed, Marla?"

"I don't know. I don't want to press charges. I just want the snuff boxes back. You may think it silly since I have so many in my collection, but my husband Jules gave them to me on our anniversary each year. It became a bit of a joke between us. Then when I married Arthur, he continued the tradition. I've outlived two husbands, and now I enjoy living with my memories. It is nice to pick up an object and remember the occasion when it was given to me."

"Of course, I understand, Marla, and I can tell you that I am very saddened that this has happened. Would you mind if I bring this to Stephanie's attention? Together she and I can do some discrete questioning?"

"As long as she doesn't make a big scene. I value my privacy and don't want to have any publicity."

"Certainly," Lupe promised.

"For this evening, my dear, let's forget about it. Perhaps I mislaid them after all. That would be embarrassing."

Lupe chided herself. How could she forget that conversation? She excused herself from her staff and rushed back to her office and called Agent Reyes.

Receiving the agent's voice mail, Lupe left a detailed message of the conversation. Frustrated, she hung up the phone and sat for a moment at her desk.

She found it hard to concentrate with all the excitement. Somehow carrying out her daily assignments seemed to take second place in her concern for Marla.

She fervently prayed no harm had come to the elderly woman. Marla always struck her strong physically, but there was no getting past the fact that she was in her 80s and bound to be a bit frail. *What if the ordeal caused her to have a heart attack or stroke? What if they weren't giving her food or her daily pills?* Lupe tried not to think about the dire possibilities.

Leaving her office, she found her staff in an uproar. Stiffening her leadership spine, she spoke loudly and determinedly. "Ok, my office, now."

Paul, Marcus, Tessa, Krisha, Ariel, and Ian gathered in her already overcrowded office, establishing themselves wherever they could find a perch.

Lupe spoke. "I know this latest news is very troubling. We have to hope for the best and that nothing has happened to Marla Howes. I know it's challenging to work on mundane matters with all that's going on, but we have a job to do. Here's what I think will be best. I'd like you all to take thirty minutes and get to a stopping point on whatever you're working on. Then we'll step out to Thompkins Square Park, review our fiscal year-end goals, and start planning for next year.

I know it seems like yesterday, but we will have to work on the budget and fundraising goals right after the gala. So, we can take a couple of hours this afternoon to look over the various drivers. It will be good to clear our heads.

We'll put all calls through to our voice mail and check in every hour."

"Sounds good, chief," said Paul. "My eyes are going a bit cross-eyed from the Harkney Foundation application."

Everyone nodded in agreement.

"And I'd like to say a few words about Tessa. She is a trusted and valued member of our team, just as you all are. I don't think I have to tell you, but I will not tolerate any rumors about her involvement in the thefts. If you hear anyone say anything disparaging, stick up for her and if it's a senior person or you feel awkward in any way, come to me. We have each other's backs. This is how a team works together."

Lupe looked over at Tessa, who had started crying again. The others gathered around to show their support. Fortunately, the mascara from the emergency drawer was waterproof.

***

An hour later, the team had sprawled on a motley assortment of old tablecloths and sun blankets in the corner of Thompkins Square Park. Lupe ordered pizza for the team from Numero 28, a Neapolitan-style place in the neighborhood. Before leaving the office, she asked Ariel to grab two bottles of very vin ordinaire from the wine cupboard. The crew relaxed and enjoyed the sunny day before the conversation turned to work matters.

"I probably don't say it enough, but I appreciate all your hard work. Contributed income accounts for over 60% of the Museum's budget, and it is through your efforts that we can meet our mission to promote healthy vegetable-forward living throughout the city. Your work changes lives. Children are healthier, families are making better food choices, and we're helping the environment by encouraging less meat consumption." Lupe didn't even meet Ian's eyes.

"I know it may seem like a drag that we work hard all year to meet our fundraising and outreach goals only to raise the goals the following year. And I certainly don't want us to tear our hair out trying to make unrealistic projections. I'd like for us to brainstorm a bit on increasing our fundraising in the next fiscal year efficiently and effectively. I know we won't work everything out today, but I'd like us to get the ball rolling and continue to develop the plan over the coming month."

Paul spoke first. "I know we have to have the government grants, but they do take a lot of time, and sometimes the grant amounts don't seem to merit the effort. I'm not trying to shift work away, but I wonder if we should cut back on those and work instead on major gift donors?"

"I agree with you that these proposals take a lot of time and have many reporting requirements. However, they do also give us increased visibility and cache. Our top donors see the government funding as a 'seal of approval,' so to speak," Lupe replied.

"Ah, well. You don't ask, you don't get," Paul said.

Lupe laughed. "Maybe we can get you some help during crunch time."

"I'm always willing to help," said Tessa. Paul smiled. A seasoned development professional, Paul had worked with countless development assistants. Lupe knew he was tired of training people only to have them leave for better jobs or return to graduate school. It was a common challenge in all nonprofits.

Lupe thought for a moment. "Remember as we do this planning to carve out time for professional development. I always keep money in the budget for conferences, and we have the Association of Fundraising Professional membership. I want you all to have whatever resources you need. Within reason. No one is going to Aruba."

The team laughed. This was Lupe's favorite remark. Whenever someone worried about soliciting donors, she always said, "you're raising money for a good cause. It's not like you're taking the money to go to Aruba."

Ariel spoke. "It's been great working with Mimi St. John's on the gala. She's really sharp at negotiating discounts. I think we'll be able to keep the direct cost to raise a dollar down to 35 cents."

"Super," said Lupe. Special events were always challenging. Unless underwriters were secured to cover the expenses – food and beverage, venue, entertainment, decorations – costs could quickly spiral out of control. Lupe liked to report the net income as the event goal but often lost in that argument to her superiors, who liked to show off the much higher gross income. Lupe's solution was to hold the one major event, the gala, each year and have hosts cover the costs for the smaller salons, breakfast events, and receptions.

"I've gotten a lot of great ideas from Mimi and will put them to use for our other functions, including the membership evenings."

"Excellent," said Lupe, glad Ariel was learning from the socialite.

Marcus cleared his throat. The development team had adopted him while the search went on for a new director of marketing.

"It's been fascinating learning more about what you all do. I have to admit it was always a bit mysterious. Sometimes you are all glammed up for a party, or you're out of the office. Now I understand that so much of what you do has to happen away from the office. I'm interested in learning more."

"I'm always happy to talk about what I do," said Paul, who, with over 25 years' experience, was the most senior of the crew. "The grant writing and proposals take about half of my time, but the part I really enjoy is the prospect research work."

"Isn't that like spying?" Marcus asked.

Lupe and Paul exchanged glances. "The majority of our gifts come from about 23% of our donors. We have to discreetly research their backgrounds to know if their interests are aligned with our mission and if they have the capacity to make a more significant gift," said Lupe.

"And we need to be sure we have a good idea about how much to ask them for so we don't low-ball the ask or go beyond their means. It's part art-part science. Data plays a big role in what we do, "added Paul.

"It's sensitive information, so we're cautious about who we share it with and how it's used. Paul makes a profile of the prospect and all our major gift donors. It's got biographical data and information about their giving history to both our organization and other similar groups."

"How do you find this out?" Marcus asked.

"Believe it or not, the first step is simply to Google the person. There is a lot of public information out there. I also have a variety of subscription-based services I use," Paul replied.

"And every three years or so, we pay to run the whole database through a wealth engine to make sure there are no hidden gems," added Krisha. "That's my favorite part of the job. The only problem is people who have very common names. Once I thought one of our members was a billionaire real estate mogul when it turned out he was a dentist."

"Speaking of profiles, Paul. I know you have been tied up with proposals, but how are you coming with updating the profiles on Stephanie's portfolio of donors and prospects?" asked Lupe.

"I should be able to finish those up next week. If you have time Marcus, I can give you a short tutorial. I had planned to show Tessa so you can join her."

"Just remember, whatever you find out should not be talked about at the water cooler. We must stay professional and respect the privacy of the individuals."

"Yes," agreed Krisha. "Donors have the right to review their records, so we are very careful how we word any information or contacts."

Lupe thought back to her last organization and a prospect who was high on their target list until the Securities and Exchange Commission prosecuted him for insider trading. Lupe kept the donor record clear of the information, merely changing the record notes to "not a major gift prospect at this time."

The team returned to the office feeling refreshed and reenergized with many ideas for increasing fundraising, especially in the burgeoning online giving area. When she checked her voice mail, Lupe was not surprised to find many messages from donors and members wanting to gossip about Marla Howes's disappearance and the thefts. Were they connected?

Sipping a cup of green tea, for Lupe had made a point of not having coffee after 3:00 pm, Lupe's cell phone rang. She recognized the number as Agent Reyes's.

"Hi, Agent Reyes. Thanks for calling me back. Was that information helpful to you?"

"Please call me Josh. And yes, I need a list of all the guests at Marla Howes on the night in question. Would you email that to me with their contact details?"

"I'll get it to you right away. Do you have any updates you can share?"

"We're pretty sure it was a man who broke into Marla's brownstone. The camera caught him, but he was wearing a hoodie and a balaclava so that we couldn't see his face. He also had on gloves, so he didn't leave fingerprints. It happened around midnight, and the camera caught the perpetrator leaving with Marla. They walked together out of the view of the camera. We're gathering whatever CCTV we can find to see if we can locate their path."

"This is so scary. We all hope Marla is ok."

"She seemed to be ok when she walked away, and she wasn't physically pushed."

Lupe thought. "Did he take anything from the house?"

"That's the weird part. According to the housekeeper, while the living room was messy, nothing of value was taken."

Ending the call, Lupe asked Tessa for the salon guest list with contact details. Tessa promptly supplied the data, which Lupe reviewed.

1. Stacy and Ralph Leibman

2. Allan Fisker

3. Ingrid and Pietro San Sebastian

4. Tang Liuqin and Sheila Denham

5. Yigor and Natasia Ilina

6. Veronica MacDonald

7. Mary Montgomery Van Clausen

8. Firoze and Raina Shah

9. Stephanie James-Howard

10. Roselle Clotier of the Musee Quai Branly-Jacques Chirac.

Lupe immediately eliminated Stephanie, Mary Montgomery, and Roselle Clotier. Operating on the assumption that the theft was somehow connected to Marla's kidnapping, she also crossed off Tang Liuqin, Sheila Denham, the Ilinas, and Ian's grandmother, Veronica MacDonald. Raina Shah also had not been in attendance on the night of the theft.

That left her with Stacy and Ralph Leibman, Ingrid and Pietro San Sebastian, Firoze Shah, and Allan Fisker. Upon reflection, she placed Stephanie and Mary Montgomery's names back on the list, although she considered it unlikely that either of the women was involved in the theft. *Why would Mary Montgomery take the paintings? Was her daughter, Charlotte, somehow involved? And Stephanie had been so upset about the loss. Could that merely be a cover? Although the detective said a man had been seen entering Marla Howe's home, could he be an accomplice?*

What was the connection between the thefts of the paintings and the disappearance of the bejeweled snuff boxes from Marla's home? And why was she kidnapped? Had Marla discovered who the thief was only to be silenced?

Lupe shuddered at the thought that the thefts could turn to murder. Without delaying further, she emailed the complete list to Josh Reyes. Hopefully, he and his team could uncover the miscreants before anything happened to Marla.

Lupe's phone rang. Charlotte said that Stephanie wanted to see her right away regarding Ingrid San Sebastian's gift agreement. Lupe grabbed a copy of the draft document and climbed the flight of stairs to the roof garden to meet her.

The garden was gorgeous, with the herbs flourishing and the squash plants beginning to flower. Ralph Leibman looked the quintessential gentleman farmer in a pair of worn khakis, chamois shirt, boots, and straw hat. He looked up and smiled as Lupe walked over to the row of tomatoes he was staking.

"The crops look marvelous, Ralph. You have a green thumb."

"Thanks, Lupe. I enjoy getting outdoors. My doc says it does me good." Lupe remembered that Ralph had taken early retirement due to a chronic heart ailment. She was glad he had found an outlet for his energies that helped moderate his condition.

"By the way," he continued. "I heard about Marla. It's terrible. Do you think it has anything to do with the missing Manets?"

"The police are investigating that possibility and asked me to send a list of those who were in attendance at the salon two weeks ago."

"Oh, I guess they will be asking us all questions." He looked concerned.

"Yes, but don't worry. Just tell them what you remember of both nights."

He still looked worried, his face turning pale. Did Ralph Leibman have something to hide?

Chapter 8
Managing Up Down, and Sideways

Lupe entered Stephanie's glass-enclosed offices and saw that Charlotte was not at her desk. Peering around the corner, she saw Stephanie's back and the Executive Director holding her iPhone to her ear. Not wishing to interrupt the conversation, Lupe stepped back into the waiting area. While she waited, she reviewed the materials on the marble-topped coffee table -- last year's annual report, invitations to the gala "Che Bella Luna" honoring Camillo Aggio, and a brochure of summer activities at the Museum. Thumbing through the program guide, Lupe was pleased to see Audry's summer camp program would be starting in a few weeks. The Museum was always at its liveliest during the summer months, with middle schoolers helping in the garden and learning about horticulture, nutrition, cooking, and art. Hearing Stephanie's raised voice, Lupe tried to avoid overhearing her remarks.

"I told you, I only deal with principals, so if you can get me a meeting with him, I'll consider it. Otherwise, you are wasting my time. There is a lot at stake here. Not just the money but the whole situation," Stephanie paused and then evidently replied. "Yes, let me know. Don't keep me waiting. I can always go to someone else. You have until the night of the gala." Another pause, and Stephanie added a curt good-bye.

What was that about? Lupe wondered.

Pausing briefly and then taking a tentative step forward, Lupe knocked on Stephanie's door. Stephanie looked up and waved her into the room. "Right, let's go over the gift agreement for Ingrid," Stephanie said.

Lupe handed her a copy of the contract and sat down with her folio. Pen in hand, Lupe prepared to make edits.

"Is the name correct, Stephanie? The Ingrid Nillson Charitable Trust?"

"No. This time Ingrid wants the gift to mention Pietro directly, so it should be Ingrid and Pietro San Sebastian."

"OK, I'll change it. The gift will cover the naming of the two classrooms for a period of ten years, with the option to renew at the end of that time. The rest of the agreement is standard. There is the usual contingency 'Bad Boy' clause in the unlikely event that their reputations are damaging to the Museum."

"Fine, fine," Stephanie nodded absently. "Ingrid wants to make the gift in one payment using Cryptocurrency. That will be our first major gift in that mode."

"Yes, but I'll talk to Pierre, and we'll get it all arranged as quickly as possible. Fortunately, the Finance Committee set an addendum to the gift acceptance policy to accept Cryptocurrency. We'll handle it like a security and mitigate the volatility as much as possible."

"Good. The board has to approve the gift, but I don't see any issues with that. Just proforma, get me an updated profile for Ingrid and Pietro to share with the board. We can have an 'action without a meeting' and take care of this."

"Paul is working on updating profiles for all the donors and prospects in your portfolio, but I'll get him to finish the San Sebastian's first."

"Fine. And speaking about your team. I still want Tessa fired. Keep a paper trail on her, so we have cause."

"Stephanie. Tessa is a great worker. She is always willing to go the extra mile, and it would be unfair to fire her over something she has no control over. And what about the Hunts? They have been members for a long time and have a lot of connections with the board. Shouldn't we just let this pass?

"Where there is smoke, there is fire, and I'm sure the Board will support me. If you don't gather the details, I'll get Charlotte on it."

"Tell you what, I'll start a paper trail, but I can't promise there will be anything negative." Lupe prayed the matter would die down and Stephanie would forget about Tessa Hunt.

"Do it, Lupe," Stephanie ordered, effectively ending the meeting. "Charlotte!" The Executive Director shouted in a voice that completely belied her upper-class breeding.

Back at her desk, Charlotte dropped three file folders, a cup of coffee, and her eyeglasses as she rushed past Lupe into Stephanie's office.

Poor terrorized Charlotte, Lupe thought. She could just picture the shy assistant attempting to stalk Tessa. She'd be as subtle as a Sherman tank coming through the lobby.

Back in the Development offices, Lupe stopped by Paul's desk. "I know we just talked about the profiles today, but would you prioritize getting the San Sebastian's updated?" Lupe asked.

"Sure, it's about as finished as it can be. Take a look at the most recent version in the drive."

"Thanks. And what do you think about having Marcus help out on the night of the gala?"

"He'd be great coordinating the audio/visual crew. I think it will be a good experience for him."

"Wonderful. I'll tell Ariel to put him on the staff list. Talk to him about renting a tux."

"I bought a new one on sale at Macy's because it was actually less expensive than renting. I'll tell him about it."

At her desk, Lupe pulled up the profile on Ingrid and Pietro San Sebastian. Much of the information about Ingrid remained the same. Ingrid San Sebastian nee Nillson was the heir to her family's energy company. The Nillson's had made a bet on alternative energy long before it was popular and had shifted their efforts to renewable sources throughout Scandinavia. Ingrid remained chair of Nillson Energy but was not involved in its day-to-day operations, preferring to make her home in a large apartment on Fifth Avenue overlooking Central Park. Her marriage to Pietro was a first, although she shared the company of many high-profile celebrities and politicians over the years.

Ingrid had met Pietro at one of his gallery showings. Thirty years old, Pietro San Sebastian had a reputation for fast living and a vivid, energetic painting style that matched his playboy lifestyle. At sixty, Ingrid donned white lace for a star-studded wedding in her family home, Eidunn Castle in Sweden. Widely covered in the tabloids, the press was not kind about the May-December match.

Mary Montgomery Von Clausen introduced Ingrid to the Museum. The two had attended the same Swiss boarding school and had remained close friends.

The profile went on to highlight prior gifts Ingrid had made to the Museum and other organizations. The most significant gift on record was a six-figure contribution to a contemporary art museum in Stockholm. Ingrid had also been involved with high-profile art institutions in New York and London. Oddly, she seemed to have severed her connection with a number of them, focusing her energies instead on promoting Pietro's work.

Lupe wondered if Ingrid had tried to push an exhibition of Pietro's work at one of the major institutions only to be rebuffed.

Of Pietro San Sebastian, there was no record of any philanthropy or volunteerism. The young artist seemed to focus solely on nightlife and working as little as possible.

He had taken to his role as regent to Ingrid with aplomb, enjoying a dazzling social life and regal comforts.

Pietro was born Pedro Sebastian Velez in Spain, but his family had immigrated to the United States when he was a child. He grew up in Miami, where his father had established a thriving import-export business. While his father wanted him to take over the family business, Pietro's teachers encouraged him to study art. He, therefore, moved to New York in his teens and became a student at Pratt Institute before spending semesters in Madrid and Paris. Early in his career he decided to change his name to Pietro San Sebastian.

A bit thin about Pietro, Lupe thought. She still wondered what motivated Ingrid to make the jump from a six-figure gift to a million-dollar contribution. It seemed out of character and raised Lupe's antennae.

Proofing the record carefully, she saved it and emailed it to Stephanie.

An alarm went off on her phone to notify her that the gala committee meeting would be starting in half an hour in the library. Lupe called Ariel and asked her to bring in the list of guests, event totals, expense list, and draft menu. Ariel replied that she had these ready and would be there in a moment.

While waiting for Ariel, Lupe took a moment to go through her emails. Leslie Palmieri of the Meyers Foundation notified her that the board had approved the $75,000 grant for education and community outreach. Lupe made a note to call her and thank her after the meeting. Audrey had sent a message asking if Lupe could make time to discuss program underwriting opportunities. Paul had sent his cartoon of the day, a head of lettuce telling a cabbage to "leaf me alone." And Women in Development were having their monthly luncheon with Lupe's mentor Theresa Hamilton as guest speaker. Lupe marked the email so she would remember to buy a table.

Ariel entered, and Lupe looked up and smiled. "How are we coming along?"

"If my projections are right, we'll exceed our goal and maybe even reach our stretch goal. I think we will raise about $850,000."

"And net?"

"Net about $550,000."

"OK. That's great. What about the menu? How does it look?"

"Aggi did a fantastic job. It's fresh yet elegant. I think everyone will be pleased."

Ariel handed Lupe a printed draft.

Lupe read. Antipasti: fresh heirloom tomato tart with cashew cream. Primi: asparagus and morel Acquerello risotto with Nova

Domus wine. Secondi: grilled vegetable Napoleons with fresh burrata and a roasted red pepper coulis.

"Vegan versions are available for both the first and second courses," Ariel added.

"Sounds delicious, but I may skip the main meal and just eat dessert. This sounds decadent." The chef had proposed a trio of Italian desserts: Torrone nougat semifreddo, the rich ice-cream-like delicacy. Almond cake with strawberries and Torta Setteveli or seven veil cake. This was layers of chocolate sponge, hazelnut Bavarian cream, praline crunch, and chocolate mousse.

"I know. I'll have to wear a stretchy dress!" Ariel exclaimed. "And with coffee, they will serve chocolate pistachio biscotti, ricciarelli, and other Italian cookie bites.

Aggi is also finalizing the list of appetizers, both vegetarian and vegan, and of course, Cipriani's will be serving Bellinis along with a full open bar." The special events manager added.

"This looks marvelous. Is there anything you need to tell me before the meeting?

"We had a slight hiccup with the entertainment, but we've secured a different dance troupe for the Soundsuits."

Nick Cave's Soundsuits were fantastically constructed outfits both colorful and engaging. The artist had crafted vegetable theme suits for the evening, and dancers would wear these while performing numbers varying from hip hop to Italian folk dances.

"And I spoke to Kaba Tadashi, and he has confirmed he'll emcee," said Lupe.

"Oh, I can't wait to see him again. He's such fun." Since becoming a television star, Kaba's schedule had become demanding, but he always made time for the annual event.

"Tessa's set up the library with coffee and nibbles. I'm going to go down now and make sure there is nothing else that needs attending to."

"I'll join you."

Lupe and Ariel made their way to the library, which retained the former factory's original wood beams and exposed brick. Lupe enjoyed spending time in the room with its large, curved windows and old-fashioned green glass lampshades. Wood and metal industrial modern tables and chairs occupied the center of the large rectangular room, and comfortable shabby chic chairs and sofas surrounded the walls between the bookshelves. In one corner was the children's reading nook with colorful cushions, books, and board games.

Three tables had been pushed together for the board meeting, and Lupe smelled the aroma of fresh coffee that had been set up on another table. She gratefully poured herself a cup with a mild admonishment that it was after 3:00 and she really should be having green tea. Oh well, she thought. *I probably won't sleep well tonight anyway.*

The committee chair, Mimi St. John, was the first to arrive, a vision in a pastel silk shift dress. Mimi was quickly followed by the other committee members, including Ian's grandmother Veronica MacDonald, Tilda Wright, a wealthy realtor, and the Grande dame of all, Dorothy Montag. Mrs. Montag ruled the gala decorations since she paid for the flower arrangements and lighting each year.

The ladies all spoke excitedly about Marla's disappearance. "No one is safe anymore," said Tilda Wright, whom Lupe knew practiced Krav Maga and would probably cause more damage to any attacker than visa-versa.

"I saw on NY1 that she just let the kidnapper into her house. It must have been someone she knew," added Mrs. MacDonald. "But I wouldn't let anyone into my house that late in the evening unless it was a dire emergency."

The group tittered nervously, expounding on various possibilities. What kind of ransom were the kidnappers asking? Where could she possibly be held? Was the perpetrator someone from Marla's past, or was she somehow connected to the mob?

Lupe eyed Mimi St. John's, who called the meeting to order. "First to business ladies, and then we can talk all about the decorations and entertainment. You'll see from the report Ariel passed out that we should exceed our goal. Thank you all for your marvelous work selling tables for the evening. Camillo Aggio was a very popular choice for the honoree.

Lupe tells me we are only missing the names from three tables, so Veronica, if you would please call Sally Hepworth and ask who she's planning to bring, and Tilda, we'll need the names of the guests from your firm's table. Lupe, it's fine to call over to Peter Nussman at my bank to get their names. Are all the invoices for the table purchases paid?"

"We still have a few outstanding, but I will make sure they are reminded to pay for the table before the night of the event," said Lupe.

"And let me know if you have any trouble. I don't like deadbeats," Mimi responded, her charming Savannah lilt becoming a shade terse. "Good. Now that that's out of the way, we can concentrate on planning a magnificent party. As you see, our dear Aggi has created a splendid meal for us. And we will have a tasting of the proposed wines at my home next Tuesday evening. When will we have the final list of canapes, Ariel?"

"Aggi promised them to me by Wednesday at the latest."

"And I will sit down with Jean Flamant at his studio to finalize the flower designs. As you know, I picture lavish Della Robbia type trailing compotes with a variety of seasonal flowers and vegetables. Can't you see it? Peonies, roses, and hydrangeas along with Japanese eggplant, baby artichokes, ornamental cabbages, rosemary, lavender, and ivy. It will be stunning.

At all the entrances, we'll have grapevines arranged alongside olive and lemon trees. I haven't decided yet whether we should just have fairy lights or go bolder with those Edison-type lights you sometimes see in outdoor bistros. I remember my husband Claude and I had the most romantic dinner al fresco on the Amalfi Coast. We had to take a motorboat from La Sireneuse to this absolutely magical restaurant only accessible by sea. They had lights like that." Mrs. Montag caught her breath, obviously intending to share more of her travel stories, when Mimi gently interrupted.

"This sounds so charming, Dorothy dear. We agreed we want elegance yet also a playful air; perhaps Jean can offer the best advice when thinking about the space considerations."

"Your vision sounds delightful, darling Dorothy," added Veronica MacDonald with only a faint hint of sarcasm. Lupe knew Ian's grandmother resented Dorothy Montag's commandeering of the flowers and lights at each year's gala. She had complained to Lupe bitterly, then begged the development director to keep the conversation confidential. Lupe was used to donors sharing all manner of confidences. She knew who was having plastic surgery, who was having an affair, and whose children were in rehab. While some of the stories were humorous, many were sad. It astonished her how much people were willing to share with her. *It's my pierogi face,* Lupe thought. *It looks so open.*

The conversation turned to the evening's program. During the cocktail hour, the silent auction items would all be arranged in an alcove near the bar. The canapes would be passed to eliminate the need for stationary food tables and leave more space for the auction.

112

A jazz trio from Julliard would play, and photos of the Museum's various programs would be shown on screens in the ballroom. The ceiling would be lit to look like stars and a full moon in keeping with the "Che Bella Luna" theme.

Speeches and Camillo Aggio's award would be kept to a minimum to allow the guests to enjoy the meal and the Soundsuit dance entertainment while allowing ample time for both the live and silent auctions. Once the bidding had concluded, Marty Vega's Banda di Ballo would play dance tunes, and after dinner drinks would be offered.

Ian entered the room in a flash of orange. Lupe closed her eyes. He was still dressed as Captain Carrot. "Hiya Grandma," he exclaimed, seeing his proud relation.

"Ian, what are you wearing?"

"Oh, it's my *Vegetable Soup* costume, Nana." The other ladies looked amused. "Sorry to interrupt your meeting, but Agent Reyes is here to see you, Lupe."

All eyes turned to Lupe. She felt a flush creep over her face. *You're not guilty of anything,* she reminded herself. *Why should you be worried? Yet, there was something about the Prada and Gucci-clad women that made her quake in her shoes.*

"Please excuse me and continue with your meeting. Once again, on behalf of all of us here at the Museum, we are so grateful to you for your hard work and dedication. I'm sure the evening will be a great

113

success." Lupe grabbed Ian and nearly ran from the room, leaving the committee eager to continue their gossip.

Chapter 9
A Good Fundraiser Knows When to Seek Outside Help

Lupe found Agent Reyes waiting for her in the lobby. His eyes twinkled as Ian stumbled past to get to the elevator.

"Hi, Agent Reyes. How can I help you?"

"Is there someplace we can talk in private?" Reyes asked.

"We can go up to my office or step outside if you'd prefer?"

He smiled, "Sometimes, the best privacy is a crowded New York Street."

The pair stepped outside into the cooling evening. Lupe realized how tired she was; it had been another long day. Not wishing the detective to see her fatigue, she pushed back her aching shoulders and widened her eyes.

"You look wiped out, Lupe."

Lupe let her shoulders sag back. "No keeping secrets from you. That's why you're the detective. Things have been busy around here. But I'm sure you've been running around too. Any updates on Marla Howes?"

"Yes, we have one lead. An Uber driver came forward saying he saw an older woman in a light blue dressing gown walking with a man dressed in a black hoodie and dark pants on the corner of Madison and

115

73rd Street. This was about 12:30 in the morning. He saw the two get into a black SUV but didn't notice the make. He didn't see the man's face but thought the older woman looked confused. He didn't report it because he thought she might have Alzheimer's, had wandered away, and was being returned home."

"Hmm., not too helpful. There are almost as many black SUVs in Manhattan as there are rats."

Reyes nodded in agreement. "We've had a number of people come forward with ransom demands, but we've followed them up, and they were all attention-seeking cranks. Everyone wants their fifteen minutes of fame."

"So sad, but true. Social media has exacerbated that problem. Must make your job much harder with everyone on Instagram and Tik-Tok."

"Everyone has a platform. Some of these people have sighted Mrs. Howe as far away as Beijing and Buenos Aires, still wearing her blue silk robe and slippers. My colleagues are involved with following up those leads, and I don't envy them."

"How can I help? Is there anything I can do?"

"Yes. You were present at Mrs. Howes's salon. Do you remember anything in particular about the evening?"

Sitting down on a bench, Lupe thought for a moment. "It was the usual kind of cultivation event. They have a sort of formula. Marla is an excellent hostess, and she had hired two waiters and a bartender for the evening. The waiters passed canapes and made sure everyone had drinks. We always try to make everyone feel relaxed.

After we socialized for about half an hour, Stephanie introduced Roselle Cloutier from the Quay Branly. Roselle presented for about forty-five minutes and then took questions. Marla then thanked everyone for coming and reminded them to support the Museum. Marla is the head of the Legacy society, so she spoke especially of her plans to leave a gift to MVC in her will."

"Did anything unusual happen? You said that after the event, Mrs. Howe found two valuable snuff boxes missing."

"Yes. I talked to Stacy and Ralph Leibman because I'm hoping to have Stephanie solicit them for a major underwriting gift soon. But I noticed Marla showed some of the guests the snuff boxes, some antique Chinese seals, and delicate figurines. They were in a glass vitrine. The lid flipped up at the top, and she had it open."

"Do you remember anyone paying special attention to the snuff boxes?"

Lupe reflected. "No, I'm afraid I was distracted. Ralph and I were petting Ingrid's dog Borgia, and I was concentrating on making sure the Leibmans would come to the opening reception. I wanted them to see the quality of our exhibitions. Ralph knows our work well, but Stacy is a newcomer to the Mission."

"What time did everyone leave?"

"The program was scheduled to end about 9:00 pm, and people did start leaving around then. If I remember correctly, Firoze and Raina Shah left early when the question and answer started. Firoze had an early flight to catch the next day. Tang Liuqin and Sheila Denham left with the Ilinas. I overheard their plans to have a late dinner nearby at Le Charlot. The Leibmans went at the same time as Mrs. MacDonald, and Stephanie and Mary Montgomery left with Roselle. They were going to have supper back at her hotel.

"What about Allan Fisker?" The detective asked, referring to the list. "When did he depart?"

Lupe smiled, bemused. "Allan didn't leave. He and Marla are a couple. I left before he did."

"I see. But Mr. Fisker wasn't there the night she was accosted." He added, "We are speaking with all the guests who were at Mrs. Howe's that evening but concentrating on those who were also at the reception the night the Manet paintings were stolen."

"So, you do think it's connected?" Lupe asked.

"Yes. We consider it a strong possibility. Perhaps Mrs. Howe saw something the night of the reception or remembered something that happened at the salon. The culprit didn't want her to come to us."

"But that means they may want to silence her permanently," Lupe said grimly,

"It's a possibility. Especially since we don't have any credible ransom requests."

"I should also tell you, Special Agent." Lupe began.

"Josh, please." He reminded her.

Lupe's eyes sparkled despite her fatigue. "Josh. Lately, we've had some thefts in our gift shop—some of the more valuable items. Silk scarves, silver chopstick rests—small, portable things. The cumulative loss is over $5,000 in retail value. Compared to the Manets and the snuff boxes, this may seem like a small amount, but it's a pattern. Our gift shop manager, Felicity Blacksmith, is distraught. She always accounts for some theft but nothing of this scale. We've put more staff in the gift shop to see if we can find the person or persons responsible."

"I'll speak to Ms. Blacksmith. We'll try to find out if anyone from the salon and reception has also recently spent a lot of time in the gift shop," Reyes said.

Lupe made a note to talk to Felicity herself. The detecting bug had bitten.

***

Home, at last, Lupe snuggled into comfortable, casual clothes. It was her turn to make dinner, and she felt decidedly low in energy. She wondered if she should treat her roommates to takeout or coax them

119

into eating an omelet and salad. Alice unlocked the door, also looking frazzled.

"You look like I feel," she said as she dropped her satchel on the floor. "The Board agreed to launch a capital campaign for renovating and expanding the clinic, but they haven't yet agreed to hire outside counsel." Alice slumped to the sofa. "I need to make a case to them that hiring a consultant is necessary and that I can't do a campaign alone. But I don't want to come across as too needy. I'm worried they'll want to hire someone who can run the department *and* handle a campaign."

"Don't be silly. They know what an asset you are. What's the campaign goal?"

"$25 million."

"Is that based on a feasibility study?"

"Of course not. That's just the amount budgeted for renovations. We raise about $1 million a year from our annual fund, and even if you triple that, we should probably be looking at a $3-5 million campaign," Alice sighed.

"Maybe not. That's why you need a solid feasibility study. I think that's where you should start. It will help the board set a realistic goal. The consultant will also advise on hiring a campaign manager. I would spend some time putting together a timeline and outlining how much time is involved. The more data you can show them about how a successful campaign is run, the better."

"I remember when I was with Whole Health. Our campaign was all-consuming, and I was only an associate then. We had extra campaign staff just for the purpose. I'm not looking forward to this."

"Relax, we'll find some data about average capital campaign staff sizes and what support is needed. I have a feeling they need a reality check. Once they see how much effort and focus is involved, they will be supportive. After all, they haven't renovated that building in forty years."

"It's a sight, that's for sure. I think our donors will get very excited once they see the improvement plans. And our families will love it."

Just then, Henry came home loudly singing, "I am the greatest of them all! I am so smart and handsome too!"

"Henry?! Sounds like you had a good day," Alice said.

"I am a genius! Mark Stein is coming to the showcase!"

"Who is Mark Stein?"

"Mark Stein is only the greatest casting director around. He specializes in representing the underrepresented. He gets great roles for people with disabilities. Did you know he represents Tom Howard?" Tom Howard was a popular British actor who, blind since birth, had a long-running detective series *Trust your Senses.*

"That's amazing, Henry!"

"I don't know if I should tell my students. They are already nervous enough. Yikes, I'm anxious for them. I feel like a hummingbird; I can't sit still. But I'm starving! What's for dinner?"

"I don't feel like cooking. How about going out to celebrate. On me! What are you in the mood for?" Lupe suggested.

"How about Ugly Baby," said Alice. Ugly Baby was a casual but absolutely delicious neighborhood Thai restaurant.

"Som Tom yummy!" crowed Henry. Green papaya salad was his favorite dish.

Over curries, spicy vegetables in glass noodles, and cold beer, the three talked about the mysteries. Lupe updated her roommates on her conversation with Agent Reyes, omitting his dinner invitation.

"As I thought, the police think there is a connection between the two thefts. I also told them about the small items going missing from the gift shop, but I'm not sure if that's related."

"I hope Mrs. Howes is safe. They say the odds of finding a kidnap victim alive diminishes greatly after the first twenty-four hours," said Alice nervously.

"Poor Allan Fisker must be beside himself. He and Marla started seeing each other socially last year after his wife died. The two are so well suited. It would be tragic if anything happens to her," added Lupe.

"Think positive," said, Henry. "The FBI is on the case. They know their stuff. I'm sure they will rescue Mrs. Howe. I have a good feeling about it."

"Here's hoping for the best," said Lupe raising her beer glass. The three toasted.

"So, what else have you learned?" asked Alice.

"Two things, I think, could be important. I was talking to Ralph Leibman, who was working in the garden. He seemed to get very nervous when I told him the police would speak to everyone at the salon and the reception. He looked decidedly anxious."

"I wonder why," said Henry. "I talked to him at the reception before it got busy while he was waiting for his wife to come. He seemed very nice. A quiet guy. He didn't strike me as a criminal type."

"Henry," admonished Alice, "There have been many 'criminal types' who look like your next-door neighbor. He could be guilty or trying to protect his wife, perhaps," mused Alice.

"Stacy just had her company listed on the stock exchange. You know, 'Tranquil-i-Tea?'" said Lupe.

"Oh, sure. The company is minting money with their new CBD products."

"Not just CBD," said Henry. "In the states where it's legal, they have some cannabis brands."

"Some people might raise an eyebrow, but if it's legal, why should Ralph be nervous?" noted Alice.

"Maybe it has nothing to do with his wife. Maybe it's something from his past. He did retire early. I understood it had to do with a heart condition, but maybe it was something else. I'll try to check it out tomorrow."

"You said you found out two things. What was the other?" Henry asked.

"Oh, listen up. And keep this among us. I was waiting to see Stephanie and overheard her having a conversation. It sounded very suspicious. She talked about wanting only to speak only to the decision-maker, and that money was involved. I didn't get a good vibe. There was something very sneaky about the call."

"Does she have any money troubles that you know about?" Alice questioned.

"I'm not sure. She's divorced and has custody of her two sons. Stephanie lives in a large apartment on Central Park West, and her boys attend private school. She probably gets child support, but I don't know about maintenance. And you know how expensive private school can be."

"What does her ex-husband do?" Asked Henry.

"Andrew Howard is an architect. His firm is Howard-Andretti, and he's well-respected. He focuses on large office and apartment buildings. Right now, Howard-Andretti's designing a luxury building in Hong Kong. It's supposed to be one of the most expensive ever constructed there. And that's saying something."

"Yes, my mother says instead of selling apartments by the square foot, in Hong Kong, they sell them by the square inch. It's that expensive." Henry noted.

"And we thought our rent was high." Alice sighed.

"If Howard is that famous, he probably left her with enough of the green stuff. She probably doesn't have money troubles," Henry conjectured.

"Unless he's over-extended?" Lupe mused. "But Stephanie comes from an affluent family, so she may not even need to rely on him. It is interesting, though. I'll keep my ears open."

Alice squealed, "Oooh, I almost forgot! I hired Ben Terrance to photograph our golf outing, and we got to talking about the thefts."

"Um, hmm. You just 'happened' to talk about the MVC?" Lupe smiled.

"Well, it is big news. Everyone is talking. And I wanted to do my part. I can't have you be the only Nancy Drew."

"What did he say? Did he see anything?" Henry asked.

"The police asked for all his photos. They especially wanted to see the ones he took early on before everyone arrived."

"Empty galleries and stacks of wine glasses? Not much to see," Henry murmured.

"Well, there was one photo, in particular the police were interested in. It was of a group of staff standing in the corner near the curtains."

Lupe sighed. It was common for staff to stand around gossiping before, during, and after events. She had broken her team of this habit by having them meet three new people at every function and carry out a 'meaningful' conversation. The next day they were to follow up with the individuals in question. While this worked for her development team, the other departments were still of the munch and skulk category, commandeering a corner of the room and ignoring the guests.

"I can see it. A picture of staff members stuffing spanakopita into their mouths and looking cranky. Sorry. It's a sore point."

"You're human, Lupe," said Alice. "But it wasn't just staff. There were some other people in the picture, some board members and donors. I asked him to email the photo to you. Maybe it will help you winnow down the suspects."

"Thanks. That's a good idea. I was so tired earlier I thought I was just going to crawl into bed. So glad we were able to spend time together."

"Yes, celebrating my genius," smiled Henry.

"To your genius!" Alice and Lupe chorused, toasting with their desserts – sweet coconut rice cakes.

Walking a few blocks back to their apartment, the roommates talked about various activities in their lives. Lupe was looking forward to the gala in the coming week. She and Alice coordinated their major evening dress purchases together to get the most mileage from the outfits.

"I think we should set up a 'rent-the-runway' just for development professionals," said Alice. "Think about it. We wear a gown once, and then it sits in the closet. No one pays that much attention to what staff is wearing, so if we shared our evening gowns with other fundraisers, no one would be the wiser."

Lupe laughed. "But I refuse to wear black to all the evening functions. I don't like being invisible. I found a great outfit on The Real Real that will look good on both of us. "It's a pale lavender, Jenny Packham. It's sleeveless with a scooped neck and light beading all over.

"Can't wait to see it. Let's look when we get home. You may need a light shawl. It can still be a bit chilly on June evenings. And you won't be able to wear the Louboutins."

"No. I learned my lesson. No one will be able to see my feet very well, so I might even wear my Nike's."

Henry was bored with the conversation and started walking on his hands while practicing a monologue.

At that moment, there was a clinking noise as coins, keys, and other items fell from his jacket pocket. Gathering the sundries up, Henry shouted in surprise.

"The cufflink! I forgot all about it," The roommates stared.

Chapter 10
Development and Public Relations are Interconnected

Lupe immediately dialed Reye's mobile phone.

"Reyes." He grunted; Lupe could almost see him glaring.

"Hi, um, Josh? It's Lupe. I'm sorry to call so late, but something has come up." She quavered.

"Sure, Lupe. Anytime. What's up?"

"On the night of the theft, one of the bartenders found a small mother of pearl cufflink in the corner near where the paintings had been placed. He gave the piece to my roommate Henry."

"And you're just telling me this now?" The detective sighed.

"Well. We meant to give it to you right away, but Henry put it into his jacket pocket and forgot about it until just now when he was walking on his hands, and it fell out." Lupe babbled.

"Of course, it did," fumed Reyes. "Alright, where are you? I'll send a car right away to pick it up. I assume you all touched it?"

"Well, yes," Lupe answered sheepishly. "But it's tiny, and there was no easy way to handle it. We'll be at home in five minutes. It's 205 Sackett Street, Apartment 4, in Carroll Gardens. I'm so sorry."

"Everyone wants to be a detective. Let me guess, you, Henry, and Alice Mayhew are trying to solve this case on your own?"

"Yes. I mean, no! We are just keeping an eye open for any clues that may help you. For example, I know that Firoze Shah likes wearing French cuffs."

"But the cufflink could have been dropped earlier or worn by any number of the guests. Even women wear French cuffs sometimes. Anyway, wait at home for the officers."

"Any updates on Marla?"

"None. Don't worry, Holmes. I'll keep you posted." Lupe thought the comment particularly snarky.

The roommates chimed in unison. "Josh!?"

"With everything that's going on, that's what you glommed on to?"

"We love some good gossip, and Alice and I don't have very interesting love lives at the moment," Henry chided good-naturedly.

"Confess. Is there anything between you two?" Alice prodded.

Lupe smiled. "He's asked me out to dinner once the cases are solved."

"Goody," Henry clapped. "He's just your type. Tall, dark, and breathing."

"Yeesh. Thanks so much, pal."

"I can't wait to meet him," chuckled Alice.

Reaching home, Alice offered to make coffee, but Lupe held firm, and while exhausted, she drank chamomile tea. Two agents arrived about fifteen minutes later. They took possession of the cufflink and questioned Henry on its finding. Henry gave the name of the bartender who had located it, and the agents departed soon after.

The trio turned into bed, and Lupe, unable to settle down, spent the night attacking her pillow. It wasn't until the first rays of dawn that she fell to an uneasy sleep.

***

It was going to be one of those days Lupe felt to be endured. Lupe had known the occasional sleepless night and had a strategy for getting through the day. First, she took a long shower, alternating hot and cold water to refresh herself. A model friend swore by Preparation-H to reduce under-eye puffiness, but Lupe trusted a cooling green tea eye gel. On days like these, she also turned to some yoga stretches and extra protein for meals. And of course, she had a stronger than average cup of coffee, but not too much as it could turn her jittery. And taking a page from Theresa Hamilton, she chose a pink dress to wear. Theresa always said, "if you're pooped, wear pink." Lupe didn't know if it was a placebo effect, but somehow these tricks helped make her feel better.

Striding up First Avenue from the train stop, Lupe took several long refreshing breaths. As she entered the Museum of Vegetable Culture's lobby, she felt all her tactics wasted. Abby Winters was standing there gazing voraciously at the director of development.

"Lupe!" she crowed. "Just the person I wanted to see. I need an update on the thefts and how they're connected to poor, dear, Marla Howes's kidnapping."

"What makes you think I can tell you anything the police haven't already?" Lupe replied.

"But Lupe," the reporter cajoled. "You always have a finger in every pie. I'm sure you've picked up something that the police missed. Confidentially, I've always felt you would make an outstanding executive director. You're wise, tactful, and good to work with."

Lupe recognized the buttering up and was not fooled. "Thanks, Abby, but we have an excellent ED in Stephanie. And seriously, I don't know anything that isn't already public knowledge." Lupe fibbed, not wishing to implicate Firoze Shah or any of the other board members or donors. "For the record, we are all hopeful that the police and the FBI will find Marla alive and well and that the Edward Manet paintings will soon be returned."

"Come on, Lupe, help a girl out. You sound like a robot with that statement."

"Abby, like everyone, I am worried for Marla's safety. That is more important than the paintings."

"Well, I have a tip for you, I scratch your back, you scratch mine?" The reporter nudged.

Lupe reflected. Abby had been a good source for her in her fundraising efforts over the years. "Let's go into the café for a quick coffee."

"I knew you'd see it my way," the art reporter purred.

The MVC's café was compact but comfortable and bright. The café was decorated with a living wall of herbs, lettuces, and edible flowers and boasted a simple menu of salads, sandwiches, baked goods, and coffees.

Lupe chose a morning glory muffin and almond milk cappuccino while the reporter asked for an espresso.

Taking an empty table in the corner, the pair settled in.

"What can you tell me, Abby?"

"You, first." The negotiations always went this way, back and forth, until one gave in. Lupe, through her fog of exhaustion, capitulated. She racked her brains for a detail she could share that would soon be in the public domain.

"Ok," she said after a few moments. "On the night of the theft, Marla Howes told me that a week earlier during a salon she hosted at her home, someone made off with two valuable antique snuff boxes."

"I knew it! It's an inside job. Someone connected to the Museum. Who was at Marla's and the reception?" Abby Winters prodded.

"Sorry, Abby. You'll have to dig that out on your own, and my staff won't be giving you the information. Now, quid pro quo. What's your news?"

"One of your board members is going under. They are about to lose their shirt."

"What? Who?"

"Sorry, Lupe." She smiled. "That's all I'm prepared to tell you."

"Right." Slugging back her coffee, Lupe wrapped up the muffin and left the reporter.

Climbing the stairs to her office Lupe pondered. *Could her mother be right? Could Firoze Shah be losing all his money through a divorce? Who else could it be? Mimi St. John? Mary Montgomery Van Clausen? Camillo Aggio? Or could it be someone else entirely?* Lupe decided to review the updated board profiles and check-in with Paul.

Waving at her team, Lupe went to her desk, followed by Tessa carrying a notebook.

"Busy day today Lupe." Oh great, Lupe thought. Of course, it is. I'm barely standing.

"What's on our plates?"

"First up, a meeting with Pierre to work out the details for the San Sebastian gift. Then you're meeting with Audry to talk about program funding opportunities. Following that, you have lunch with Theresa Hamilton. After lunch, we'll start looking at the table assignments for the gala."

"Ok, would you have Paul meet me after that? I'll need about half an hour."

"Gotcha."

Grabbing the updated gift agreement, Lupe went to the CFO's office. Pierre was staring at a report on his computer screen but turned when Lupe came in.

"Lupe! Ton est fatigue?"

"It shows? I tried covering the circles with makeup, but I didn't sleep well last night."

"Only a little. It gives your face character."

"You Frenchmen, what a way with words."

Pierre smiled, his brown eyes sparkling. "So, we are getting this gift through crypto, eh?"

"Yes, it will be our largest. Are you set to receive it? I have to give the code instructions."

"Oui. We have a cryptocurrency brokerage exchange and will sell the gift as soon as it comes in. We use the same policy as with gifts of stocks and bonds and don't hold these assets. Mrs. San Sebastian will have to have the cryptocurrency appraised, so we should advise her to ask her CPA for a referral."

"Just like any noncash gift over $5,000?"

"Yes, The IRS considers crypto property. Her accountants will also have to file form 8283 for noncash charitable donations. It's worthwhile because she gets the deduction for the fair market value of the crypto and doesn't have to pay capital gains taxes on the appreciation. Depending on when she purchased the currency, this could be quite a lot of money."

"Alright, it's already in our standard gift agreement. I'll just add the type of instrument. I think cryptocurrency donations will soon become common practice."

"A number of organizations got into receiving crypto donations long before us. It's fairly straightforward, but Mrs. San Sebastian should instruct her broker to send a test transfer to our wallet, so we are sure the funds are coming to the right wallet."

"Will do. Stephanie is going to hold an action without a meeting to get the board to approve the gift. By the way, I know I owe you the next fiscal year budget. I promise to get to it this week."

"Do you see any major changes?"

"Of course, I would love to offer some of my team raises beyond the standard cost of living adjustment. Is there any chance we can put in for more professional development funding? I've done the research, and staff are more productive and happier when they have professional development opportunities. We had a brief offsite the other day, and I talked about it with them."

"Well, Cherie. All you can do is put it in and hope for the best. If you show that it positively impacts fundraising, you might be able to make a case."

"Thanks, I will." Lupe was frustrated but understood. She always tried to pair her dreams with data. "By the way, I was stopped by Abby Winters in the lobby this morning. She was trying to dig for dirt on the thefts and Marla's disappearance. Have you learned anything new?"

"We had a Financial Committee meeting yesterday and Allan was distraught. He feels responsible somehow for Marla's kidnapping. He keeps saying, 'If only I'd been there, she would be ok.' Poor man. I don't know if he would have been able to protect her."

"He was a Navy Seal in Vietnam. I think he still sees himself as 21 and fit to take all comers."

"Yes. Firoze was able to soothe him. The FBI thinks they may have some DNA evidence. But it takes time for it to be processed and will only help if the perpetrator is in their database."

"Maybe they will ask everyone present at the salon to give a swab? But I don't see how that will help."

"Neither do I, unless the person who took her was not at the salon?"

"That's possible. Connected to one of the donors but not actually at the event?"

"Oui. D'accord. That could be the case. But I don't know how it will bring them closer to a solution. By the way, entre nous, the insurance company is outraged that the pressure sensors were not working and may not pay the claim. We may have to seek permission from Allan Fisker to break the endowment."

Lupe remembered Allan's insistence that part of the funds from the spiralizer patent go to a permanent endowment. A percentage of the interest from the endowment had provided a steady income stream to the Museum over the years.

"Oh, dear. That will be horrible. Allan will be angry, and I don't think the board will be very jolly about it either. How is Stephanie taking it?"

"Our conversations have been very terse of late. Stephanie wants to blame Moe and fire him."

"The board won't let her get away with that!"

"I don't know. She has her allies."

"Yes, but some of the old guard will side with Allan and Moe."

"And we thought all the politics happened in Washington."

Lupe smiled and left for her meeting with Audry.

Audry, silvered-haired and dressed in a gauzy dove grey linen tunic and flowing trousers, exuded charm and authority. She had been an educator and program officer for her whole career and never tired of the role. Always looking for new ways to attract the public to the Museum, she encouraged her staff to be bold in their project ideas. Most of her team's efforts were popular and revenue-generating. From summer camps to senior lectures, outdoor concerts, and street fairs, Audry felt variety was the spice of life.

Lupe knocked on Audry's door, a mirror image of her own on the other side of the floor.

Audry smiled and beckoned her in. "Lupe. I was looking forward to our time together. I have some brilliant ideas to run your way."

Lupe smiled in return. She loved Audry's vigorous spirit. She had known people who barely kept their seats warm. Audry set the room on fire with her energy. For not the first time, Lupe reflected what a tremendous executive director Audry would make. She wondered if the older woman was ambitious in that direction.

Audry continued. "Summer camp is fast approaching, and we have exceeded the financial goal. Even so, I know we could manage a few more children and still have a low student-to-teacher ratio. I'd like to offer scholarships to some of the low-income neighborhood children. I have enough in the budget to offer five full scholarships and wondered if you could find enough to match that. It's such a splendid opportunity to be out in nature, learn about science and health, and have fun."

Clever gal, thought Lupe. She had positioned the "ask" just right, giving Lupe the goal of doubling the number of students who would benefit.

"Of course, Audry. I have just the person in mind to ask." Lupe had a regular donor, a retired teacher who had managed her TIAA-CREF investments well and was now comfortably off. Mrs. McGuiness loved supporting the Museum's educational programs.

"Good. I'm so glad. Also, we have a big project in mind for next spring and will need some major sponsors. To go along with next spring's show 'Art in the Garden,' it's a series of lectures and performing arts performances. I want to call it 'Digging Deep: The Artist Within.' The lecturers will come from some top Universities, and the performers will cover a broad array of disciplines from jazz musicians to contemporary dancers, poets, and even a comedian. I want this to be big and put MVC on the map as a performing arts venue."

Last summer, Lupe remembered when Audry and members of her team traveled to performing arts festivals in the Berkshires and Aspen to scout vibrant artists.

"I'm sure it will be wonderful, Audry. I'll need details as soon as you can get them. We'll write up a brief statement, and if you have the names of any of the performers and speakers, that will help too.

As soon as you have a draft budget, please share it with me. I might also be able to get underwriting for hotel rooms and air tickets."

"I knew I could count on you. I'll get something to you right away. I can see it. The family programs that will tag along with this. And classes for adults too. We all have an artist within."

"Sign me up," laughed Lupe, thinking of the sad, misshaped bowl she made in pottery class.

Returning to her office to prepare for lunch with Theresa Hamilton, Lupe was surprised to find Henry sleeping on the chaise longue, donated to the silent auction. Nudging her roommate, he woke up with a start.

"Lup-ay-ay. I was having such a nice dream. I dreamt that I didn't have to rush anywhere and that I could sleep all day in a hammock by the beach."

"I think you invaded my dream. I barely slept last night."

"Neither did I. I kept thinking your Special Agent was going to arrest me for withholding evidence. If I thought my parents were mad now....aye, ee!"

"Relax. I think it will be fine. What brings you here?"

"I'm meeting with Tom Unger to go over the contract to rent the auditorium for the showcase. Thanks for helping us get the friends and family discount. Temple Emanuel has been very nice to let us use their community room for rehearsals, but it will be much more special

141

for my students to be in an actual theater for the performance. Tom's even throwing in two nights for rehearsing on the stage so they will get their bearings." Henry added.

"I'm so glad. We like to support other nonprofits whenever possible, and Hephaestus Theater Corps is so important."

"Yeah, it's hard enough getting gigs when you are non-disabled. But my crew is all tough. And some of them really have what it takes. I know it's an uphill battle, but I'm especially proud of Daniel LaGrange. He brings a new dimension to Richard III. He's so good-looking, but when he turns into the King, he becomes pure evil." Permanently injured in a rugby accident, Daniel had continued to build his upper body strength. He regularly participated in adaptive sports competitions but also loved acting. "And I have Anya Vaderesque playing Lady Anne opposite Daniel. She's very compelling. Attractive yet strong." Anya had been born without a right forehand, and despite the handicap, she had become a respected yoga instructor and occasional print model.

"I can't wait to see them all. Alice and I are looking forward to the show. You should put a poster up in the break room, and I'll send an email around. It will be great to have a big audience."

"The more, the merrier. I have fifteen people in the company. They're all bringing family and friends, and I have their agents and directors as well."

"I have to rush. I'm meeting my mentor for lunch in midtown. Are you planning to nap on the chaise all day?"

"Just a little longer. Don't mind me. I'm softening up the leather," and with a long cat stretch, Henry curled up.

Chapter 11
It Pays to Have a Mentor and to Mentor Others

Lupe found Theresa Hamilton already seated at a table at Sushi Yasuda near Grand Central. Lupe loved dining there with the fresh seafood and impeccable service. It was nice to enjoy a leisurely lunch with her friend and mentor rather than shoveling down a meal at her desk.

Theresa, who had retired the prior year from her role as executive director of a major cultural center, was now working as a consultant and appreciated the flexibility the new life allowed. Lupe had met Theresa years earlier through a Women in Development program designed to connect young professionals with seasoned fundraisers. Lupe loved Theresa's devil-may-care attitude, confidence, and fundraising acumen.

Lupe noticed a small carafe of sake was already at the table and suspected her mentor didn't have too many meetings scheduled for later in the day.

"Lupe, you look marvelous in that outfit. But pink? Is it one of those days?"

Lupe sank gratefully into her seat. "It was a tough night. We've had so much going on with the thefts and Marla Howe's disappearance."

"Yes, that is a challenge. Did I ever tell you about the time we found a body buried in the basement of the cultural center?"

Lupe's eyes widened. "No! When was this?"

"Oh, it was a long time ago. I was the director of development. We were converting the basement into a black box theater, and it was my first capital campaign. The construction team had to clear up some broken concrete flooring, and there was a body just lying there."

"What did you all do?"

"The police sent in a cold case unit and found the man had been murdered by the center's former director of programming. She had strangled him with a gold chain belt. It turned out to be a crime of passion. The problem was many of our older donors had worked with her, and they were naturally horrified. It wasn't good for our image as a wholesome, family-friendly organization."

"What did you do to get past that?"

"We had a very wise executive director. She got on the phone with all the donors and board. She didn't let up. One by one, she listened to them and addressed their concerns. Then with the current programming director, we created a host of free family-friendly programs. It took a while but eventually, the notoriety let up."

"Were you able to build the black box? What did the capital campaign donors do?"

"Some did ask us to forgive their pledges or return their gifts but most stuck with it. The lesson to me is that you can't please everyone. I never understood how they could hold the center accountable for the deeds of one employee. But there it is. We finally built the black box and years later something crazy happened."

"What was that?"

"The son of one of the former donors asked to give tours of the basement as part of a haunted Manhattan tour!"

Lupe and Theresa laughed. Theresa poured a small glass of sake. Lupe toasted her with matcha tea.

"You will get through this. And I promise there will be better days ahead. And worse too. Remember what the sage said, 'this too shall pass.'"

Lupe trusted her mentor's discretion and told her about the possibility of the insurance company not paying the claim on the two stolen pieces.

"We may have to ask permission to break the endowment. Those paintings are so valuable."

"Do you think Allan Fisker will agree?"

"I don't know. He was one of the Museum founders and has a vested interest in its success. He's been there from the beginning when the Museum was just an abandoned shoe factory. He's been so generous over the years. Who knew you could make so much from a spiralizer? The endowment now has over $40 million, and we use about 4% a year. It's invested in some really great impact funds."

"If he doesn't, you'll have to get a Cy Pres and get the court to remove the spending restriction. It could get gruesome. Certainly, it will make it much harder for you to get restricted gifts if your donors think their intentions might not be followed. I'm sure Stephanie has already sought the advice of counsel, but you should check."

Lupe picked up a piece of yellowfin tuna sushi with her chopsticks, "I will," she answered before popping the morsel into her mouth. Chewing carefully, she then added, "Stephanie is not taking this well at all."

"She shouldn't. The buck stops with her. She is the ED, after all. I would be surprised if the board didn't put her on notice or worse. But onto fun things, how about some mochi ice cream for dessert?"

"I'm trying to stay away from sweets before the gala. The dress just fits if I use Spanx."

"Half a piece of mochi is not going to set you over. Did I tell you about my experience with mochi in Japan?"

"No, what happened?" Lupe asked between sips of strong tea.

"For dessert, I asked for mochi, and my host was very confused. Evidently, that's the generic name for a rice cake. He thought I wanted to eat bland rice paste. Mochi ice cream is more of a children's treat."

"That happened to me when I was on exchange in Italy for my Master's. I asked for a latte and was given a glass of milk. Latte is Italian for milk."

147

Theresa smiled. "So many things can be lost in translation."

***

Back at the office, Tessa rushed up. "I'm so glad you're back. Charlotte made a mistake. You're to interview the first of the three marketing director candidates in ten minutes."

"Goody. Do you have the candidate's resume? Who is it?"

"His name is Porter Larson. I put his resume on the top of your desk. Would you like a coffee?"

"You read my mind," Lupe smiled and went to her desk.

Porter Larson's resume read like a textbook marketing professional. The candidate had a BS in Marketing from the University of Pennsylvania. He had many years of experience in marketing and communications and had risen progressively up the ranks. Lupe was surprised that he had only worked in the for-profit medical sector.

A few moments later, Tessa entered with a medium-height blond man in his early forties standing behind her.

"Lupe, this is Porter Larson. Porter, this is Lupe Reinowski."

"Thanks, Tessa. Porter, please have a seat. I'm sorry it's so crowded in here, but we're getting ready for our gala, and these are some of the silent auction items."

Porter looked around. Did Lupe see a sneer on his face?

"It's no big deal. It's *cozy* in here."

"That's one way to put it. I looked over your resume, and it's very impressive. You have a lot of strong marketing experience. But it's all in the medical field. I'm sure you've been asked this question, but why are you interested in working for a museum?" Lupe asked.

"Working for a nonprofit has long been a dream of mine. You will have noted on my resume that I serve on the board of my club in Scarsdale. I can tell you when I came to the board, the organization was in the red. Through my marketing efforts, our programs started attracting more members, and those members stayed to use the food and beverage services which also impacted the bottom line. Now we are clearly in the black, and I know it is through my work."

So humble, thought Lupe.

"Why are you interested in the Museum of Vegetable Culture specifically?"

"I fights to the finish 'cus I eats my spinach." Porter crooned. Lupe plastered on a smile at the corny Popeye reference. "Seriously, I see great promise here. Your programs are not well marketed, and I think the Museum desperately needs a branding campaign." Lupe took a sip from her 'Mr. Smiley' mug. "Seriously?" He admonished, pointing at the tomato logo. "That is so childish. You need something hip and stylish. Something that conveys the power of vegetables in society. You nonprofit folks could really benefit from some strong corporate insights."

Hmmm, Lupe thought. The handsome hero is coming to save the day. This was not the first time she had heard such patronizing rhetoric.

"Our members are diverse in age and demographics. How will you tailor your marketing spend to maximize its effectiveness? I should tell you that the total budget is about $250,000 per year." Lupe challenged.

Porter grew a shade paler under his early summer tan.

"Well, the first thing I would do is get more money in the budget. Surely everyone will agree that spending on advertising is better than wasting it in some of the other departments?"

"Perhaps. But it may take time to get that kind of change. Sometimes, there can be politics to consider."

"It's a zero-sum game." He smiled. Sometimes you win, and sometimes you lose. Well, others may lose. I don't."

In my book, you do, Mr. Larson, Lupe thought.

The interview was drawing to a merciful conclusion. "Do you have any more questions?" She asked pro forma.

"Yes, I do. Who was the idiot who didn't make sure the pressure sensors in the gallery were working the night of the theft?"

Lupe suppressed a sigh. Some people were determined to commit career suicide.

"Who are you meeting next?"

"I'm off to see the head cheese. I have lots of great ideas she'll want to implement."

"I'm sure she'll be delighted to hear all about them. She appreciates constructive criticism. Please don't let me keep you."

Lupe closed the door after him and laughed. She hoped the next two candidates would be better.

Tessa entered. "How'd it go?"

Lupe rolled her eyes. "I'll send my notes upstairs. Are you and Ariel ready to look at the table layout?"

"Yes, we're in the conference room. I made up those circles you suggested and have lots of post-its."

"Super!" Kissing her 'Mr. Smiley' mug she led the way to the conference room.

"We have a couple of tables turned back, so we'll be able to invite some prospects as our guests, and the staff table will be covered," Ariel greeted her boss.

"Sounds good. I'd like to invite Mrs. McGuiness. I'll be asking her to sponsor some students for the summer camp. We can seat her with Audry."

Looking over the table, Lupe noted that the Platinum tables and Aggi's guest of honor table were already placed in the premium positions.

"Do we have any seating challenges?"

"Only one. A wife and a mistress are both coming to the event. We'll have to make sure their tables are far apart."

"Par for the course."

Krisha entered in a rush. "Marla's been found!"

"What? Where? Is she alright?"

"She was found walking in Central Park by the Alice in Wonderland statue. She was still wearing her pajamas and slippers. They've taken her to Lenox Hill Hospital for observation."

"But no word on her condition?" Ariel asked.

"She must be ok if she was able to walk?" Krisha responded.

"Thank heaven," Lupe said. "I'm sure we'll learn more soon." She was having a hard time controlling herself and wanted to call Reyes for the details. "Let's get back to work. I'll leave you to finish the table layout. I have to speak to Paul and interview the next marketing director candidates."

Lupe found Paul at his desk. "You heard about Marla?" The researcher asked.

"Yes, I'm so relieved. I wonder what was behind it all?

"The police haven't said anything more. They will question her, I'm sure."

"I'm sure that will be soon. Listen, I need you to do some research strictly on the QT."

"What is it?"

"I got some intel that one of our Board members is going to be facing a major financial upheaval. I need you to do some digging and see if you can figure out who it is."

"No small job, Boss. We have twenty members."

"I know. Start with Mimi St. John and Firoze Shah. Oh, and you also add Aggi."

"Aggi?"

"He may have overextended himself when he opened his latest restaurant. This is to remain between us, OK?"

"Of course. I'll get to work on it right away. By the way, what do you call a table you can eat?"

"Oh, Paul. That's terrible. A vegetable!"

Lupe grabbed one final cup of coffee and prepared for the next candidate.

Sheila Jackson's resume was unusual. The woman had handled marketing for an ashram in upstate New York and for a naturalist society. Lupe wondered if that was a nudist group. She had a degree in naturopathic medicine which made Lupe wonder how and why she ended up in marketing. She noted she had been a volunteer at the Museum for several years, but Lupe couldn't put a face to the name for some reason.

Tessa entered a few moments later and introduced Sheila Jackson, a petite woman in her mid-fifties. Sheila was dressed in low-rise leggings and a midriff revealing top which showed off her lithe figure. Her hair was tied up in a floral scarf.

Am I getting old? Lupe thought. I don't expect people to interview in a dark suit but at least cover your belly button!

Lupe smiled. "It's a pleasure to meet you, Sheila. Have a seat."

"Please call me Amani. It means peace. It's crowded in here."

"Yes, we're getting ready for our gala next week."

"Crowded spaces indicate cluttered minds. I think you need a cleanse. Isn't there anywhere else this can go? You need to change the Feng Shui right away. I sense your safety is threatened."

"Thank you, Amani. I will consider it." *Another winner*, thought Lupe. "So tell me, why do you want to work at the Museum of Vegetable Culture?"

"I've been volunteering here for quite some time. I help out in the green market almost every weekend. I think a vegan lifestyle is the key to longevity and inner peace."

"There may be some truth to that, but not all of our members and visitors are vegans or even vegetarians. Our goal is to encourage a healthy lifestyle through the consumption of more vegetables. How will you support people at every stage in their journey?"

"I would help them see the importance of veganism."

"Yes, but do you have any specific ideas for how you will engage a diverse member and guest base?"

"I'm feeling very threatened by your questions. This is adversarial. Is this a hostile workplace?"

Lupe took a sip of coffee before answering. "I'm sorry you feel that way. I'm merely asking about how you intend to do your job as marketing director."

"It's always about outcomes with you people. You always want more. I choose to live like my name -- in peace. You are giving off an black aura of anger."

"Thank you for coming in, Amani. Who else have you seen today?"

"You are my first, and I might say, I'm not sure if this is a good fit for me if your vicious attitude is anything to go by."

"Yes, well, I wish you good luck with the rest of the interviews."

Lupe put her head on her desk. What the what?

After a moment's hesitation, she pulled out her mobile phone and dialed Josh Reyes's number, deciding to hang up if she received his voice mail.

He answered on the first ring. "Reyes."

"Hi Josh, it's Lupe. I heard that Marla has been found. Is she ok?"

"Yes, she was dehydrated, but the doctors say she's fine otherwise."

"Have you been able to see her?"

"Yes, but she won't tell us anything about what happened."

"Is it amnesia?"

"No. I think it's fear. She's afraid to name her abductors. I don't know what they are holding over her, but we can't convince her that she's safe."

Lupe sighed. The poor woman. To be terrorized so.

"And before you ask, Holmes, there are no new leads on the missing paintings. It's like they vanished into thin air. None of our usual sources have given us any meaningful leads."

Lupe thanked the detective and hung up the phone as Tessa returned with the third and final candidate for the marketing director position.

Tessa introduced Malcolm Maye. A tall, striking-looking man with coffee-colored skin, Malcolm smiled warmly and extended his hand.

"I've heard a lot about you, Lupe. I used to work with Theresa Hamilton at the Hadley Center." Lupe had not had a chance to glance at Malcolm's resume, or she would have picked up on that fact right away.

"Malcolm, you have the advantage of me. Unfortunately, the day has flown by, and I haven't had a chance to look at your CV. Would you like a coffee or water while I take a minute?"

"No, I'm fine. Take all the time you need."

"Have a seat; please excuse the mess."

"I bet you have a gala coming up. One time, someone donated a pinball machine for our auction, and we put it in my office. I was very popular for a few weeks. Everyone came to 'just make sure it worked!'"

Lupe swiftly reviewed the resume. BS in marketing with a double major in communications from Fordham. Halfway through an MBA at Baruch's Zicklin School of Business part-time program. Ten years relevant experience, most in nonprofit cultural settings. *Looks very promising*, Lupe thought. *And if he's not a good candidate, we'll be back to the drawing board.*

"Thanks, Malcolm. Your resume is strong and relevant. Why are you interested in the Museum of Vegetable Culture?"

"I grew up in one of the poorest congressional districts. Life was tough, and getting good, healthy food was not always easy for my mother. Though she tried, in many poorer communities, there are limited resources; you'll find plenty of bodegas but not enough actual grocery stores. I was lucky. Mom sacrificed so I could get a good education. Through her hard work and scholarships, I attended Cardinal Hayes in the Bronx. They taught us the importance of giving back to the community. I've made it a point of being of service through my work and as a volunteer. I am a success story and want to make sure others can benefit as well."

Lupe smiled in relief. Passion for the mission, check.

"Our guests and members range in age from three to ninety-five and come from all walks of life. How will you engage these people given a limited marketing budget? It's about $250,000."

"There's one thing we nonprofit professionals know how to do is stretch a dollar. I would look at how the spend is being used at present and measure the effectiveness of each channel. Sometimes the best methods are the cheapest. Borrowing email distribution lists from other organizations and keeping up with community calendars, for example. There is no need to blow it all on large print ads if that's not going to move the needle."

"Do you have any questions for me?"

"Yes, the Museum has been in the media lately because of the thefts and Marla Howes. Have you seen a negative impact on attendance?"

"Surprisingly, no. People are coming from all over to stare at the blank wall where the Manets were."

Malcolm smiled. "Yes, no news like bad news."

"You said it."

Chapter 12
Special Event Management for the Weary

The next day, Lupe took an Uber to the office since she had to carry her gala outfit. She would love to be able to take a long shower and groom for the event, but she knew from experience she would be dressing in the cramped staff bathroom in a rush before leaving for the venue.

Her office phone was ringing as she arrived.

"Lupe Reinowski," she answered in her usual upbeat tones.

"Good morning, Lupe, it's Allan Fisker."

"Allan! How are you? How's Marla?" Lupe breathed.

"She's upset naturally and won't say anything about what happened to her. I'm taking her to my farm in the Berkshires to rest and recuperate. I think some time in the country with long walks and trail rides will help her relax and recover."

"Excuse my asking, but do you think you'll be safe? The kidnapper is still out there." Lupe questioned.

"I've asked my grandson and some of his friends from Williams to come stay with us. Between them and my farm crew, we'll protect Marla. It's very peaceful there, and Marla will enjoy all the farm produce and seeing the wildlife."

"That's wonderful, Allan. I'm sure it's just what the doctor ordered."

"Yes, so we're leaving today and won't be at the gala. Would you have someone host our table?"

"Certainly, I'll ask Pierre Renard and his wife, Elyse. Your guests all know Pierre, and I'm sure they will have a lovely time this evening."

"Thank you, Lupe. I can't wait to get Marla away. My farm in Stockbridge is only three hours from New York, but it feels like a different world."

"Marla is lucky to have you, Allan, and I am so glad she is safe and in your care."

"I can tell you; I am so relieved. The past few days have been dreadful. She is my world."

Lupe suddenly felt sad. *Would she ever know such love?*

The day progressed rapidly, with Lupe attending to hundreds of last-minute details. Over a quick group email discussion, the directors and Stephanie all agreed that Malcolm Maye should be offered the director of marketing and communications role. Lupe breathed a sigh of relief at that news.

***

Arriving at Cipriani's at 3:30, the team set up the silent auction and connected with the sound and light technicians and the florist. Jean Flamant had outdone himself with gorgeous trellises loaded with grapevines thick with fruit, entwined with fairy lights and lemon and olive trees in terracotta pots sprayed with gold designs to pick up the lights.

Lupe noted that Mrs. Montag had decided on both fairy lights and the Edison lights. The place looked elegant and sumptuous. Lupe was also glad they would repurpose the decorations after the event with the flowers sent to the hospice center and the vegetables taken to an East Village soup kitchen.

Despite the hard work, Lupe enjoyed galas and dressing up. She also loved seeing her team in their finery. Marcus looked proud and confident in his new dinner suit with a skinny tie, and Paul's tuxedo was a definite change from his usual Birkenstocks and faded jeans. The ladies all looked elegant in their gowns. Krisha had opted to wear a gorgeous saffron-colored Salwar Kameez, loose trousers with a long, embroidered silk tunic and sheer scarf. Lupe had recruited Felicity and Silke to also assist with the guest check-in and the auction. Felicity wore a simple black sheath with a long strand of fun pearls, but Silke was still holding out hopes to sing with the band and had dressed in a gold beaded gown with a feathered fascinator in her flaxen hair.

They all look wonderful, Lupe thought. It's like a Hollywood set. Lupe took copies of the speeches and put them on the podium in order of speaker. Stephanie was to welcome the guests and introduce the evening's emcee, Kaba Tadashi. Kaba would warm up the crowd with some impressions and then introduce Mary Montgomery van Clausen who would give the Outstanding Advocate Award to Camilo Aggio. There would be a quick photo opportunity, and Aggi would give a brief speech and offer a toast. Dinner would follow with the band playing Italian songs in the background. After dinner, the dancers would perform in Nick Cave's whimsical Soundsuits. Then they would screen a short video about the Museum's various programs. The live auction and dancing would follow this.

Stepping from the stage, Lupe saw Ben Terrance, the event photographer.

"Ben! How are you?" Lupe asked.

"Fine, Lupe. The venue looks wonderful. I already took some great shots of the setup and even did some glamor shots of some of the committee."

Lupe laughed. "I'm sure you made their day! Paul will go around with you during the event to make sure we get the names. It's sometimes a problem to figure out who's who later."

"By the way, did you get the photos from the evening of the theft?" Ben queried while snapping a few quick shots of Lupe.

Lupe hit her head with the palm of her hand. "I can't believe it. In all the rush of the gala, I forgot to look at them. They're in my inbox. I'll make a point of reviewing them tomorrow."

"The police were especially interested in one photo I took of some of the donors and staff before the reception started. They were all standing near the curtain where the pictures were supposed to be."

"Thanks, Ben. I'll look for it. Maybe I'll see something that can help the police."

"Do they have any leads?"

"Nothing as far as I know. We are just relieved that Marla was found safe and reasonably well."

"Yes, it would have been tragic if she had been hurt or...?"

"Or." Lupe agreed soberly.

Lupe walked over to where Marcus was chatting with the technicians.

"You've checked the slides, Marcus?"

"Yes, we'll project images of the live auction items and larger silent auction items in a loop. That's interspersed with photos of people enjoying the education programs and visiting the galleries. I also have slides to acknowledge all the top donors."

"Great. I'm glad we're cutting down on paper waste by not having a program, but I was worried we'd lose revenue by not having journal ads. I repackaged the levels, and the companies seemed pleased with this exposure."

"Yes, they've been on our website for three months and on all emails, in addition to Kaba's shoutouts from the stage and the slides running on a loop for the cocktail hour and through dinner," Marcus replied.

From there, Lupe walked over to greet the trio from Julliard. She noticed a tall, handsome red-haired young man helping them set up.

"Ian?" Lupe asked in astonishment.

"It's me, Lupe. Captain Carrot has the night off," he grinned.

Ian was wearing a plum-colored velvet smoking jacket and paisley ascot tie. He had gelled back his usually unruly hair and looked as if he had snuck away from a 1930s British country house party. On the mercurial young man, it suited.

"You look dashing, Ian. I mean it."

"I clean up well, don't I?" He preened.

"Yes."

"Lupe, I have an idea to raise some more money this evening."

"Yes?" Lupe answered with slight hesitancy.

"You know that Jaeger-LeCoultre Reverso Classic Monoface watch in the silent auction?"

"Yes?" Why was Lupe growing nervous?

"You know how you usually end up with only fifty percent of the value of items in the silent auction?"

"Yes, silent auction bidders tend to want value and live auction bidders want to make a splash."

"The watch is valued at $5,000. Here's what I would do. I'll take Silke with me, and we'll take a deck of cards and go around selling each card in the deck for $100. It's a one in fifty-two chance of getting the watch, and we would raise the full value of the donation. I'll wear the watch and show it off, and Silke will handle the money. We'll make a smashing couple."

Lupe thought for a moment. She had seen something like this at another event where glasses of champagne were sold for $50. Each flute had a small rhinestone placed in the bottom. One glass had an actual diamond, and the winner received a diamond bracelet.

"Sounds good, but you need to do three things. Ask Marcus to change the watch slide to showcase the 'cards', ask Ariel to take it off the auction list on the iPads, and be sure she doesn't need either of you when you start selling cards. She may need your help with check-in."

Ian gave a dazzling smile. "I'm on it!" He literally leaped away in happiness.

The Juilliard students quietly settled in, and Lupe was delighted at the professionalism of the Cipriani staff. She had never had a bad experience there and was looking forward to the evening.

By 5:00 pm, all was ready. The committee had done a great job positioning the silent auction items in tempting arrangements amidst the flowers. Lupe walked over and put in her bids on an iPad. Each guest was registered and given a unique number connected to their credit card information. This spared the staff having to chase people down for their information. It also simplified the silent auction process. Lupe bid on the Four Seasons spa day, which she hoped she'd be able to nab as a birthday gift for her mother and a family portrait to give her sister, Rosario, once the new baby arrived. Lupe found auctions were a great source of interesting gifts. She remembered being the winning bidder to an aerial yoga session and loved the experience of turning herself upside down in the "silks."

Ariel approached her, iPad in hand. "All is set, chief. The early bird guests will probably be arriving soon." Although cocktails were to begin at 6:00 pm, some guests invariably turned up much earlier.

"Are you ok with having Ian and Silke do that card-selling stunt?"

"Sure. The biggest crush will be at 6:30. I'll have them come back and help for the rush, and then they can go back to their card game." Ariel laughed.

"Any crises I should be aware of?"

"No, I have Charlotte van Clausen and Tray Nevins helping with the dancers. They are being given sandwiches in a 'green room' I had set up. Marty Vega's band is there too. They've finished their soundcheck."

"Great. You can tell the trio to start playing anytime. And be sure to have some canapes before the crowd gets here. You'll need your strength."

'Ha! I'll stand by the kitchen entrance and waylay the waiters," joked Ariel.

Lupe picked up a flute of sparkling water with lemon. One of her hard and fast rules was to drink plenty of water at events. The extra exertion and adrenaline always made her parched.

Lupe slipped over to the dining area and saw the members of the committee all seated at one of the tables, obviously trying to save their feet before the evening ahead. Mimi St. Johns waved her over.

"Lupe! You look scrumptious. That dress looks lovely on you." Mimi gushed.

Lupe smiled in pleasure. She was so glad the mail-order dress fit well, and she hadn't had to rush around finding something else to wear. The pale lilac suited the early summer season, and the beadwork added flair.

"You look lovely too, Mimi. All of you ladies do. Thank you so much for all you've done. We're sure the evening will be a wonderful success."

Dorothy Montag piped up. "And the flowers and vegetables work, don't they? I was really trying to capture the spirit of the Italian countryside. Like that wonderful movie, 'Enchanted April.' Do you know it? It's about these four English women who rent a castle on the coast of Italy. The scene when they wake up their first morning and open the windows to the magnificent foliage and the view of the sea. Ah, it's breathtaking. I told Claude I had to go to that exact spot in Portofino. And you know what? It's there. It's called Castello Brown. Ah, such magic." Reaching into her evening clutch, she withdrew a tiny lace handkerchief into which she sniffled softly.

Lupe caught a quick exchange of glances between Tilda Wright and Veronica MacDonald. Mimi smiled indulgently. Feeling protective, Lupe reached for Mrs. Montag's hand.

"It's so wonderful you experienced all these places and turned your memories into such a garden of delight this evening. We are so grateful to you. I would love to hear more about your travels, perhaps over coffee next week?"

"You are a darling, Lupe. That would be lovely."

Mimi cleared her throat delicately. "And now we must greet our guests. Shall we?" Mimi rose with grandeur and lifted the sheer layers of the train that covered her floral slip dress."

Lupe then found Stephanie and assured her introductory speech was set up on the podium. Stephanie looked chic in a midnight blue Armani gown.

"I decided to go with an Italian designer to follow the evening's theme," she confided. Lupe fought back the urge to roll her eyes.

"If you could spend some time this evening with Stacy and Ralph Leibman, I would appreciate it. I think we can ask them for a gift in the high six figures, and I want them to develop a relationship with you."

"Ralph is so dull. He never wants to talk about anything but gardening."

"You should chat up, Stacy. Talk about her IPO, entrepreneurship, and successful women in business. Talk about our program to provide STEM-related courses to at-risk girls. That might interest her. We might even be able to sell them on endowing Audry's directorship."

Lupe could tell she was coming close to the line. Stephanie wouldn't want anyone to have a named directorship until she did first.

"I'll consider it. Let me go greet Aggi now."

A waiter passed at that moment and offered Lupe a canape of grilled artichoke and leek on crispy polenta. Lupe quickly bit into the morsel and marveled once again how delicious vegetarian food could be. She had to control herself from chasing the waiter across the floor for a second helping.

In the final few minutes before the throng began, Lupe reflected on the Museum's last event. Tonight, would be an opportunity to see many of the same guests, including many suspects. What might she be able to find out?

Lupe shook herself out of her reverie as several guests entered at once. She went up to meet them. This was the part of the job Lupe loved the most. She greeted Ingrid and Pietro San Sebastian and the ever-present Borgia and took them over to Mary Montgomery and Stephanie. She instructed Ben and Paul to make sure they got photos of the group. As she turned back to the entrance, she saw Josh Reyes and Detective Collins, both dressed for the evening. The Special Agent wore a sharp evening suit and tie, and Collins was dressed in a black satin pantsuit with jet beading on the lapels. She wore high heels that made her even taller than her normal 5'9". Lupe felt herself turning into a cheese pierogi next to the svelte detective.

"I'm surprised to see you. You're on duty; I take it?" Lupe asked.

"Yes, we'll keep a low profile," Reyes responded.

"All of the people who were at Marla Howes's salon and the reception at the museum will be here tonight. We've cleared it with Stephanie." Collins added.

"I'm sure it will be fine. Let's get your seats for dinner."

"That's not necessary. We can stand in the back." Josh asserted.

"Then you will be conspicuous. Don't worry. I'm sure we have a couple of spare seats. The menu is delicious. It was planned by the evening's honoree, Camilo Aggio, and it's already been paid for." Why am I gushing? Lupe thought.

"If you're sure. We would appreciate that. We don't get to sit down to too many nice meals in this job."

"Yes, thank you," added Collins. "We'd also like to see where the guests we're interested in are sitting."

"We try to do things with our iPads, but I'm sure Ariel has a printout. Let's go ask."

Lupe took the two officers over to the registration table and got the special event's manager's attention.

"Ariel, would you find places for Agent Reyes and Detective Collins?"

Lupe loved how her manager always stayed calm under pressure. Years of experience had kept Ariel completely unruffled even in the most trying of situations. Two last-minute seats were a piece of cake.

"Certainly, I have two seats that Pavillion Bank turned back. It's table 70."

"I'll take you over and introduce you to the other guests when dinner starts," Lupe offered. "The officers also need a guest list. Do you have a printout you can spare and a highlighter?"

"Sure. Here you go."

The Cipriani venue had once been the Bowery Savings Bank and was an exquisite setting. The cashiers' windows were fitted with brass tracery and now served as cocktail highboys. Lupe led the detectives across the marble floor to one of the windows. There, the three highlighted the names of all those who had attended both functions. Lupe mentally noted to seek out each of them at some point in the evening.

"Alright. We'll look for these people. I promise we won't cause a scene. We just want to see them in their natural habitat, so to speak." Reyes promised.

"They probably won't even notice you in the crowd," Lupe replied.

"Yes, we fit in," said Detective Collins smugly. *But you're hardly inconspicuous*, Lupe thought, gazing a bit balefully at the statuesque detective.

"Let me show you to your table." Lupe led the way through the glittering tables to number 70, which offered a good view of the entire room and stage. "This should work well for your purposes. I hope you enjoy the meal. I know you're on duty, but the wines are excellent. Mimi St. Johns, the chair of the gala committee is an aficionado and selected some special vintages. It's a step up from the usual event wines."

Josh looked at Lupe and smiled with his eyes. "I think we can manage a taste."

Chapter 13
Events: Details, Details and more Details

After introducing the detectives to their tablemates, Lupe went to visit her own table. She found it challenging to sit still at events, but she made a point to at least greet those seated at her table.

Her guests were all donors whom Lupe was cultivating for deeper commitments. They included a lawyer, Thomas Danek and his wife, Judy, and a retired businessman Mason Tolland and his wife, Marlo Hunt, who ran a flourishing staffing agency. Also at the table were the dean of Diversity, Equity, and Inclusion at Trotman College in Westchester, Sylvie Jackson, and her partner, Candace Tyler; two sisters, Stephanie and Joyce Feldman, who loved to attend all the museum events; and a recent widower, Harlan Meyers. He owned a chain of popular bakeries.

Lupe was happy to see all her table guests engaged in conversation and walked around to say hello.

"Sylvie! I'm so glad you managed to make it." The dean was always in hot demand to represent the college and sometimes found herself attending several functions in one evening, eating multiple meals on the same night.

Candace laughed. "One dinner tonight. It's a luxury. And you're serving something healthy. Sylvie usually has to beg for a fruit plate at some of the events."

"I've gained so much weight with this job. It's always breakfast, lunch, and dinner, receptions. Promise me, Lupe, when you come after me for money, don't make it over a meal!"

The three laughed. "Promise," Lupe responded. It was essential to know how donors wanted to be solicited. She felt the same and tried to avoid meal meetings.

Stephanie and Joyce Feldman were in deep conversation with Harlan Meyers, and Lupe suspected he would not be alone for long. Hopefully, the sisters won't fight over him, she prayed.

The Daneks and Tollands greeted Lupe with broad smiles. "Lupe, the reception was wonderful, and we loved the canapes. So inventive." Marlo stated. "Would it be possible to get the recipes?"

"Some of them came from Aggi's new book, and you'll each receive a copy at the end of the evening." Lupe sometimes struggled to find interesting items to place in the SWAG bags. She wanted to represent the Museum yet not spend unnecessarily. Fortunately, Aggi had donated the books, and the logoed canvas tote bags showcased the Museum's mission.

With a quick drum roll, the crowd settled. Stephanie stepped up to the podium and smiled. As she looked down at her speech, Lupe saw the smile freeze on her Executive Director's face. *Oh, dear* Lupe wondered. *What happened?* She could see Stephanie was trying valiantly to control her anger.

"Ladies and Gentlemen, thank you for joining us this evening for our 30th annual gala event, 'Che Bella Luna.'" She paused for applause. Then Stephanie rapidly and haphazardly thanked a variety of people. *This was not her speech*, Lupe thought. *Ugh.*

"And of course, I want to acknowledge this evening's presenting sponsors, Gopika and Ashish Balasubramanian and Balasubramanian Industries. Aap donon ko dhanyavaad, Thank you both." Stephanie stumbled over the Hindi words which she had so carefully practiced. Lupe could see the sheen on Stephanie's brow. The Hindi sounded painfully like Klingon. "But now, it gives me great pleasure to introduce this evening's master of ceremonies and a great friend of the Museum of Vegetable Culture, Kaba Tadashi!"

Stephanie smiled gratefully at Kaba, who ran up the steps to the podium.

"How are you tonight? Did you all bring your credit cards?" Everyone laughed. Kaba had a naturally engaging presence and a rubber face which he used to comic effect. Lupe relaxed as the rest of the program went along as planned. Slipping from her seat, she walked around to the left side of the stage. Stephanie was standing behind some of the potted trees.

"Lupe!" The director hissed. "You told me my speech was on the stand. Where did it go? I just made a fool of myself out there!"

"I don't know what happened, Stephanie," Lupe whispered back. "It was there. I put it on top with Kaba's remarks underneath, followed by Mary Montgomery's and Aggi's."

"Well, I will get to the bottom of this. I think I know what happened, and I will not let this go unanswered."

Lupe tried to soothe the irate woman. "Stephanie, no damage was done. I'm sure no one really noticed. But perhaps you could say something to the Balsubramanian's?

"Gopika and Ashish won't forgive me!"

"No, of course, they will. They will understand once you explain. I'm sure you're not the first person to mess up their name." *Or butcher an acknowledgment in Hindi*, she thought.

Mary Montgomery van Clausen had introduced Aggi by then, and it was time to present him with the award. Stephanie straightened up, reset her polished smile, touched her hair, and mounted the steps to join the others for a photo.

Lupe turned to return to her table and almost ran into Mimi. Her face glowed in triumph. A horrible feeling came over Lupe. "Mimi, did you have something to do with Stephanie's missing speech?" She asked quietly.

"Oh, my goodness, no," the aging belle drawled. "But it was fun to see her floundering up there. She's always so high and mighty about her upbringing. She doesn't exactly show grace under pressure. I'm going to buy a cocktail for whoever did it."

"It's an open bar," Lupe replied.

"Even better!"

Just then, Stephanie and Mary Montgomery came down from the stage. Seeing Mimi's satisfied face, Stephanie's own turned red.

"You! You did it. You never did like me," Stephanie stormed. She looked ready to come to blows with the gala's chair. "You're caging for my job. I know you are behind the thefts. You keep going out of your way to make me look bad."

"I did no such thing," Mimi huffed. "And you don't need my help looking bad, my dear."

Mary Montgomery stepped forward, equal to the occasion as usual. "Ladies. This is not the time or place. In fact, I don't know if there ever is a time or place for this type of character assassination. We will discuss the matter tomorrow morning at the Museum. I expect to see you both in the conference room at 10 am. Until then, you will each go to your 'corners' and stay there for the rest of the evening."

Bless Mary Montgomery, Lupe thought. She wore the mantle of leadership well.

"Now, Mimi, please go enjoy the evening with your guests. You should savor your success. Lupe, please take Stephanie to freshen up.

You still have to visit all the tables." With that command, the matron strode off to her table.

"I'll get your purse and meet you in the ladies' room," Lupe said.

Back in the ladies' room, Lupe was relieved to see the director had regained her composure. Neither woman spoke as Stephanie refreshed her lipstick and mascara.

After a moment, Stephanie spoke. "Let's start with the platinum tables. I suppose I should apologize to Gopika and Ashish first. Better get it over with."

Lupe found Ben Terrance and Paul and took them along as she followed Stephanie from table to table. Gladhanding was where her director shone. She was warm and welcoming to all the guests, no matter what level of support they had given—stopping by the tables and offering a few words of greeting made everyone feel special. Ben took group photos along the way, and Paul carefully noted the table numbers. Seeing all was well, Lupe returned to her table to have a few bites of her first course.

Her table was ebullient, and all seemed to be looking forward to the live auction. Lupe had learned to keep the live auction short with no more than five exciting packages on offer. This evening, in keeping with the Italian theme, Kaba would auction a stay at a luxurious villa in Tuscany for ten, a three-day racecar driving course with the use of a Ferrari 488 GTE, a shopping spree at Prada, and dinner prepared by Aggi at his Hamptons beach house.

Sipping a glass of the wine paired with the first course, a Pietracupa Greco di Tufo from the Campania region, Lupe sighed in contentment. There were perks to the job. She glanced up and saw Firoze Shah speaking with a lovely blond woman wearing a grey silk gown cut dramatically low in the back. Who was she, Lupe wondered? And where was Raina? The pair slipped away behind one of the cashier's windows. Hmm, Lupe thought.

"May I have this dance?" Josh asked.

Lupe looked up and smiled. Marty Vega was crooning, "That's Amore." Many guests were dancing between courses.

"I'd be delighted." She stood up, and Josh led the way to the floor. Josh took Lupe's hand and twirled her into his arms. The pair danced gracefully in a tight circle.

"Have you picked up on anything?" Lupe asked.

"A few useful tidbits. But if I tell you, I'll have to kill you." Josh teased.

"I saw something interesting, but I don't know if there is anything to it? I'll tell you mine if you tell me yours?"

"Is it about Firoze Shah and the blond?"

"Drat! I thought I was so observant. The rumor is that he and Raina's marriage is in difficulty, and he may be facing an expensive divorce."

"Yes, I heard that," Josh replied.

Josh was an excellent dancer, and for a moment, Lupe wanted to forget about the investigation and just enjoy the experience.

Marty Vega finished the old standard with a flourish, and the tempo shifted. Suddenly everyone was bopping to "Mambo Italiano." Laughing, Lupe joined in the fun. She was pleased to see so many of her donors and major gift prospects on the dance floor having a good time. Pierre was escorting one of the Legacy Society members, and looking over to his table, she could see others eagerly awaiting their turn. The CFO would get his exercise this evening. Near the dance floor, Ian was showing off the watch to guests at Stephanie's table. Silke was passing out the last remaining cards in exchange for crisp $100 bills or Square payments. Ingrid and Pietro were laughing with Stacy and Ralph.

Perspiring lightly, Josh and Lupe ended the dance, and he walked her back to her seat.

"You never told me what you learned," Lupe chided playfully.

"Ah. I won't go into it now, but it has to do with the terms of Stacy Leibman's IPO."

Lupe's eyes widened. "I will hold you to it. I planned to ask them for a big donation."

Josh grinned. "She'll be good for it, don't worry."

"I'm a development director. I always worry."

Laughter sounded through the great hall as the guests chattered and enjoyed their meals. Lupe's risotto had grown cold while she was dancing, but she didn't mind. It was delicious at room temperature. She fell into conversation with a distinguished-looking man sitting on her right. Thomas Danek was a lawyer with a prestigious white-shoe law firm who had judicial aspirations.

"Thomas, I'm so sorry I've been up and down all evening. I know everything is going smoothly, but I feel more comfortable keeping an eye on things."

"Is that what you were doing on the dance floor? I should be jealous." Lupe chuckled because she knew how much Thomas Danek adored his wife, Judy.

"A girl's gotta have fun. Are you enjoying the evening?"

"Lupe, it's all marvelous. I always love this setting, and Aggi's food is delicious. I may have to take home a bottle of this Barolo."

"Famous attorney stealing charity wine. Let me send you a bottle instead."

"Hmm...might be a conflict of interest."

"What?" Lupe asked

"My firm is representing the Musee D'Orsay and the Wallraf-Richartz in recovering the cost of the stolen Manets."

Lupe let out a deep breath. "We are hopeful the police will find the paintings undamaged, and they will be restored to both institutions."

"Yes, we all hope for that. But if it doesn't happen, they will seek compensation."

"Understood." Lupe took a longer sip of her wine. She felt powerless and thought of Allan Fisker. Would he allow the MVC to break the endowment?

Lupe excused herself to check in on her team. She walked to the outside of the dining area to avoid crossing the crowded room. In the shadows, she saw Stephanie talking to a fully bald man. He wore unusual eyeglasses with pale blue rims, and his suit was European tailored for it fitted him beautifully. Lupe did not recognize the individual but could read power and wealth in his demeanor. Stephanie was engrossed in the conversation and seemed to be captivated by the stranger's words.

Curiouser and curiouser, Lupe thought, but refrained from eavesdropping. At the staff table, Lupe found Ariel and Tessa going over some notes.

"How are things so far?"

"The silent auction is rocking. We've hit the goal, but no one bid on the college coaching session." Ariel said.

"Happens sometimes."

"But the night on the town was a big hit as usual." Tessa chimed in.

"Any trouble seating everyone?" Lupe asked.

"You won't believe it. Judit VonKolbe tried to sneak in. That woman drives me crazy."

"She probably gave a lame excuse as usual?"

"Yes, she said she was a guest of Mary Montgomery's!"

"What did you do?"

"You know how Mary Montgomery is. She didn't want a scene, so she offered to buy Judit a ticket."

"We can't let her do that," Lupe stated.

"No, indeed. I had an extra seat at the mix-match table and put Judit there. And you know what? She complained she didn't have a good view of the stage!"

The women sighed. Lupe vowed to deal with the interloper the next day.

Ian and Silke jumped out of their seats and raced up to Lupe.

"We did it!" Ian broadcast. "We sold all the cards. Stacey Leibman bought the last one."

"That's fabulous. Great job. And you seemed to have fun?"

"It was wonderful, Lupe," said Silke. "I felt so glamorous. But the night will be perfect if…."

"I know – if you could just sing with the band. Maybe at the end of the evening. We'll see." Lupe replied.

Silke and Ian grinned. Marcus stepped over.

"All ready for the video and the live auction. No problems at all. We checked everything earlier."

"How are you enjoying yourself? She asked the young man, who was only one year out of college.

"It's great. When I was a kid, I would walk past places like this, but I never thought one day I would be here with a seat at the table."

"Trust me. You deserve a seat at any table. You are smart and hardworking. Set your goals and follow them. This is just one of many exciting experiences."

After checking that the dancers were all set, Lupe returned to her table, where dessert was being served. Oops. I missed the main course; she thought—an occupational hazard.

Kaba came to the stage and welcomed the dancers in the Nick Cave Soundsuits. The color and movements were delightful, humorous, and thoroughly engaging. Lupe was so glad the committee agreed to the off-beat entertainment. After much applause, the three-minute video was shown. Stephanie and Mary Montgomery provided the narration while footage of various activities played. Although the production cost was higher than Lupe liked, she felt the video was worthwhile in helping donors better understand the depth and breadth of the Museum's reach.

Kaba quickly moved on to the live auction, which he kept lively by joking with some of the heavy hitters. With everyone warmed up, the packages went quickly. To offer opportunities for everyone to be involved, they provided a "fund an item." Lupe was still trying to secure funding for the short winter exhibition on Gregor Mendel's pea plant experiments, so this was posed as the evening's opportunity. She knew if anyone could sell a 19th-century polymath, it would be Kaba.

Kaba shouted from the stage. "Lupe's made me work for my dinner tonight. Our "fund an item" is underwriting the winter exhibition on the work of Austrian scholar, Gregor Mendel." Kaba gave an exaggerated yawn, and everyone laughed.

"But we're going to make this fun! On the screen, you'll see three text-to-pledge numbers. And we will have three horses in a race here on the stage. Aggi, Firoze Shah, and our Board Chair, Mary Montgomery von Clausen, have agreed to be our celebrity jockeys!"

The crowd roared as Aggi, Firoze, and Mary Montgomery came to the stage with hobby horses and wearing colorful jockey caps and numbered bibs.

"Choose your favorite jockey and pledge to have their horse win! *Something's Cooking, Money's in the Bank*, and *Lady in Red*. Jockeys to the starting gate." Aggi pranced around making snorting noises. The crowd was hysterical.

As the dollars were raised, Kaba called out the race. "It's *Lady in Red* in the lead by a nose, followed closely by *Money's in the Bank*. *Something's Cooking* has yet to leave the starting gate. Woohoo! A flood of speed for *Something's Cooking*, the course favorite. He's determined to beat out *Money's in the Bank* and the *Lady in Red*."

Lupe smiled in relief as the pledges exceeded her internal goal.

"And it's *Something's Cooking* by a full length! Thank you all for your contributions, and thank you to Aggi, Firoze Shah, of course, our board chair, Mary Montgomery von Clausen, for playing along. Everyone's a winner! Tessa, Silke, and Ariel presented each with a bouquet. Stephanie awarded them with trophies.

"The silent auction closes at 9:00, and now we'll draw the winning card for the Jaeger-LeCoultre Reverso Classic Monoface men's watch."

Silke and Ian came to the stage. Silke held a fresh deck of cards, and Ian showed off the elegant watch box.

"Ok. Does everyone have their card? I'm going to shuffle the desk like so." And with surprising dexterity, the performer made several intricate shuffles.

"Ask me how I got through acting school." He joked. "Now, Silke, please choose the winning card. And remember I bought ten cards. No pressure."

Silke reached out and drew a card and shouted. "It's the seven of hearts!"

"Lucky number seven!" Kaba cheered.

Lupe's table burst out as Thomas Danek shouted. "It's mine!" He bounded up to the stage.

"Congratulations!" Kaba handed the watch case to the lawyer, and Ben took a photo of the four.

Returning to his seat at the table, Thomas smiled as he opened the case to show off his prize.

The case was empty.

Lupe sighed. The evening had gone too well.

Chapter 14
Grace Under Pressure: a Fundraiser's Maxim

Lupe quickly gathered her thoughts and reached for the watch case. "Thomas!" She exclaimed. "I think I know what happened but let me go check with my colleagues. I'll be right back."

She rushed through the crowded ballroom to where Ian and Silke were dancing. "Ian," she whispered urgently. "I need to see you now."

"Sure, Lupe, what's up?" Asked Ian, after twirling Silke in several dramatic revolutions.

"Not here. Follow me." Lupe led Ian over to one of the cashier's booths. "Ian," she asked frantically. "Where's the watch?" Lupe opened the box to display the empty velvet lining.

Ian shrieked and fell histrionically to his knees. "OMG, Lupe! Where is it? I put it in there half an hour ago."

"Shush," Lupe admonished, making sure no one had noticed his outburst. "Did it leave your side? Think, think, Ian, think."

"Ah, yeah. I put it down at the registration table for just a minute. Oh, Lupe, I'm so sorry, it's all my fault. If I hadn't come up with this stupid idea…."

"Don't worry, Ian, we'll think of something. Come with me. Let's go to Pierre."

Lupe and Ian raced back to the dance floor, where Pierre was sedately dancing with a bejeweled matron. Lupe stepped up and tapped Pierre on the shoulder, stopping the two.

"I am so sorry to interrupt your dance, Mrs. Kraus, but unfortunately, I need to borrow our CFO for a few minutes. Ian will be happy to dance with you. Won't you, Ian?"

Ian flashed a dazzling smile and captured Mrs. Kraus in a hearty embrace.

"Pierre. The Jaeger-Lecoultre has been stolen. What is wrong with this Museum? Are we cursed? The rider will cover the theft, right?"

"Yes, Lupe," Pierre replied calmly. "We will need a police report."

Lupe sighed heavily. "Of course. OK, if you take care of that with Detective Collins, I'll talk to Thomas. I'm about to tell a great big fib." Lupe said grimly. She had an awful vision of being stricken from the Association of Fundraising Professionals membership.

Lupe straightened her shoulders and strode purposely back to her table, where her guests were all chattering.

She plastered a smile on her face. "It's just what I thought! My intern gave it to one of the security detail. Unfortunately, the officer mistakenly took the watch back to the Museum for safekeeping. I'll hand-deliver it to you first thing tomorrow." Thomas looked like he didn't quite believe her but said nothing.

***

Lupe dragged herself into the office the following day, eager to clear up the latest theft. She had told her staff to sleep in after the long night and was surprised to find Marcus already at his desk, looking bright and energetic.

"Marcus. I told you; you didn't have to rush into work this morning.

"I know, Lupe, but last night was so extraordinary I couldn't wait to get to work on the acknowledgments. Ben Terrence has already sent me photos that I can use in a collage to send out to all the donors."

"That's wonderful, Marcus, and be sure to send it to those who didn't attend as well. They should also have the opportunity to contribute. It's important to get the acknowledgements out quickly while the event is still on people's minds. Listen, I have to step out for a bit to run an important errand. If anyone needs me, they can reach me on my cell phone. I should be back in about an hour and a half."

Lupe caught the subway to midtown to go to the Wempe store to buy a new watch. *My corporate card is going to be maxed out,* she thought grimly.

While traveling, she reflected on the night before. *Who had taken the watch? Was that somehow connected to Stephanie's missing speech, or were the two completely unrelated?* Lupe wondered how the meeting was going between Mimi and Stephanie. How on earth would Mary Montgomery achieve a peace treaty between the two warring Type-A personalities?

Lupe had brought a photo of the stolen watch to show the salesman. Fortunately, there were several in stock, and the salesman merely had to change out the strap to match the one that had been raffled off.

Breathing a sigh of relief, Lupe stepped out of the store and realized she was near Bergdorf Goodman. Buying a fresh lipstick was a treat that always helped lift her spirits. Lupe walked the few blocks up 5th Ave to the landmark store and took the escalator down to the basement.

Paradise, she thought blissfully. Cosmetics and exquisite perfumes of all kinds. Just being there gave her a lift. At the Charlotte Tilbury counter, she spent ten minutes happily conversing with the elegant saleswoman. She chose a lipstick for the summer in a rosy shade called *Love Liberty.*

After making her purchase, she decided to sample the latest Diptyque scent. Out of the corner of her eye, she saw Ingrid San Sebastian and was about to greet her when she realized Ingrid was not alone. Standing with the donor was a tall, very fit young man with short dark blonde hair. The two seemed captivated by one another. Lupe realized they were not casual acquaintances, and when the young man's hand slipped low on Ingrid's back in a tight embrace, Lupe caught her breath. *Is everyone having an affair?* She thought with some irritation.

She reflected on the previous night at the gala – *Firoze Shah and the attractive blonde woman; Stephanie and the sophisticated bald man; and now Ingrid? Why, she had only been married a year!* Lupe thought it better to draw the veil and get the watch delivered to Thomas Danek at his law office, but she didn't want to be seen. Sidling around a Hermes display, she snuck over to the elevators in the back and made it out the door to 5th Avenue.

Fortunately, Thomas was in a meeting when Lupe arrived at his firm. His assistant signed for the package, and Lupe was spared further scrutiny by the sharp-eyed attorney.

Lupe hurried back to the office where Ariel and Tessa were busily ensuring the last remaining auction items were delivered.

"I'm glad we had the auction items online ahead of the event. We got some high bids from people who didn't attend. I should have a final tally for you in an hour or so," said the special events manager. "It was a great night."

"Yes. I was happy with the 'horse race' that worked out well."

"Everyone enjoyed it. Ian told me about the watch. Is everything OK now?

"I bought a replacement and hand-delivered it to Thomas Danek. Pierre assured me we could file a claim with the insurance rider."

"I'm glad you checked on the extra event coverage."

"So am I. It's so important when you're dealing with expensive luxury goods and also for liability if anything happens to a guest."

"What do you have left to deliver?"

"Just the art deco lamps and the chaise. I'm sending Ian in a taxi."

"Will today's outfit pass muster?" Lupe asked.

"He was so happy with last evening's feedback that he's upped his game. Today he's decided he's a French yachtsman. Striped shirt and white linen pants, and a beret with streamers."

Lupe laughed out loud. "You made my day. Let me check in with Pierre about the insurance claim."

On her way to Pierre's office, Lupe stopped for a quick coffee. Sisi and Audry were also in the break room chatting about the prior evening.

"Lupe! We were just talking about last night. What a great event. And you went over the goal. I'm so glad you got Mendel covered." Sisi gushed, referring to the winter exhibition.

"Yes. We're very pleased. I was thrilled that the horse race worked."

"Where do you come up with your ideas? Was it hard to get Firoze, Mary Montgomery, and Aggi to play along?" Audry asked.

Lupe poured a cup of coffee. "I knew Aggi would go along. He's so fun-loving and spirited. Once he agreed, it was easier to get Mary

Montgomery and Firoze to participate. I thought Firoze would be very stoic about it, but he seemed to have a lot of fun."

"Yes, and Mary Montgomery looked majestic riding her hobby horse in her Dior gown," Sisi added. They all laughed.

"What happened to Stephanie? She seemed to have lost her place in her speech?" Audry asked.

"She actually lost her speech. It was taken from the podium. She was not amused."

"Oh, no! She's so sensitive to appearances." Sisi said.

"No one at my table seemed to notice," Audry stated. "And thank you for introducing me to Margaret McGuiness. She is wonderful and has agreed to pay for the camp scholarships. I'm going to talk to the principal of PS19 later today."

Lupe thanked the two directors for their participation in the success of the event. Having an engaged leadership team made her fundraising efforts more impactful.

Pierre was talking with the bookkeeper when Lupe entered. Pierre quickly signed off on a report and welcomed Lupe to sit.

"How are your feet this morning, Pierre?" asked Lupe.

Pierre laughed. "Those ladies kept me on my toes. I think my wife was a little jealous. I only got one dance with her, and it was to 'Volare.'"

Lupe smiled at the image. "Pierre, I'm sorry to interrupt your morning, but I took care of buying the new Jaeger-LeCoultre and delivered it to Thomas Danek at his office. I want to make sure there are no snags with the insurance rider."

"Nothing to worry about, Lupe. We'll get full replacement value. And in the scheme of things, this is as you say, small potatoes."

"Yes. Any updates on the insurance claim for the Manet thefts?"

Pierre sighed. "It's not looking good, I'm afraid. We will, in all likelihood, have to ask Allan to break the endowment to cover the loss. Mary Montgomery, Firoze, and Stephanie are going to have a video call with Allan to sound him out."

"I wouldn't want to trade places with them. Allan will be livid."

"Yes, he's very paternal about the Museum and wants it to be sustainable. That's why he established the endowment in the first place."

"I spoke to Agent Reyes last evening, but he didn't tell me much about the investigation. He did mention that I should be aware of something to do with Stacey Leibman's IPO. What do you think that could be?"

"Pfft." Pierre shrugged. "It could have something to do with the first-quarter earnings. That has a big impact on the stock prices. They had a big fire at their main warehouse and lost a lot of inventory. It will probably have an impact on their supply chain. They should be issuing that report next week. I'll keep a lookout. TQT is the ticker."

"Thanks, Pierre. We're prepping for a major gift conversation, and I want to make sure my estimated ask range is correct."

"They would probably hold off on a response until after the earning's report and remember she's got a six-month lock-up, so won't be able to give her actual gift until later in the fall."

"That's fine. I didn't expect it for this fiscal year anyway. By the way, I was talking to Ralph last week, and he looked nervous when I told him the police would be questioning everyone who was at the reception and Marla's salon. Why do you suppose that was?"

"Ralph is a naturally nervous person. A lot of people get anxious when they have to speak to *les flic* even when they've done nothing wrong."

"That's true. It could be nothing more than that. But-"

"No, Lupe. Before you ask, I am not going to spy on our members. You are the only detective we need."

"Word gets around. How did you know?"

"Detective Collins let it slip last evening. I think she's a bit jealous of the attention Agent Reyes is paying to you."

"Nothing is going on between us," Lupe spluttered, feeling the color rise on her cheeks. "I just want to get the pictures back."

"As we all do. But you have a knack for investigating."

"It comes with the job. All the research. But I make sure to use my powers for good, not evil." Lupe smiled.

Realizing she was hungry, having skimped on breakfast, Lupe grabbed her wallet and went down to the café for a quick snack. Although early for lunch, she took a hummus and sprouts wrap to have at her desk. Looking to the corner of the café, Lupe saw Mary Montgomery and Mimi in intimate conversation. I wonder how the meeting went, she thought.

Mimi saw Lupe and waved.

"Hi Honey, thank you for a lovely evening last night." Mimi looked relaxed and comfortable in pink. *Was that her anti-fatigue strategy too?*

"I should be thanking you both. We've exceeded our goal, and I should have a final total for you shortly. I'll send you the photos to look at too."

"I can't wait to see them." Mimi smiled.

"You just want to see me parading around on my hobby horse," Mary Montgomery jested. "The things a board chair has to do."

Mimi and Mary Montgomery exchanged meaningful glances. Lupe was sure she enjoyed the "horse race" better than dressing down her executive director or finding millions of dollars to pay two international museums.

Back at her desk, Lupe munched on half her sandwich, putting the remainder in her desk drawer for a mid-afternoon snack.

How had the meeting with Stephanie gone? She must be really feeling the pressure from the thefts. After all, the exhibition was the biggest to happen at the MVC, and Stephanie counted on the positive publicity to burnish her name as a leading director. Lupe was certain Stephanie wanted bigger things. While many would be proud to head the small Museum, Stephanie exuded ambition. She dreamt of moving uptown to a more prestigious institution. *Bigger budgets, grander names, and not having to deal with aging hippies,* Lupe thought.

Lupe's phone rang. Swallowing quickly, she answered on the second ring.

"She wants to see you," Charlotte whispered. "And it's not good."

"Can you give me a hint?"

"The meeting with Mimi and my mother didn't go very well."

Lupe sighed. *What was she supposed to do about it?* "I'll be right there."

Lupe ran up the stairs stopping at the roof garden to catch her breath. Charlotte was frantically sorting papers at her desk in a mad attempt at seeming efficient. Unfortunately, her activity looked manic. Not a good sign, Lupe thought.

Smiling with a bravura she did not feel, Lupe, knocked on her boss's door.

"Lupe! Mimi swears she didn't take my speech, but I want to know who did. I want you to get to the bottom of it."

"I'll do my best." She wondered why the executive director was so obsessed with the speech when her museum faced financial distress.

"You will do better than your best. I will not be made a fool. Whoever did this should be censured or maybe even fired—and speaking of fired. What have you got on Tessa Hunt? Do you have enough of a paper trail?"

Lupe stood as tall as her 5'4" would allow. "No, Stephanie. I do not have any reason to fire Tessa. She and Ariel worked really well together at the gala, and we have gone above our goal. I think we should focus –"

"You think?! I told you if you did not gather evidence to fire that girl, I would have Charlotte do it. Charlotte!" Stephanie bellowed, and Charlotte ran into the room.

"Charlotte, we need to fire Tessa Hunt, and I want you to gather the support we need. Log all her mistakes and anything she does that's out of line. I want her gone by the end of the month."

Instead of merely looking like she was going to cry, Charlotte began to tear up.

"Your allergies are acting up, Charlotte," Stephanie snapped. "You want to run a museum eventually. This is a necessary part of the job. You always have to have honesty, integrity, and loyalty from your people." Stephanie stared at Lupe as she said, "loyalty."

Lupe remained composed. She had worked with difficult personalities before, and her way of managing them was to diffuse their anger. Sometimes changing the subject did the trick. Here goes, she thought.

"Allan told me he was taking Marla up to the Berkshires to recover from the kidnapping. He told me she's OK but needs rest."

The abrupt change seemed to work. "Yes, he said as much to me too. I'm sure Pierre told you about the endowment. We're hoping Allan will agree to let us break it. Otherwise, we will have to go to a judge for permission. The media is hounding me all the time about the theft. Our lending Museums have given us ninety days to make payment arrangements. We have five years to make full restitution, but they have to agree on our payment plan. This has all been a nightmare. It was meant to be such a grand exhibition. Remember what happened at the Isabella Stewart Gardner?"

In 1990, 13 priceless masterpieces were stolen from the Boston museum. The paintings had yet to be returned, although the Museum continued to offer a $10 million reward for information leading to the paintings' recovery.

"The authorities will find the paintings. The technology the police and the FBI use is much more sophisticated. I'm sure there will be a break soon." Lupe was thinking about Marla's disappearance and the multiple thefts. She felt they were all connected. She just had to figure out how.

"I'm not as sanguine. If we can't break the endowment, we may have to face restructuring. That means massive layoffs and program cuts. We would be ending MVC and all I've built these past five years."

"Should we call Jane Mehra? She can help us with messaging to engage members during this time?"

"Yes, and Malcolm Maye will be starting as Director of Marketing and Communication. He is competent."

"For now, attendance is better than ever. I wish people were coming for better reasons than to see the empty wall space, but at least they are getting in the door. Ariel told me membership applications at the front desk have increased by ten percent year over year. They may have come for the drama, but they are staying for the mission."

"Perhaps." Said Stephanie. "For now, I want you to find out who took my speech. That was inexcusable."

Chapter 15
Dealing with Difficult Bosses

Lupe stepped out of Stephanie's office to the waiting area and Charlotte's desk. Charlotte sobbed quietly.

"Come with me," Lupe whispered as she guided the unfortunate assistant out of the room and over to the greenhouse across the roof garden.

"Don't let her get to you, Charlotte. You don't have to spy on Tessa. I will talk it over with the other directors, and we will make sure nothing happens."

"It's not that, although that's bad enough." Fresh tears pooled in Charlotte's pale blue eyes. She looked even mousier than usual.

"Buck up. Remember, you can always talk to your mother if things get too tough."

"That's the last thing I can do. My mother won't stand for any weakness from me. She's always telling me that strong women don't cower, but that only makes me want to hide more."

"What is it then? Perhaps I can help." Lupe felt sorry for the young woman who was obviously feeling assaulted from many fronts.

Charlotte pursed her lips. "You're the last person to help. "

"Charlotte? What can you mean? What have I ever done to hurt you?"

"It's what you could do."

Mystified, Lupe thought for a moment, and then the pieces of the puzzle seemed to fall in place.

"You hid Stephanie's speech, didn't you?"

Charlotte's eyes blinked rapidly. "Nnnno." She stammered and then admitted. "Yes. She's so mean to me. I just wanted to make her suffer a bit, but I can't have her find out. She'll tell my mother, and maybe I'll get fired."

Lupe patted the secretary on the shoulder. "I won't say anything about it. But don't pull any stunts like that again. Stephanie is difficult to work with, but getting back at her won't make things better in the long run. You are at the beginning of your career, and you will work with some great people and some challenging personalities. I suggest you learn some assertiveness skills to communicate better with people like Stephanie." *And your mother,* Lupe, wanted to add but refrained. "Tell you what. I can mentor you if you'd like. But you have to promise me to knock off the passive-aggressive behavior."

"Thanks, Lupe, but what will you say to Stephanie?"

"She's not going to let this go. She's trying to regain control because she feels powerless. The theft of the paintings and Marla's kidnapping have her extremely stressed, and she's acting out. It's not professional, but we are all human. I don't condone her behavior, but I understand it. Your understanding of the situation may help you deal with her."

"I do understand, but it's hard being in the line of fire."

"Yes. Once, early in my career, I worked with a director who had a fiery temper. He expected his major gifts officers to be on the phone from dawn to dusk talking to prospects. When email came into vogue, he got so frustrated he picked up a computer and threw it across the room. Fortunately, the board chair gave him a stern lecture, and he was sent for anger management training."

Charlotte dried her eyes and smiled. "I wish Stephanie would do that."

"For now, I want you to try this. When she starts storming, take a deep breath and imagine you have a protective cloud encircling you. Give the cloud a color, whatever you like best. That cloud will keep out her bad mojo. And remember, you have friends."

Lupe went back to her desk, where Tessa was waiting.

"You'll never believe this one," the development assistant laughed.

"What is it?"

Tessa handed a letter to Lupe, written on the letterhead of a large law firm. In sum, one of the Legacy Society members who had recently passed away had remembered the Museum. Her specific gift amounted to a Kissimmee timeshare, an uncatalogued stamp collection, and two hundred Hummel figurines.

Lupe sighed. "That was kind of Mrs. Lombardo. But it presents a few issues. Timeshares can be a pain to sell, and we'll have to get the stamps and Hummels appraised. I'm not sure of the 'value' of this gift, however generous it was intended to be. Sometimes people think their collections are more valuable than they actually are. But still, it was good of her to remember us.

"Can't you encourage people to give more practically?" asked Tessa.

"We try with our 'lunch and learns' and through our communication pieces and of course we encourage people to take the advice of counsel when making or revising their wills. But we can't be sure of their plans unless they tell us outright, and sometimes even then, it's not accurate."

"Is it difficult to talk to donors about gift planning?

"The reasons people want to leave a legacy gift are the same reasons they support the organization, in general. I enjoy asking why someone is involved with us and how long they have been giving. It's also interesting to learn about their other charities."

"Have you ever been surprised by a bequest?"

"Besides this one?" Lupe laughed. "I'm always pleased when a modest annual fund donor remembers us. It shows our impact. I once held a luncheon for a group of ladies who had regularly given between $500-$1000 to the annual fund. Audry and Sisi came in and spoke about the programs and collections, and most of the women subsequently asked to join the Legacy Society. We try to hold special talks for the members, and they enjoy spending time together."

Lupe asked Tessa to research appraisers for the objects and check options for selling the timeshare. In Lupe's experience, some timeshare "brokers" took hefty fees, leaving very little for the seller. Lupe then reviewed the acknowledgment letters for major gift donors and the gala committee for Stephanie to sign. The committee members would each receive a lovely Italian ceramic salad bowl. She took the letters to Stephanie's office personally and was happy to note Charlotte's countenance had improved. She no longer looked like she was next in line for the guillotine and actually smiled when she saw Lupe. Stephanie's door was closed, but Lupe could see she was on a video call at her computer. *Was she speaking to Allan*, she wondered?

Returning to her desk, she then reviewed the email Marcus had created with the gala highlights. With his usual knack, he had made it visually engaging and informative. She reminded him to double-check that the links to the donation page worked and approved distribution.

Gathering her thoughts for a moment, Lupe reviewed the rest of her day ahead. She needed to call Jane Mehra to have her begin to work on the crisis communications plan. Then Lupe would meet with the team for a quick event post-mortem and work with Paul on the New York City Cultural Council grant. But first, she decided to take a few minutes to reflect on the many thefts and Marla's disappearance.

Were the thefts of the paintings and snuffbox related? The pictures were worth tens of millions of dollars, and the snuffbox, while valuable, was worth about $30,000. The recent thefts of items from the gift shop and the watch amounted to very little in comparison. Perhaps the gift shop things and the Jaeger-LeCoultre were the work of another person or persons? Perhaps, as Marla conjectured, she had mislaid the snuffbox. But why was Marla so secretive? Was she afraid for her life or that of Allan's or a member of her family? Allan said she was unharmed but had she been emotionally abused or threatened? Lupe was furious at the thought.

Josh Reyes gave her no relevant information the previous evening, but he hinted that he had new intelligence. Lupe hated not being in the know. Everyone has a weakness, she thought, *and this is mine.* Besides embodying the rare combination of an extraverted personality with attention to detail, Lupe had a stubborn, competitive streak which she tried to curb. She remembered her childhood and how her siblings hated playing Monopoly with her.

If professionals stole the Manets, there was little Lupe could do to solve the mystery. But if the thefts were connected, her suspects were limited to those who attended the de Legumes reception and Marla's salon. Stacy and Ralph Leibman, Pietro and Ingrid San Sebastian, Firoze Shah, Mary Montgomery van Clausen, and Stephanie. After a moment's hesitation, added Marla and Allan. What if Marla had, for some obscure reason, faked the kidnapping? It seemed far fetched, but for now, she left them on her list.

She considered each suspect in turn. Josh hinted that something was going on with Stacy's company now that it had gone public. *Did she need cash?* The masterpieces were not really liquid assets unless she also had an ultra-high net worth buyer to make a quick sale. Wouldn't the FBI catch on to that quickly? *Not if the transaction was in anonymous cryptocurrency,* she thought. The same could be said for Firoze Shah if he needed money because of an impending divorce. He obviously was interested in a woman other than his wife Raina, if last night was any indication.

Lupe wrote a note by both Stacy and Firoze's names. It read: follow up with Paul on finances.

Ingrid didn't seem to have money woes since she planned to make a seven-figure gift to the Museum. But who was the young man she was with at Bergdorf's? Was she also planning a divorce? Ingrid was a savvy businesswoman, and no doubt had an iron-clad prenuptial and probably postnuptial agreement.

Lupe reminded herself that the gift agreement was finalized. *I wonder if I can hand deliver it to Ingrid's apartment,* she thought. This would give Lupe a chance to see the doyenne and perhaps her regent in their natural habitat.

Pietro had a playboy reputation and seemed to enjoy the esthetic comforts of marriage to Ingrid. He had never flirted with Lupe, preferring long-legged models. Perhaps he had tried to woo Silke, Lupe thought. Would Pietro have stolen the paintings out of jealousy because his work lacked the same vigor and prestige of the

209

impressionist master? For some reason, Lupe doubted that. Since his marriage to Ingrid, Pietro's art career had taken a back seat to a vibrant social life. He always seemed content to worship at Ingrid's feet, caring for Borgia, and traveling to their many homes, especially the villa on the Riviera.

Lupe skipped over Mary Montgomery because she really couldn't see the august board chair as a criminal mastermind. *I can't see a reasonable motive,* she thought.

Yet, Stephanie had been acting suspiciously. The conversation Lupe overheard was decidedly odd. The bald man could just be a prospect Stephanie was chatting up, but wouldn't Lupe have known him? Was Stephanie trying to create not a golden parachute but a platinum one? Selling the paintings would set her up for life. No, Stephanie's anxiety over the thefts seemed authentic. She was behaving precisely like the paintings had been stolen under her watch, and her job and reputation were on the line. Having worked with Stephanie for five years, she knew she wasn't a good enough actress to fake her concern.

That left Ralph Leibman. Was he the gentle gardener he pretended to be? Or was there something nefarious about his past? Was he being blackmailed and had to take part in the thefts to protect himself or Stacy and her company, Tranquil-i-Tea?

For a moment, Lupe set aside motive and thought about means and opportunity. How had the criminal known the sensors were not working? How did they get the artworks out of the building unseen?

The time frame was short, barely two hours. Lupe concentrated on that period and tried to remember anything unusual that had transpired. Looking down on her sheet, she saw she had inadvertently started doodling. Art was not her strong suit. She had started drawing a pepper with eyeglasses, but it looked more like a pear with a unibrow. Crossing it out, she put the notebook in her desk drawer and saw her unfinished sandwich. *Not very appetizing*, Lupe thought as she gazed at the stale wrap. She was tearing off the more dried-up pieces of the tortilla when Ariel entered.

"Great news! The horse race put us over $1 million."

"That is good news. It tells us our donors and members still have faith in us as an institution and aren't blaming us for the thefts."

"And it tells us we came up with the right mix of engaging activities. Kaba is such a great host."

"Kaba! How could I possibly forget him! We need to send him something special as a thank you."

"I've already thought about it. He is so passionate about the Green Market. I thought we could choose one Saturday next month and call it Kaba Tadashi Day? We could make a contribution in his name to purchase some extra special food items. Audry told me they never have enough spices --even something as simple as salt and pepper to make the food taste better."

"That's a good idea! If he can be there, all the better, but if not, we can stream some of *Creature Comforts*."

211

"I'm sure he would love it."

"I'll call him now, and would you get everyone to the conference room for the post-mortem?"

Ariel nodded and left the room as Lupe called the actor. She was surprised that he picked up the phone on the first ring. She'd expected him to be busy performing.

"Lupe! It was great last night. The crowd seemed to enjoy paying it forward," he chuckled.

"Yes, you have a knack. If you ever want to give up on this acting biz, I can use a major gifts officer."

"Let me guess. It will be like auditioning. Lots of 'no's' before you finally hear 'yes?'"

"You got it in one. It's exactly the same. Some of the best fundraisers are former actors. They have thick skins and are very resilient. Thank you so much for last evening. You were wonderful. Everyone had so much fun, and you were great with the auction. We hit $1 million, which is more than 30% over our goal. You really made a difference."

"You know it is my pleasure, Lupe. I'm so glad things turned out well. Who knew so many people were interested in Gregor Mendel?"

Lupe laughed. "Haven't you heard? 19th Century monks are all the rage. We'd like to thank you by having a Kaba Tadashi Day at the Green Market next month. We'll have some special treats for our clients and maybe screen some of the *Creature Comforts* programs for the kids. Would that be ok with you? I know your schedule is busy, so I don't expect you to make it."

"Lupe! Of course, I'll be there. It would be an honor."

"Wonderful! I'll connect with your assistant on the details and date."

"Perfect. By the way, I know you all have been so worried about the paintings. I overheard something last night you might want to pass along to the investigators."

Lupe's ears perked up.

"I was sitting at the lead table with Stephanie, Aggi, the San Sebastian's, and the Leibman's. That kid Ian came by to show off the watch. He should consider acting lessons. He's quite a character. We all looked at it, and some of the men started showing off their watches too. At first, they were trying to be discreet, you know, checking the time? Then it was like a little battle of who had the best man jewelry. It was a strange game of one-upmanship. Soon they moved on to Lamborghinis and Maybach's and then to art. That's when the women got into the act. Stacy talked about a Degas sketch she had bought at Sotheby's last month, and Aggi's date mentioned a Renaissance bust attributed to the school of Tintoretto. I've heard these types of conversations with celebrity types, but it seemed a bit out of character for MVC patrons. I always thought they were less flashy."

"That is unfortunate. But what can that have to do with the thefts? Unless you think one of them stole the paintings to have something the others couldn't possess?"

"It did cross my mind. I know it could be an outside gang, but I heard the theft occurred within a two-hour window. Surely someone would have noticed if strangers came in and took the paintings away?"

"One would think so, Kaba. Unless the thieves were disguised as waiters but even then, how would they know the pressure sensors weren't functioning? They would be taking a big risk to steal the paintings while the room was being set up for the reception."

"I certainly don't want to get anyone in trouble, but I just wondered. Could the thief or thieves be closer to home?

With this food for thought, Lupe thanked the actor and ended the call.

Ignoring the afternoon hour, Lupe poured a fresh cup of coffee and treated herself to a large splash of creamy cashew milk. A minute on the lips, she sighed. Her team was assembled in the conference room, chatting happily about the previous evening's success.

"First off, thank you all for your hard work in making the gala so successful. Thank you especially to Ariel and Tessa for their outstanding efforts with the auctions. Ariel tells me we have hit $1 million, which is a new record for this event. I'm so proud of you all and humbled to work with such a resourceful and energetic team."

The group shared a round of applause, and Ian cried out, "encore, encore!"

"I like holding post-mortems for our more significant events so we can learn how to continually improve our fundraising and event operations and see what we want to continue doing and what we might not want to have as part of the event.

"The food and decorations were all amazing," said Marcus a bit shyly.

"Yes, we started at a very high level. Did anyone try the fish option, or did you all stick with the vegetable napoleon?"

"I had the grilled snapper,' said Tessa. "It was excellent, and Pierre was delighted we had a pescatarian choice."

"Yes, Pierre likes fish. Do you know how many people took advantage of it?"

Ariel consulted her notes. "We were pretty spot on. 20% of the guests asked for fish, and we were about equal on the dairy and vegan versions. Tom Unger was disappointed there was no filet mignon."

"Of course, he was. The wines were exceptional, and we have Mimi to thank for that. She has such good taste and knows how to get value."

Ariel smiled wickedly. "I was able to snag the leftover wine for our stash."

"Waste not, want not!" Ian chortled. "I'm still upset about the watch being taken. Do you think it has anything to do with the paintings and Marla's disappearance?"

"I think it does," Paul affirmed. "I've been doing some after-hours digging, and I'm pretty sure I know who's responsible."

All eyes turned to the prospect researcher in astonishment.

Chapter 16
Be a Practitioner, not a Theorist

"Paul!" The group chorused. "Who is it?"

"I don't think I should tell you all before I speak to the FBI."

"That's not fair," Ian whined.

"No. We won't tell a soul," Marcus echoed.

"I'll give you a couple of hints, and then you have to figure it out for yourselves."

"Will you share the reward if we do?" Ian asked.

"You wish. Ok. So the cameras didn't show anything unusual during the two hours in question. Everything checked out. Agreed?"

"Yes, get to the point," Krisha admonished.

"And the FBI hasn't found any leads to an organized gang of thieves, so it was probably someone connected to the Museum."

"Yes, yes." Lupe was ready to join the others in shouting.

"But the person who took the paintings had to know the pressure sensors weren't working. So that limits the suspects to Moe and the other security guards."

"And me," Lupe said. "Moe told me about the problem. Who knows who else he spoke to or who the guards might have told?"

"True. But I have spoken to the guards, and there was only one who knew about the Wi-Fi issue because Moe asked him to stay close to the Manets."

"Andreas!" They all shouted and then looked around to make sure no one outside the conference room had heard them.

"Yes, Andreas. He's an artist and would not only know the value of the paintings but has a chip on his shoulder about his work not being appreciated like the masters."

"But how did he manage to get the paintings out of the gallery?" Asked Ariel.

"And where did he hide them from the agents?" Added Tessa.

"I think he just put the paintings in a trash bag and put it in the garbage can and rolled them out back to the dumpster at Sitar of India next door. He probably snuck back in the early morning hours and got the garbage bag back. I bet he's got the paintings in his apartment or a storage locker."

Lupe reflected for a moment. "It's a possibility, but if you're wrong, it will be hard on Andreas."

"I know, and I don't say this lightly. I like him, and I think he's a good guy. But somehow, I think he had an irresistible urge and couldn't control himself. The motive, means, and opportunity all aligned at the last moment, and he gave in."

"Don't you think the FBI has dug into his background since they know he's an artist?" Krisha inquired.

"Yes, but I don't think they put it all together, or he would have been arrested by now."

"What will you do next?" Ariel asked.

Paul sighed deeply. "Much as I hate to do it. I'm going to call Reyes and tell him what I know. He'll either tell me I'm wrong and they have already investigated and found Andreas is clear, or they will call him in again."

Lupe still believed the culprit was someone connected to both the salon and the reception and somehow didn't see the art student as a kidnapper and master criminal.

"Tread carefully, Paul. If you're wrong, the criminal is still out there. It could get dangerous. Let's wrap up. I'll need your summer vacation plans by the end of the week. And no, you can't all leave in the same two weeks. Please put your first- and second-time off choices. I call director privilege. I have to go to Texas for my cousin's quinceanera in the first week of August." *Won't that be fun*, thought Lupe, thinking of the big family party in the appalling heat.

***

The next day, Lupe reviewed the draft NYC Cultural Affairs grant application and noted a few questions for Paul. Stepping over to his desk, she was surprised to find him absent.

"Where's Paul?" Lupe asked Tessa.

"He hasn't come in yet; did he text you he was running late?"

"No, but I'll check. Probably a subway delay." The bane of all New York commuters.

Her phone rang, and Lupe answered with a cheery greeting. It was Charlotte.

"Lupe," she whispered. "I need your help. It's urgent." The assistant sounded terrified.

"Charlotte? What's wrong?

"Randall and Milo are here, and Stephanie wants me to watch them. I can't. They are so unruly. They keep threatening to tie me up and stick me in the compost pile."

Lupe laughed. Stephanie's two sons were a handful. Occasionally their nanny had an appointment, and Stephanie was forced to bring the young boys to the office. At six and eight, they were already holy terrors. Lupe suspected the nanny made up her "doctor" visits just to get some peace.

Ian sauntered by dressed once again as Captain Carrot. Evidently, his resolution to "dress to impress" had ended.

"Ian, I need you to do me a favor."

"S'up?"

"Stephanie's boys are here today. I need you to spend time with them. Charlotte is overwhelmed."

"Gotcha. I'm on it." And with an exaggerated lunge, he rushed off.

Lupe's cell phone rang. It was Reyes.

"Josh, how are you?"

"Fine, Lupe, but I have some bad news. Paul Howley was mugged last evening and has a concussion. We just found out now because the mugger took his wallet and cell phone, and Paul has just regained consciousness."

"Oh, Lord. Where is he? Is he in the hospital?"

"Yes, he's at Bellevue. They are keeping him for observation, but he's communicative. He had left me a message last evening, and I wasn't able to return the call. This morning he told me his suspicions about Andreas Konstavides."

"Have you been able to check that out?"

"Yes. There is no footage of Konstavides leaving the Museum at all during the time in question, so Paul's theory of how he might have taken the paintings doesn't hold water."

"Another dead end. Poor Paul. I'll get right over to the hospital to see him."

"I'm sure he'd appreciate that. Are you doing ok otherwise?"

"Yes, I wish I had some clues to share with you. I really want to get this case solved."

"We all do, but remember, the person or persons responsible could get desperate as we close in on them. It might become risky. Take care of yourself, Sherlock."

"I promise."

After telling the team what had happened, Lupe grabbed her purse and caught a cab to the hospital.

She was relieved to find Paul sitting up in bed, changing channels with the remote to find something interesting to watch.

"Paul!" Lupe exclaimed. "We're all so worried. How are you feeling?"

Paul tapped on his head. "Solid as a rock. They ran tests and, as expected, found nothing. I could have told them that."

"Oh, Paul. You always find humor in every situation. I'm sure the police asked but do you remember anything that happened?"

"I was walking home from the Museum, and I heard footsteps, but almost like a child running. They were very light. That's the last thing I remember. I keep trying to rack what we laughingly refer to as my brain, and I can't think of anything else. The doctors told me not to press. Evidently, it's pretty common with head trauma."

Street crime was down in that area of the city but still known to happen.

"I'm so sorry. Is there anything I can get you?"

"I could murder a Grande cappuccino with almond milk."

"Done. I'll get it right away." Lupe paused, Reyes's comment on the criminal returning to her mind. "Did you mention your theory to anyone else but the team?"

Paul looked sheepish. "It slipped out. Everyone likes to be 'Big Man on Campus,' I told Tom and Moe yesterday."

Lupe's brow creased in a frown. She certainly didn't suspect the Operations Director and Chief Security Officer. "Where were you when you told them?"

"We were up on the roof garden. And yes, others could have overheard. Ralph Leibman was finishing up, and Stacy had come to meet him. Pietro San Sebastian was there with Borgia waiting for Ingrid, who was chatting with Stephanie."

Could Ralph, Stacy, or Pietro have mugged Paul? Could Pietro have told Ingrid and she had attacked him? If so, to what purpose? Did they think he would stop his sleuthing? Why would one of them want to protect Andreas? So many questions unanswered, thought Lupe in frustration.

***

223

Lupe returned to the office and reassured her team that Paul would be ok. She climbed the steps to Stephanie's office to check in with her. The development director and executive director had a regular weekly meeting to review donors and prospects.

Charlotte smiled brightly when she saw Lupe. "Lupe, thank you! Ian took the boys away to play, and peace is restored."

"Are you doing well otherwise?" Lupe's eyes shifted to Stephanie's office.

"A day at a time. My forcefield is bright orange and keeps me safe."

"It works, doesn't it?"

'Yes, can I bring you a coffee?"

"Absolutely!"

Lupe stepped in and greeted Stephanie, who gave Lupe a warm smile she usually reserved for patrons.

"Lupe, thank you for sending up Ian. I know my boys are challenging, and Charlotte is just not up to the task. It's difficult being a single parent."

"Yes, childcare coverage must be difficult." Lupe thought of all the working parents who did not have Stephanie's social clout. No matter how open workplaces purported to be, it was still hard to balance family and work.

"I want to review your top prospects. I think we have cultivated the Leibman's enough and can go to them for a major gift. I just think we may want to consider the timing of the ask." Lupe told her boss about the Tranquil-i-Tea warehouse fire and the "smoked" cannabis. "The loss was high if you pardon the pun, but insurance will cover most of the loss of inventory. The share price did take a hit because they lost so much product. Stacy and Ralph's net worth is tied to the Tranquil-i-Tea stock."

"So, when do you think we should approach them?"

"I think we should wait three months and then make the ask, assuming nothing else untoward happens to the company. From preliminary conversations, I think they will be open to making the gift, and it's just a question of when."

Stephanie agreed. "Ingrid and Pietro came by yesterday. They were in the neighborhood. Is their gift agreement ready?"

"Yes, it is. I wish I had known they were here; we could have had them sign it. But no worries, I'll hand-deliver it this afternoon."

"Good idea."

Lupe then shared the news of the legacy gift.

"Why do people do that?" Stephanie moaned. "At my last Museum, someone left us their sporting trophies. I think they thought they were sterling silver but they were electroplated."

Lupe laughed and quickly realized her mistake. Stephanie's warm smile vanished, and she stared stonily at her chief fundraiser.

"Lupe. Allan Fisker does not want to break the endowment. That means we will have to go to court. You'd better start planning for layoffs, starting with Tessa Hunt. You were the one who came up with this stupid idea in the first place. If we hadn't gotten in over our heads, the Museum would be fine. This fiasco happened on my watch, and I will not go down without a fight. If those paintings are not recovered, the Museum will have to cut its budget drastically, and your department will be the first to go. You are an expensive overhead. We certainly don't need so many people to raise money. I will just work with our major donors and not waste time with small donors and foundations – and certainly not the Legacy Society.

Just then, Stephanie's cell phone rang. She looked at the number, frowned, and gestured to Lupe to leave the room.

As she closed the door behind her, Lupe overheard Stephanie bark, "so, what's the answer?"

Lupe felt depressed. First the paintings, then Marla and now Paul. The FBI and police had no answers. She was out of fresh ideas. She had plenty of suspects but no evidence. Now her team was facing dismantling, and massive budget cuts might take place. It was disheartening. She never understood why the one department every organization needed was often first on the chopping block – development.

Before stopping by Ingrid's palatial apartment on Fifth Avenue, Lupe had called to ensure the businesswoman would be at home. Lupe's eyes widened at the array of art on display in the grand foyer. Many were obviously Pietro's work, but others spanned generations of outstanding artists. She saw a late Matisse, what was surely a Magritte and a Rothko. One entire wall was given to renaissance and baroque works featuring the holy family and biblical scenes. *Hmm, a great place for the next salon,* she thought.

Ingrid's maid asked if she wanted a beverage and left to get Ingrid. At that moment, Pietro entered with Borgia at his heels.

"Lupe! Como estas, mi vida?" The handsome artist asked.

"I'm well, Pietro. I just stopped by to give you and Ingrid the gift agreement. We greatly appreciate your generosity. This means so much."

He smiled ruefully. "It's all Ingrid, but I'm happy to take partial credit. Come, Borgia wants to play."

Of course, he does, thought Lupe sardonically, reflecting on how much time she had spent tossing a ball to the spoiled poodle. Today, Borgia's fur had been dyed pale blue, and she sported matching toenail polish. She was wearing a lapis-lazuli collar.

Lupe smiled brightly. She could fake it with the best. *Thank you, Theresa Hamilton!*

"Hey girl, who's a smart girl?" Lupe tossed the blue ball. *Aren't we matching today?*

Borgia yipped and ran about the room excitedly.

"How did you enjoy the gala the other night, Pietro?"

"It was fun. We stayed until the band stopped playing. Then we went clubbing. Ingrid came home, but I went with Aggi and his date and Silke and Ian." *Ah, ha! You are hitting on Silke*, Lupe thought with irritation.

Ingrid entered wearing Lululemon workout clothes, and Lupe noticed her hair had been tinted the same color as her canine companion. She had obviously just finished a workout. She misted her face with rose water with one hand and sipped a glass of mineral water with the other.

"Lupe! So good to see you. I'm sorry we missed you yesterday."

'So am I. I was just telling Pietro how glad we are that you made such a kind gift. We're so glad you are partnering with us. Your gift will ensure—"

"Yes, yes. I'm wonderful. Lupe, you don't have to go through your appreciation spiel with me. We are happy to assist the Museum. Mary Montgomery is a close friend, and I want to support her."

"That's a marvelous way to honor your friend," said Lupe as Borgia's tiny toenails started tearing into her pantyhose.

"Pietro, darling. Come here. Let's sign the gift agreement for Lupe. Lupe, I see you have the Crypto exchange information. I will have my assistant send the funds this afternoon."

"Would you ask him to send a test first to make sure it goes through correctly?" Borgia had left Lupe calves to go to Ingrid's side.

"Of course." Ingrid signed with a flourish and gave the pen to her spouse. Pietro signed quickly, and both smiled at Lupe. "There. That's done. Thank you for bringing this to us, Lupe. I wanted to tell you how much we enjoyed the gala at Cipriani's. Aggi is such a tremendous asset to the Museum. His menu was fabulous."

"Did you eat any of it, my pet," crooned Pietro. This was the first time Lupe ever heard the swain say anything less than adulatory to his wife.

"Of course, I did. It's just I have such a light appetite, my sweet." Lupe looked at the toned matron. She was very skinny, but her arms looked powerful. Perhaps she took a page from Wallis Simpson, the Duchess of Windsor's book. *"A woman can never be too rich or too thin."* Lupe mused.

Lupe wondered how to bring the conversation around to the thefts and Marla's kidnapping.

"Well, we especially appreciate your support after the thefts. Some of our funders have expressed concern over our security standards."

It was swift, but Lupe didn't miss the exchange of glances between the couple. Ingrid spoke first.

"It was no one's fault. Stephanie told me about the Wi-Fi. The building is old, and it is difficult to attend to such things. I should know. My castle in Denmark is ancient and needs constant maintenance."

"Yes, I'm sure. The FBI hasn't figured out if it was a planned crime or one of opportunity. We may never know."

Pietro interjected. "Remember the Munches that were taken in Oslo? One of the versions of "The Scream" and his Madonna?" In 2004, Edvard Munch's priceless paintings were taken in a bold daylight robbery when two men wearing balaclavas threatened the unarmed museum security guards with guns. The pictures were later recovered.

"But the police believed that crime was intended to distract from an investigation in the murder of a Norwegian policeman," Ingrid interjected.

Lupe wondered. *Could that be the case here? Was the theft intended to cover up another crime? If so, what could it be?* Lupe's mind was racing. She didn't want to go off on another tangent, but what if Ingrid was right and the thefts and Marla's kidnapping were just a cover-up of some other more major crime?

Thanking the pair once more, Lupe caught the subway back to the office. On the ride there, she considered what she had learned. Ingrid and Pietro were hiding something, but did it have anything to do with the crimes?

Entering the Museum lobby, Lupe decided to look into the gallery once again. *Perhaps I'll get some insight if I just look at the setting.* Much was unchanged; the table settings augmenting the various other works looked beautiful with a wide variety of arrangements and linens. While not as prized as the Manets, the other impressionist pieces that comprised the exhibition were undoubtedly stunning. Sketches by Edgar Degas and Alfred Sisley competed with minor works of Mary Cassatt, Marie Bracquemond, and Berthe Morisot.

Lupe was pleased to see the room was crowded but saddened that many people were snapping shots of the empty wall to the dismay of the gallery guards. Nothing outwardly had changed, although Lupe knew there were more guards on duty, and a second router had been installed to keep the Wi-Fi constant for the pressure sensors.

Mentally measuring the distance, Lupe guessed there was about two and a half feet of space between the edge of the table setting and where the paintings had once been positioned. Not much room to maneuver, she thought. The person who stole the images had to be thin and nimble. That knocked out Mary Montgomery, who was queenly in her proportions. Lupe realized Allan and Marla could not manage to quietly slip behind the velvet curtain and lift the paintings off the wall.

Right. That left Ralph, Stacy, Ingrid, Pietro, and Stephanie. Ingrid was definitely the thinnest, so she went to the top of the list.

Chapter 17
In Nonprofit Management, Creativity is Key

Lupe left the gallery and stepped into the library to sit for a moment in peace. How to proceed, she thought? Lupe couldn't tell Reyes she had "a feeling" about Ingrid and the others. She needed proof. Getting the evidence was the hard part.

She entered the room and heard Ian speaking in the children's corner.

"And then the zombie cucumber came out of the patch and attacked the tomatoes. It was grisly. There were seeds and juice everywhere. I have never seen such a massacre!"

Randall and Milo lay on the large colorful pillows in rapt attention.

"What happened next, Captain Carrot?" asked Milo.

"Yes, did you kill it with your paring knife?" chimed in his older brother Randall.

"Do cucumbers bleed?"

"I dug into my magic pocket and pulled out my giant vegetable peeler. He tried to run away, but I caught him and skinned him alive, ah, ha, ha, ha!" Ian lashed out wildly with his mitts. The boys screamed in glee.

Lupe smiled and left the room. Perhaps Ian should be a manny. Crossing the lobby to the elevator, Lupe shrunk back in astonishment. Entering the gallery was the blond man she had seen with Ingrid. *Who was he, and what was he doing here?* Lupe waited until he was out of view and then went to the front desk.

"Do you happen to have the name of the blond man who just went into the gallery?" she asked the coordinator on duty.

"What? Do you mean the tall one? Very fit? He's cute. Are you stalking him, Lupe?"

"No, he just looks like a former classmate of mine," Lupe fibbed. *I'm getting good at this,* she thought.

"Let me see. He paid his admission fee by credit card. His name is Sam Tolland. Is he the same guy?"

"No. My mistake. Thanks anyway." But she had a name. And in fundraising, a person's name had value.

Lupe raced up the three flights to her office, determined to find out something about Ingrid's admirer.

As she got to her office, Tessa raced in. "Lupe, have you forgotten the time? There's a senior staff meeting in five minutes.

"The meeting. I completely forgot." Lupe felt meetings ran her whole life. The agenda for this one was to review the coming year's exhibitions and programs. *Mendel again,* Lupe smiled.

The day was warm, so Lupe poured a glass of lemon thyme iced tea Krisha had made and went to the conference room. Tom was the only one there yet.

"Hi Tom, how's it going?"

"Still having trouble with the Wi-Fi in the gallery. I've told Moe to keep it quiet. We don't want a repeat of the Manets."

Lupe felt ill. "Could that happen? Is it common?"

"Thieves may think we're an easy mark."

Audry and Sissy entered, followed closely by Pierre and Malcolm, who had just started as Marketing Director. Stephanie was the last to arrive.

"Let's make this fast. I have a meeting that has come up," Stephanie announced. "Some of you might not have heard from the telegraph, but the meeting with Allan Fisker did not go well. He is not permitting us to use the endowment to pay back the museums' for the lost Manets. Our lawyers are working on a plea to the attorney general's office, but we have to prepare for the contingency that we will not be successful. I want you to go back to your budgets and cut out 25% on expenses. We also need to increase revenues as planned, so you will have to be creative."

Malcolm glanced at Lupe. *Great way to start a new job*, she thought.

Pierre was the first to speak. "I suggest we look at staff who might be willing to accept an early retirement package." Lupe saw Stephanie's eyes sparkle. *She's thinking of Moe.*

"Yes, that's good. And for some of those positions, we won't be restaffing. You'll just have to get your people to take on more work. Tell the junior staff that the additional responsibility will look good on their resumes."

"Stephanie. That's disingenuous. They will smell a rat. Extra work without extra pay and a change in job title?" Audry challenged.

Stephanie stared at the program director. Lupe could almost read her mind, for Audry was close to seventy.

Pierre suavely interjected. "Perhaps we should review our technology. There might be ways to cut back on staff by using more technology. We could use kiosks instead of having to have front desk coordinators?"

Sissy looked mutinous. Lupe knew she felt strongly about the human touch in curation.

"I'm already getting by with a skeleton crew. I can't cut my people," she stated flatly.

"You can, and you will. All of you will find a way to cut the fat from your budgets without compromising program quality, security, fundraising, and general maintenance. Tom, figure out what can be deferred within the building. I need a punch list of capital needs and their priorities. I don't know how long we will be in this situation, but we need to prepare for the long haul."

Hardly a rallying cry thought Lupe miserably. Her mind drifted to the thefts. How could she solve the case and get the paintings returned? That would solve everything. She decided to find a way to interview Ralph and Stacy to gain insights. And Stephanie? Was she guilty? Just then, she heard her name.

"Lupe is going to start the ball rolling by getting rid of Tessa Hunt," Stephanie exclaimed. "We don't need people with that kind of background at our institution. We need to be like Caesar's wife, 'above suspicion.'"

Lupe had hoped the other directors would stand up for the assistant, but they were all mute, obviously concerned about their own department needs.

"Understood?" Stephanie concluded. All nodded. "So, let's discuss the next exhibitions. Sissy, give us an update."

Sissy discussed the Gregor Mendel exhibition, and Audry added details about the complementary programming.

"I also want to talk about next spring's show, 'Art in the Garden.' I've spoken to Lupe and want to coordinate a series of outstanding performing arts performances and experiences. The working title is 'Digging Deep: The Artist Within.'" The Programming Director continued.

"How much will this cost? I need Lupe to focus on general operating support and not run around for special funding. Do you have a budget yet? Don't come to me with bright ideas without hard numbers to back it up."

"Yes, Stephanie," Audry said while passing a spreadsheet. *She had seen this film before.* "Pierre and I have gone through the budget, and based on conservative projections, we will be able to increase program revenue by 20% year over year with strategic events and activities."

Nice, thought Lupe. *Stephanie loves the word "strategic."*

"The performances and lectures will also elevate the Museum's profile," Sissy added.

"And I have a list of foundations and qualified prospects who have shown interest in similar projects," Lupe interjected.

Stephanie read over the report quickly. "Malcolm, I want a marketing plan from you for this. If the advertising costs can be kept down, we may consider it. Also, test these projections. Audry, get me the full program list asap. No boring professors or authors." She glanced at her Franck Mueller wristwatch. "I have to leave for a meeting, but we'll need the revisions to Pierre by early next week at the latest." She stood and strode purposefully out of the room. The rest sighed.

Sissy turned to Pierre. "Is it really going to come to this?"

"We need to be prepared. Hopefully, we will get permission from the AG's office to use the endowment but just in case…"

Audry spoke. "It's a challenge, but we're up for it. I remember before we had the endowment, and my 'staff' were all volunteers. We managed to create some outstanding programs then, and we'll find a way now."

That's what Lupe loved about Audry. Nothing held her back.

"And welcome aboard the Titanic, Malcolm," Tom added.

Malcolm laughed. Relieved, everyone joined in.

As Lupe left the room, Charlotte rushed up to her.

"I have something to tell you." She said in a conspiratorial whisper.

"What is it, Charlotte?" Lupe whispered back dramatically and with a smile.

"I know who Stephanie is meeting."

"You're her assistant; I expect you do."

"No. She had the appointment marked confidential in Outlook, but I know her password."

"And you will keep the confidence she expects of you. No matter what you think of your boss, it doesn't do to go behind her back. Remember what we learned from the speech incident?"

Charlotte looked disappointed. This was a piece of gossip she was dying to share. She looked like she was going to explode in excitement.

"She's meeting David Kalkan!" She burst out.

That's who the mystery man at the gala was, Lupe thought. Of course, she realized. Kalkan was a billionaire hedge fund investor, art lover, and philanthropist. Was Stephanie wooing him for a leadership gift? If so, why didn't she tell Lupe? She would have prepped her with a full briefing.

"OK. That is interesting, but I want you to keep it to yourself, Charlotte. She is probably trying to get a big gift from him to help the Museum."

Charlotte looked doubtful. She obviously thought there was something more, but Lupe didn't want to delve into the young assistant's theories.

***

Back at her computer, Lupe decided to return to her own sleuthing. She planned to do some digging on Kalkan and why he might be meeting Stephanie. Was she going to sell the paintings to him? First, Lupe wanted to find out something about Ingrid's blond man, Sam Tolland. Trying a variety of Boolean searches, Lupe finally found a photo of Sam Tolland. It turned out he was a personal trainer and sometime boxer. *He's probably Ingrid's trainer,* Lupe thought. She wouldn't be the first woman to fall for her trainer. *But why would he be at the gallery? Perhaps he was just intrigued by the notoriety of the thefts?*

Lupe's cell rang, and she answered it. "Lupe Reinowski."

"Hi Lupe, it's Paul."

"Paul! How are you feeling?"

"I'm back home, and I feel fine, but I've been told to take it easy for a couple of days. I guess that means Matzo Ball soup and binge-watching foreign detective series."

"Yes. Follow doctor's orders. I don't want to see you here for the rest of the week. Do you need us to get you anything?"

"Lupe. This is New York. I can get everything delivered."

"True. Any after-effects of the mugging?"

"They gave me something for my headache."

Lupe couldn't resist asking. "Have you remembered anything else?"

Paul hesitated. "Well. I'm not sure if it's an actual memory or if I just dreamt it. I keep thinking I heard a voice whispering to me. After I was knocked to the ground and before I was hit on the head."

Lupe caught her breath. "Were you able to make out the words?"

"Yes. The voice said. Don't get involved in the thefts. This is a warning."

"Paul. You have to tell Reyes."

"Yeah, but what if I just dreamt it?"

"It doesn't matter. Was the voice male or female?

"You know, I think it was a woman."

"Call Reyes now."

"I will."

"And check your locks. Have the delivery people leave your soup at the door."

Lupe hung up with her prospect researcher and grabbed a pen. Sometimes when she was nervous or thinking about a problem, she would twist a pen in her hand. Once, she was so focused on an issue; she broke the pen in half, getting black ink on her hands.

She tried to assemble the clues and suspects as she knew them.

Was the cufflink significant? This indicates the thief could be a man. Could it have been dropped earlier?

How did the thief get the paintings out of the Museum? Lupe didn't have access to the camera footage. I wonder if Moe has copies, she thought.

Who kidnapped Marla and why? Did it have something to do with the theft of the snuffbox? The cameras picked up a male figure in a hoodie. This was further evidence that the crook was a man.

Were the theft of the Jaeger-LeCoultre and the items from the gift shop related to the other crimes?

Who mugged Paul? He said the voice was female. Was it an actual memory, or did he dream it?

Could it be a team?

She considered each of her remaining suspects, Ralph, Stacy, Ingrid, Pietro, and Stephanie.

Captain Carrot made an appearance at her door. "Lupe! The kids' nanny arrived, so I am ready for a new assignment. And I've got big news!" He closed the door.

"OK, Ian. What's your news?"

"Stephanie is interviewing to be Executive Director at the Moulton Museum uptown."

"Ian? How on earth could you know that?"

"Milo let the cat out of the bag. He said, 'Mommy dressed up today because she's seeing the big boss at the Moulton about working there.'

Lupe felt like a broken record. "Keep it to yourself, Ian. It's none of our business."

Ian smiled knowingly. "Mums the word."

Lupe looked down at her list. David Kalkan was the chair of the board of directors at the Moulton. She crossed Stephanie's name from her list. *And then there were four.*

Lupe took the stairs two at a time to the roof garden. Ralph was tending a patch that had been "adopted" by Miss Prentiss's third grade at the nearby charter school. Looking up, the quiet man smiled as he pulled a weed from a patch of baby lettuces.

"Hi, Ralph. The summer crop is coming along well."

"Yes, our compost is so fertile. I'm spoiled for any other type."

Lupe had raced up to the roof with no real plan of how she would get Ralph to confess or implicate Stacy. Now she racked her mind, trying to think of an opening.

"Ralph. I don't know if you heard, but Paul Hawley was mugged the other day on his way home from the Museum."

"I heard. Tom told me. That's terrible. Is he OK?"

"Yes. He's resting at home and should be back to work next week."

"It reminds me of the old days in the city. Muggings were a way of life. It's sad when it happens, especially to someone you know."

"Yes. On top of the thefts and Marla Howe's kidnapping. We have had more than our share of crime lately."

"Do you think they are connected?"

Lupe weighed her words carefully. If Ralph was the criminal, he could harm her like Marla and Paul. Or worse. She stood taller and looked him in the eye.

"Yes. I don't think there is any question. Paul told me that the person who attacked him warned him to stay out of the thefts."

Ralph looked terrified. *He can't be that good of an actor,* Lupe thought. It was genuine fear.

"Criminals can be ruthless. When I was a teenager, I got in with a bad crowd. Drugs, petty theft. Then we graduated to car theft." He sat on the folding stool he kept to rest. "I was caught and sent to juvenile detention. Fortunately, I had been a good student, and the teacher, Mr. Alfonso, mentored me. He helped me fill out college applications and reviewed my essays. I was able to turn my life around. I'll never forget him. When I'm not gardening, I still tutor at Crossroads Juvenile Center in Brooklyn."

Lupe felt her eyes well up at this confession. This was not what she expected.

Back at her desk, she crossed out Ralph's name.

"Lupe, Lupi, oh, no, me gotta go. Aye-Yi-Yi-Yi." Henry belted as he danced to her desk.

"Henry! What are you doing here?"

"How quickly they forget. My troupe is practicing in the auditorium this evening."

"Of course. Yes, it slipped my mind."

"Come see us after you finish work. We'll be there until 9:00."

'Sure. I was planning on staying late this evening. I have some proposals to finish since Paul is out of commission. Do you have a minute?"

"What's up?"

"I need a sounding board. I'm pretty sure I know who's behind the thefts, but I don't really know why, and it's a bit complicated."

"Tell me! I need to be in on the kill."

"OK. I have it narrowed down to three people. Stacy Leibman, Ingrid San Sebastian, and her husband Pietro. The only motive I can think of for any of them is greed, but there is such a variety in the stolen things. Paintings worth millions. An antique snuff box is probably worth about $30,000. Then there is the Jaeger-LeCoultre watch valued at five grand and the things from the gift shop."

"Well, the smaller things could be unrelated."

"That's what I thought at first, but somehow, I feel they are connected. I can't shake the gut feeling."

"In acting, instinct can be beneficial. Use it." Henry's phone pinged. "Yikes. I have to rush. I'm sorry. I want to help."

"It's OK, Henry. I'll check in on your rehearsal later. Break a leg."

Realizing the time and that the Cultural Development Fund grant deadline was that evening, Lupe focused on her work. But in the back of her mind, she had a nagging feeling she was so close to the solution.

Chapter 18
The Full Cycle of Development

Through sheer force of will, Lupe managed to finish the grant proposal just minutes before the deadline. Try as she might, the rush to meet grant application deadlines happened more often than she would like. Grants represented about 11% of her total budget and were an essential component of her development plan, but they required careful analysis. Lupe could hear the echoes of board members and staffers who waxed lyrical about foundations being the solution to all the Museum's fundraising needs. Lupe gently but firmly disabused them of this idea. Yes, grants could be one source, but they could also be time-consuming with reporting requirements that were disproportionate to the size of the grant.

Ensuring the foundations understood the cost to administer a grant was a constant challenge. Sure, it was wonderful to receive program funding, but if the staff had to spend excessive hours collecting data points and monitoring the projects, it was not always worth it. Fortunately, Lupe was seeing a growing trend on the part of funders in understanding this issue.

With the city grant finished, Lupe took a moment to review this week's development plan items. The annual report was ready to be posted, the appeal had gone out online, and the returns looked promising. All the acknowledgments were finished for the gala. She had some personal notes to write, which she enjoyed.

Theresa Hamilton insisted on the personal touch, and since handwritten notes were no longer common practice, this was an area where savvy development professionals could stand out with donors. Lupe had worked hard to improve her handwriting. When she was in high school, she took a speed writing class, and it dramatically altered the precise cursive script she had been taught in the third grade at Holy Name School. Her usually legible handwriting turned to long lines and curves, and it took years for her to lose the speed writing habit.

Lupe smiled and wondered. Could she still do speed writing? Doodling on her pad, she wrote out: *Who is the culprit?*

Stretching her shoulders, Lupe pushed back in her chair and flung her feet onto her desk.

Who is the culprit? She repeated aloud. A name kept coming back to her. Ingrid San Sebastian.

Yet, Ingrid did not need to steal the Impressionist paintings; her Fifth Avenue apartment walls were filled with scores of priceless works. Could she have another motive? What if she just wanted to do it for kicks? It could happen. There were many stories of affluent people looking for new experiences. She had lived a charmed life. Maybe she was bored with the villa and the castle and parties?

But a man took Marla from her house. Could Pietro be involved too? Or Sam, her trainer?

Lupe picked up her phone but hesitated. She wanted to call Josh Reyes and tell him her surmises, but she thought it unlikely he would act without hard evidence.

She had filled her page with doodles. Cufflink, kidnapper, reception, salon, watch, scarf, snuffbox, photo. The photo! She pulled up the .jpg of Ben's photo of the gallery before the reception. She peered at the image closely. Moe, Andreas, Pietro, Stephanie, Firoze, and Ingrid were standing in a group. Borgia was at Pietro's feet. Lupe magnified the photo and realized what she had missed, what they had all missed.

Her mind was in a flurry. *Could it be possible? Yes. So audacious, yet simple.*

She called Reyes but got his voicemail. Leaving an urgent message to call her back, she hung up. She felt antsy and decided to walk over to the auditorium until the agent called her back.

Lupe slipped through the gallery and into the auditorium where Daniel La Grange and Anya Vaderesque were performing their scene from Richard III. *Possibly one of the most unusual of "romantic" scenes,* thought Lupe. Richard III wooed Lady Anne over the funeral bier of her husband Edward, whom Richard killed as well as Anne's father-in-law, the king. Anne is filled with hatred and disgust for the soon-to-be crowned king. Richard uses all manner of silken arguments to explain his motives. The cunning Richard goes so far as to offer her a knife to kill him, knowing the God-fearing woman will never retaliate.

"Teach not thy lip such scorn, for it was made for kissing, Lady, not for such contempt.

If thy revengeful heart cannot forgive, Lo, here I lend thee this sharp-pointed sword,

Which if thou please to hide in this true breast and let the soul forth that adoreth thee,

I lay it naked to the deadly stroke. And humbly beg the death upon my knee."

Lupe was mesmerized by the classic language made fresh by Daniel's acting. Anya was a haunting beauty and showed fire in her expressions and vocal cadence.

"Nay, do not pause, for I did kill King Henry—But 'twas thy beauty that provokèd me.

Nay, now dispatch; 'twas I that stabbed young Edward—But 'twas thy heavenly face that set me on. Take up the sword again, or take up me."

Anya, as Anne replied, "Arise, dissembler. Though I wish thy death, I will not be thy executioner."

Through the slyness of his voice and action, Daniel's duplicitous face changed to one of love and kindness. Anya physically wavered at the sight of the handsome and beguiling murderer.

Lupe looked over to where Henry was sitting. His face glowed with pride. Lupe smiled. The other actors, who no doubt had seen the scene many times, were just as rapt.

Daniel and Anya continued as Richard and Anne.

"Vouchsafe to wear this ring," cooed Richard.

"To take is not to give," replied Anne.

"Look how my ring encompasseth thy finger; even so, thy breast encloseth my poor heart. Wear both of them, for both of them, are thine."

Lupe joined in the heartfelt and genuine applause as her phone rang. Slipping quickly out of the auditorium, she answered.

"Josh, thanks for calling me back. I think I know who stole the paintings and kidnapped Marla Howes, but I don't really have any hard evidence."

"Tell me what you think, and I'll see if it checks with our information."

"I think it's Ingrid San Sebastian, but I don't know why. She does not need to steal the paintings, and the only reason I can give is that she wanted the thrill of committing a major crime."

"Hmm. Interesting theory. It has been known to happen. What makes you think she's the culprit?"

"Several things, taken separately don't sound like much but together? First, the person who stole the paintings had to be slim to fit between the dining table and the wall. It was only about two and a half feet wide."

"Good point. But she wasn't the only slim person at the reception."

"Yes, but she was at the reception and Marla's salon when the snuff box was stolen."

"But so was her husband, who's also fit, and Stacy and Ralph Leibman, who are both trim."

"It's definitely not Ralph, but I can't tell you why."

"He told us about his juvenile record if that's what worries you. But that leaves Stacy and Pietro. And Paul Hawley said it was a woman who threatened him before hitting him on the head."

"Yes, and Stacy's business did have a setback with the fire at the fulfillment center. But I think it was Ingrid because of Borgia's carrier."

"Borgia's carrier. You think she put the paintings in the carrier and pushed the stroller out of the Museum?"

"Yes! There is a photo Ben Terrance took before the reception. Everyone is standing around, and Ingrid is talking to Stephanie. Ingrid's holding on to the carrier, and Borgia is by Pietro's feet."

"It's so simple. They left the Museum to have drinks before the reception. We'll ask Stephanie if Ingrid or Pietro left to put the carrier in their car."

"Good. Thanks so much. I know I might be wrong, but I appreciate your follow-up."

"Well, since our other leads haven't panned out. Thanks for the idea, Lupe, but as I said before, be careful. If it is Ingrid, she's shown she's not afraid of hurting someone. Paul got lucky that the concussion wasn't worse."

"I will. Promise. Hospital gowns aren't my favorite fashion statement."

Lupe entered the darkened gallery to go back to her office and get her purse. She was tired. The adrenaline of her suppositions wore her out, and she wanted to go home and make some cauliflower rice with spicy beans and catch up with Alice.

Lupe was aware of an individual dressed in dark clothing crossing the room. The person carried two large parcels. Lupe reached for the lights, and as she did so, the intruder dropped the packages and raced toward Lupe. Her first instinct was to scream, but in the moment of terror, her voice was gone. Strong arms grabbed at her, and this time, Lupe was ready. With a swift kick to the individual's groin, she let out a yell surprising the attacker. The attacker placed a gloved hand over her mouth and whispered in a fierce voice.

"You've meddled enough. This will teach you a lesson." Lupe was pummeled with a powerful fist and sank to her knees, stunned. Just then, the room filled with people as Henry's theater troupe raced in from the auditorium.

"Stop him!" Henry ordered as the attacker tried to hit Lupe again.

Daniel took the lead. "Scrum!" He shouted. Even if the actors had never experienced a Rugby game, they understood the command and flung themselves enthusiastically on the intruder. With fifteen actors slammed against the miscreant's body, he had no chance of escape.

"Hold up!" Daniel commanded as he pulled his wheelchair to a stop. The group held still as if they were playing an acting game of statues.

"Keep a hold of him but get up one at a time. Sally, keep Ben back. Sally was a middle-aged, visually impaired woman whose service dog was barking vigorously in excitement.

One by one, the performers pulled themselves out of the human pileup. At the bottom was a man in a black balaclava and hoodie. Aggressively, he began to stand to resume the fighter's stance. With a swift uppercut, Daniel sent the attacker flying back to the ground unconscious.

"Lupe? Are you ok?" Henry asked as he sat down on the floor beside her.

Lupe held her jaw. "Acck. My mouth." She exclaimed as she looked at the blood trickling onto her dress. "I think I might have lost a tooth. Who is it?"

One of the actors reached down and pulled off the face covering and hoodie.

"Sam Tolland!" Lupe exclaimed.

"Who is he?" Henry asked.

"He's Ingrid San Sebastian's personal trainer. He was here earlier today. I saw him in the dark and tried to scream for help. He had something in his hands. Look over there." Lupe pointed to the other end of the gallery.

Two actors rushed to the other side, with Daniel following quickly in his wheelchair. They brought over two brown paper-wrapped parcels, one of which had torn, revealing a painting.

Lupe caught her breath. "Put them down slowly and carefully. Henry, my hands are bloody from wiping my mouth. Can you open these?"

Henry gently tore the paper off the first smaller parcel to reveal *The Stalk of Asparagus*. This time, Lupe screamed with glee. The others joined her. Henry giddily opened the other package to review the second stolen Manet.

Lupe stood; her painful mouth forgotten. "Ok. Daniel. I want you to guard Sam until the police get here." Several performers joined Daniel in a tight circle around the recumbent trainer.

"Henry. I need you to find out what happened to our guards. Andreas should be on duty inside, and there should be someone in the security booth. It's weird that Sam could just walk in with the paintings."

Anya spoke. "I called 911, and the police are on their way. I also asked for a paramedic to look at you, Lupe."

"I'll be fine, but I'll have a big dental bill," Lupe replied mournfully. "Don't touch anything else. We'll need evidence, even though we opened the paintings." Someone handed her a wad of tissue which she unceremoniously stuffed in her mouth.

Lupe looked around and found her phone in the corner of the room. Calling Reyes, she was pleased he answered on the first ring.

"Josh." She mumbled through the bloodied tissue. "I was right. It is Ingrid. Her trainer just brought the paintings back to the gallery."

"What!?"

"Yes, they are both here and look undamaged, but I'll call Sisi Truman-Ngao to check them out."

"Wait. We have a lab and will check to make sure they are ok. We also need to look for fingerprints and DNA. I'll be right there."

Lupe's mind whirled. *Why would Ingrid steal the paintings only to have them returned? Why wouldn't she just leave them someplace and inform the authorities anonymously? How did Sam get in without security catching him?*

Sam grunted and started to stand only to have the actors jump on him again. "You're not going anywhere, buddy. Want some more of what I just gave you?" Daniel inquired with an unconscious flexing of his robust frame.

Sam looked hunted. At that moment, Henry returned with two police officers and an EMT.

"What happened here?" A tall police officer whose badge read "Wilson" asked, looking down at Sam, who was being growled at by Sally's German shepherd.

"Officer Wilson, I'm Lupe Reinowski, and I am the Director of Development here at the Museum. These are actors with the Hapaestus Theater Corps, and this is Sam Tolland. Sam is personal trainer to Ingrid San Sebastian and snuck in here tonight to return our stolen Manet paintings. Josh Reyes of the FBI art crime unit has been informed and is on his way."

"What happened to your face?" Asked the shorter officer.

"He attacked me when I entered the gallery. I started to scream, and the actors came in to protect me."

"I'm Henry Tsai, and I'm the director of the Hephaestus Theater Corps. We were using the auditorium tonight.

Wilson turned to the group on the floor. "We'll take over. Please get off this man." The actors reluctantly climbed off the trainer. "Do you have anything to say?"

"Not until I get a lawyer," Sam said gruffly. The other officer cuffed Sam just as Josh Reyes and Detective Collins entered the room.

"Officers take this man into custody," stated Collins.

"We'll book him on felony assault and criminal possession of stolen property, anything else?"

"There will be federal charges as well," added Reyes.

"What!?" Sam Tolland shouted. "I'm not going down for anything. I just returned the paintings for Ingrid San Sebastian."

"So, she stole them. But why did she want to have them returned?"

"Not her, Pietro. He's a kleptomaniac. Can't keep his hands off anything. Ingrid spends all her time cleaning up his messes. But this was too much. she just wanted to put the paintings back and try to get help for Pietro."

The scales fell from Lupe's eyes. *How could she have missed it? The small items taken from the gift shop: the watch and snuff box. But the paintings seemed too big.* Then Lupe thought back. If she knew about the problem with the pressure sensors, maybe Pietro had overheard as well. Could it be just a crime of opportunity? *Pietro slipped behind the curtain while we were all running around trying to catch Borgia?* Pietro grabbed the paintings from the wall and put them under the toy poodle's cushions. All he had to do was push the carrier out of the Museum and then hide the paintings in his car.

"How did you get in here?" asked Collins.

"It was Ingrid. She came to the side door and waited until one of the security guards came out for a smoke. She knew him and offered him a coffee doctored with a roofie. When he started to pass out, I came out of the alley and helped bring him in. The other guard saw us carry in the first one and came to see what was wrong. I knocked him out and left Ingrid to keep an eye on both. I was supposed to go to the security room and take the film after leaving the paintings by the wall."

"Why didn't she just leave the paintings somewhere outside and leave a tip?"

"Ingrid likes the drama. That's why she fell for Pietro, to begin with. She liked the adventure of being with a thief."

"Yes, but a kleptomaniac is not the same thing," observed Reyes.

"You're telling me. I get paid extra to 'put back" the things Pietro has taken, but I have a huge backlog."

"And what about Marla Howes? Did you kidnap her?"

"I was just returning the snuff box. No one was to be at home. The housekeeper was away, and Mrs. Howes was supposed to be with her boyfriend that night, but I got there, and she was asleep in her bed. She woke up, and I couldn't hurt her. Mrs. H. looks just like my grandma. I told her she needed to come with me, and she did. She didn't make a fuss at all. It was a little weird. I took her to a hotel on the Thruway, and we stayed there for a couple of days. She didn't like the food, and I got worried because she wasn't eating and cried all the time. I took her back to the city and dropped her in Central Park."

"And you threatened her."

"Just a little. I told her we would go after her boyfriend if she told anyone what happened. I like the old lady and wouldn't really hurt her."

Lupe felt ready to scream at the trainer, but Collins interjected and charged him, reciting the Miranda Warning to him.

Epilogue
Development Best Practice - Celebrate your Victories

The next few days were filled with a flurry of activity as the investigation continued. The FBI lab confirmed the paintings were in perfect condition to the immense relief of the lending museums and all at the MVC. Ingrid, Pietro, and Borgia were caught at Teterboro trying to leave the country on their private jet and taken into custody. Henry was thrilled that his small theater company had garnered much positive press for their part in capturing the culprits. Lupe felt rushed off her feet as she dealt with donors and ensured the San Sebastian gift was returned. Fortunately, Malcolm dealt with the press with the sage advice of Jane Mehra.

Lupe was sipping on her third-morning coffee when Charlotte entered her office. The young woman looked pink with happiness.

"Hi Charlotte, you look radiant. What's up?"

"Stephanie is leaving to become executive director of the Moulton Museum uptown!"

"Really?" Lupe feigned surprise.

"Yes, and I'm hoping the board will put Audry in as interim director during the search for a new director."

"That would be great."

"There will be a directors meeting in half an hour. She'll make the announcement then."

Charlotte happily raced off to tell the others.

Lupe's phone rang, and she answered it with a smile. It was Allan Fisker.

"Allan! How are you? How's Marla?" Lupe asked in genuine concern.

"We're fine now that this ordeal is over. Marla told me everything that happened and has spoken to the police and FBI. She's such a darling person. She even asked for leniency for that terrible young man who kidnapped her."

"That's just like Marla."

"Yes, I'm so grateful she is well and safe. We've decided to marry at my farm in Stockbridge. She's really taken to it."

"Oh, Allan mazel tov to you both! That is wonderful."

After hanging up the phone, Lupe called Tessa into the office. "Tessa. Marla and Allan are to be married. Would you send flowers and champagne to his farm from all of us here at the Museum?"

Tessa smiled widely and rushed off to complete this happy task.

Lupe went to the conference room where the other directors had gathered expectantly. Charlotte had obviously shared the news with them as well.

Stephanie entered with Mary Montgomery van Clausen and Mimi St. Johns at her side.

She began with no prelude. "I am taking on the role of executive director of the Moulton Museum uptown at the beginning of next month. I am proud of what has been accomplished at the Museum of Vegetable Culture during my tenure. The programs and exhibitions have brought in record audience turnouts, and fundraising has doubled. The facilities are in better condition than ever, and our financial management and governance are stronger and more secure."

Stephanie went on extolling the various successes that had taken place under her watch. When she finally ended her laundry list of achievements, she turned to Mary Montgomery, who spoke.

"We are very grateful to Stephanie for her visionary leadership and thankful to you all for your work in carrying out the strategies that have made the MVC such a success. We will be conducting a nationwide search for a new director, and some of you may be asked to join members of the board on the search committee. For the time being, Mimi St. Johns has graciously agreed to step up and serve as interim executive director."

Lupe glanced at Audry, who seemed calm and content. Maybe she didn't want to be an executive director after all. Perhaps she was happy to serve as programming director and make that her life's work. But Lupe wasn't so sure of that.

Mimi spoke with her characteristic treacle-filled voice. "I am so honored to serve as chair of the gala committee and now as interim executive director. I want you to know that I plan to make no major changes during the search period. I will be a sounding board to you in your day-to-day work, and we will follow the plans that are already in action. I will dedicate myself to handing over a strong institution to the next executive director."

That sounded reasonable, Lupe thought. Mimi continued.

"I am a hands-on kind of leader, so don't be surprised if you see me around working with you," Mimi archly added while staring pointedly at Stephanie. "I prefer not to spend time in my office but rather troubleshoot as things happen. And of course, my strength is fundraising and negotiating for the best prices for everything. So, I'm sure I will work closely with Lupe on soliciting our donors and with Pierre and Tom on negotiating with our vendors."

"For now," Mary Montgomery interjected. "Mimi will spend time with Stephanie and me during this transition time. Do you have any questions?"

Audry spoke first. "It has been a valuable experience working with you, Stephanie, and I'm sure the other directors join me in wishing you every success in your new role." *Audry had such a splendid manner,* Lupe thought. She made graciousness look easy.

"Brava!" Pierre echoed, lifting an invisible wine glass to the air.

Everyone applauded on cue whether they believed it or not.

***

Lupe was excitedly looking forward to her long-awaited first date with Agent Josh Reyes. He was to pick her up at the Museum that evening, and Lupe had dressed for the occasion with a day-to-night dress and peep-toe pumps. A trim black sheath with a pink-lined ruffled skirt and pink piping around the square neckline, the dress made Lupe feel sexy and sophisticated. She decided to let her bronze highlighted hair hang loose. She took her spare curling iron from her desk to freshen up the soft waves at the ends of her shoulder-length hair. Touching up her makeup to cover up the fading bruise on her cheek, Lupe checked her mouth, where the dentist had cemented in her broken tooth.

At 7:00, she met the FBI agent in the lobby with a bit of trepidation. It had been a long time since Lupe last had a date, and she had so many fantasies of how this evening would pass. Had he selected the charming Italian restaurant of her dreams, or would he take her to a quiet French café? Possibly they would go to an exotic Moroccan restaurant decorated like a casbah with colorful brass lamps, ornate rugs, and floor cushions. He would delicately feed her by hand various mezze. Lupe could almost taste the cumin-scented carrots and dilled beets and smell the freshly baked bread. It would be magical.

"Lupe. You look wonderful," said Josh as he reached out for her hand.

Lupe smiled broadly. She was keyed up in anticipation.

"Shall we go?" He asked"

"Yes!"

"The restaurant is just a few blocks from here. I've wanted to try it for a long time. I hope you will enjoy it."

"I'm sure I will. I promise not to talk shop all evening, but do you have any updates on the investigation?"

"Yes, we had a search warrant for the San Sebastian's home on Fifth Avenue and found many stolen items, including the Jaeger-LeCoultre and the snuff boxes along with several things from the Museum's gift shop. Pietro was a busy boy."

The pair strolled through the city streets in the mild evening. Josh continued. "The San Sebastians have a top law firm representing them, and I'm pretty sure Pietro will be sent to a posh treatment center. They've even let him keep Borgia as an emotional support pet. I hope Ingrid doesn't get off as lightly. They both are trying to put all the blame on Sam Tolland, but that won't fly."

Lupe hadn't been paying attention when Josh stopped. "We're here!" he said happily.

Lupe looked up. *Veselka*, the east village classic Ukrainian restaurant. *So much for a romantic evening*, she thought as she looked at the diner-like setting,

"I thought you would enjoy this. I've always wanted to try their kielbasa."

"Yes," Lupe laughed. "I can never get enough of those favorites."

The pair entered the restaurant and were seated at a table in the center of the brightly lit room.

Lupe selected the vegetarian plate of cheese and vegetable pierogies and a vegetarian stuffed cabbage with a bowl of cold borscht to start. Josh decided he was a lumberjack and ordered the deluxe meat plate of veal pierogies, kielbasa, pork knuckle, and stuffed cabbage. Josh started with a bowl of kasha, and Lupe wondered how he would manage to eat so much. The wine list was limited, and Josh chose a bottle of Croatian dry red wine. Lupe did not have high hopes on how it would turn out and was pleasantly surprised that it wasn't bad.

Josh gazed into Lupe's eyes. "I'm sure you expected a more romantic setting for our first date."

"To be honest? This is a bit unconventional."

"Part of my training. I confess I've gotten in the habit of seeing how people react when they are out of their comfort zones."

"So, this is a test? I would have thought the past few weeks would have shown you how I respond out of my 'comfort zone,'" Lupe responded with more than a hint of irritation.

"Force of habit. I promise it won't happen again. You can choose the next restaurant."

If there is a second date, thought Lupe, discouraged that the handsome agent would think he had to test her. She forced a social smile on her face.

"Let's make the best of this evening, shall we?" she said as she lifted her wine glass. They clinked glasses.

"Lupe, mi Corazon!" Came the unmistakable fluty tones of her mother, Lucia. Lupe's head popped around in horror as her parents swiftly crossed the restaurant to their table.

"Maly ptak, we didn't expect to see you here," said Pavel as he pulled over a chair from another table and sat down heavily. "Your mother had a regional realtors meeting, and I decided to come in to join her. You know this is my favorite restaurant, even if it is Ukrainian and not truly Polish."

Lucia looked at Josh expectantly. After checking the room to make sure no more Reinowskis were there to interrupt her date, Lupe spoke.

"Mami and Papa, this is Josh Reyes. He's the FBI agent who was responsible for the Museum's case. Josh, these are my parents Lucia and Pavel Reinowski."

Josh, who had stood when Lupe's mother appeared, extended his hand in a warm greeting. *Now, let's see about "comfort zones,"* Lupe thought wryly.

"I'm pleased to meet you both. Lupe and I just ordered. Will you join us?"

Better and better, thought Lupe as she gazed down at her little black dress. *I could have worn a mu-mu.*

"We'd love to," smiled Lucia as she took a seat. The waiter came by and took their orders. Pavel was delighted that the agent shared his love for kielbasa.

"I grew up in Queens, and my best friend was from Poland. His Babcia made all kinds of great dishes. It was a real treat to have dinner at his house."

"And you, Josh? What is your family background?" Lucia would have made an excellent detective, thought Lupe.

Josh poured Lupe's parents glasses of wine. "I'm a typical American mutt. My mother is Irish, and my father is Puerto Rican."

"So, you're Catholic!" Lupe wanted to sink under the table.

"Well, yes. I was raised in the Faith."

"That's wonderful. And you have siblings?"

"I have three brothers and one sister. They live in Queens and Long Island."

"And your parents are well?" Lucia prodded on with the inquiry.

269

Suddenly Lupe wanted to laugh. Josh seemed utterly unperturbed by Lucia's questioning. She decided he was worth a second date.

"If Lupe hasn't already invited you, you should come to a family dinner on Sunday in Parsippany. I make the best smoked brisket."

The End

Acknowledgments

Lest anyone fear, the characters in this book and the Museum of Vegetable Culture are entirely of my invention!

This idea for this book came to me in the summer of 2021, during Justine Clay's Creative Business Accelerator and I am grateful to her and my teammates, Sisi Recht who also designed the clever book cover, Tracey Lam, Ashley Johnson, and Ericka Scott. I will be forever grateful to my editor, DeAnna Sanders for keeping me to schedule and for her wisdom, and to my friends and family for their encouragement. These include my husband Nash Madon and son Andrew Birnbryer, Helen Lowe, Judith Danek, Josephine Law, Melody Dickerson, Liz Fanning, Dr. Brian Aslami, Jamie McCormack and so many others who inspired me to write this first novel.

Research materials on museum operations and security come from the American Association of Museums, Sotheby's Institute, Security Informed, and the Electrical Contractor Magazine among other sources.

Additional information on development points is taken from the Association of Fundraising Professionals, Board Source, CFRE, and Nonprofit Source among others.

In creating the Museum of Vegetable Culture, I developed a full contributed income budget and development plan. If you are interested in seeing a copy, reach out to me at smadon@minervamgt.com.

About the Author

Susan Madon is a certified fundraising executive who enjoys helping nonprofits acquire the resources they need to be sustainable. She holds a BA in Theatre from Jacksonville University and an MBA from Columbia University's Graduate School of Business. In addition to consulting chiefly in the areas of education, poverty alleviation, faith-based organizations, and the arts, she is a voice actor and singer. She splits her time between Manhattan's upper west side and the Berkshires in Massachusetts. This is her first novel.

www.susanmadoncfre.com

www.minervamgt.com

Lessons for the Reader

An Effective Development Effort Involves Many Stakeholders

Early in The Disappearing Donor it is obvious that Lupe relies on the many people to help promote the MVC's mission and garner resources. She has her team each working independently and collectively on various aspects of the work, she has rapport with her fellow directors to push through projects and she has great relationships with the board, donors, and volunteers.

Even a professional working in a one-person development office must engage with multiple publics. Fundraising is not a solo sport. Each phone call, email, meeting, visit, or event is an opportunity to increase the capacity of an organization. While Lupe benefits from having a dedicated team, that many smaller organizations may not be able to afford, I am sure she would be creative in finding ways to get help. Many organizations, small and large rely on interns and volunteers to help with projects and activities.

Don't Put Your Eggs in One Basket

It is easy for an organization to turn to one or two key funding streams and ignore the other aspects of a robust fundraising program. While it is important to be strategic and not go after every channel in the fundraising universe, it is important to engage a wide variety of donors. If, for instance, the MVC relied solely on the gala for its fundraising and was faced with a black swan crisis like the pandemic, it would have very real and potentially debilitating consequences.

273

I believe all development programs should have at minimum three sources of revenue and four if you are including investment income from an endowment. If one stream falls short for any reason, you have the chance to make up the loss through another area. Notice who Lupe has appeals, institutional giving, sponsorship opportunities, special events, and a well-constructed major gift program. Her board is also deeply engaged making their annual gifts at a mutually agreed-upon level.

Make Time for Planning Away from the Day-to-Day Grind

Lupe takes her team to the park to review their annual goals and create a workplan. This is an opportunity for team building and for refreshing and regaining objectivity. I am sometimes asked how I can stay fresh in fundraising after nearly 30 years in practice. Each year I review what worked well, what could be improved, and most especially, what tools I can use to make my work easier and more efficient. It is far too easy to get caught on a treadmill never really stopping to regroup. I think staying close to the mission really helps me in maintaining energy, enthusiasm, and passion.

Make Technology Your Friend

Some development professionals dread data management. Being comfortable with your CRM is critical in managing data not just for your work but for other team members and future staff. Making time to write out call reports is a drag, but crucial in record keeping. There are few things more damaging to an organization that to have the institutional knowledge walk out the door with the exit of a key staffer.

Beyond CRM's the research tools available for effective fundraising in institutional giving, prospect research, and a host of other functions make everything from mailings to gift processing simpler. Be sure to assess your tools on a regular basis to make sure they are up to date and efficient. If you think a process could be improved upon, chances are it can. Often the initial outlay is minor considering the benefits. Don't be afraid to ask or look for solutions.

Build your Network

I've been as guilty of this as anyone. When I returned to the US from Hong Kong, I basically put my head down into the ground like an ostrich. I had regular clients and didn't feel like doing the adding work of getting out and building or rebuilding my network. This was shortsighted. Effective development professionals are continuously building their networks – and not just with other fundraisers. A great network allows you to be a trusted leader. Referring doctors, attorneys, even a window washer, or marriage officiant can put you in good stead with donors, your board, and of course your friends!

Endorsements

"Fundraising is more than a profession; it is the art of connecting passionate people who seek to create change. What an enjoyable way to learn about such an important and vital role in our society."

- **Gail L Freeman**
President & Founder
Freeman Philanthropic Services, LLC

"Witty dialogue and wry humor offer a seductive tour of museum intrigue in front of and behind the scenes. The Disappearing Donor serves equal parts fine art and workplace culture. This romantic mystery is laden with gastronomic references and epicurean delights to thrill the most avid foodie or devoted connoisseur. Madon's debut novel is a wholly entertaining whodunit, entertaining and educational and as priceless as a great work of art."

- **Judith Corridan Danek**
Director, Office of the President and Government Relations
Health New England

"If you think the world of nonprofit development is all about another fundraising campaign, new donor initiatives and gimmicky sales pitches, then you haven't met Director of Development Lupe Reinowski. You haven't walked into the galleries of the Museum of Vegetable Culture. This story takes you behind the scenes and into the personal lives of nonprofit management.

276

Author and seasoned nonprofit management expert Susan Madon weaves her masterful insight through this story and offers you her wisdom. She serves it to you in a whimsical, humorous way. You are in for a treat. Enjoy the journey that awaits."

- **DeAnna Sanders**
DLS Communicator for Global Good

Josephine's Famous Black Bean Brownies (without the hash!)

These brownies are nutritious and delicious. Soft and gooey, gluten free and can be made vegan with an easy swap.

Prep Time 10 minutes

Cook Time 25 minutes

Total Time 35 minutes

Servings 12 brownies

Calories 141 kcal

INGREDIENTS

- 1 (15 oz) can of black beans, rinsed and drained
- 2 eggs or flax eggs (add an additional egg if you like cakier brownies!)
- 1/2 of a large ripe avocado
- 1 tablespoon melted coconut oil
- 1/2 cup unsweetened cocoa powder plus 1 tablespoon
- 1/2 teaspoon baking powder
- 1/4 teaspoon baking soda
- 1/4 teaspoon salt
- 1 teaspoon pure vanilla extract
- 2/3 cup coconut sugar or sub brown sugar (or sub 1/2 cup pure maple syrup)
- 1/3 cup chocolate chips + 2 tablespoons for topping

INSTRUCTIONS

1. Preheat oven to 350 degrees F. Grease a 8x8 inch baking pan.

2. Place all ingredients besides chocolate chips into blender or food processor. Process or puree until ingredients form a smooth batter. If the batter is WAY too thick and won't process then add in a teaspoon or two of water. This batter needs to be very thick in order to produce fudgy brownies.

3. Add in 1/3 cup chocolate chips and fold into batter.

4. Pour batter into prepared pan, sprinkle with 2 tablespoons of remaining chocolate chips. You can also fold in nuts or swirl in peanut butter.

5. Bake for 25-35 minutes or until knife inserted in center comes out somewhat clean and top of the brownies begin to crack. Cool pan completely on wire rack then cut into 12 delicious large brownies!

NOTES

To make vegan: Sub 2 flax eggs for the regular eggs. To make brownies more cake-like: Use 3 eggs instead of 2.

Alice's Mushroom Bourguignon

- 3 tablespoons butter or extra-virgin olive oil, plus more as needed
- 2 pounds mixed mushrooms, such as portobello, cremini, white button, shiitake or oyster, cut into 1-inch chunks (about 10 cups)
- 8 ounces peeled pearl onions (2 cups), larger ones cut in half
- Kosher salt and freshly ground black pepper
- 1 large leek or 2 small leeks, white and light green parts, diced (1 1/2 cups) – Alice sometimes substitutes onions)
- 2 carrots, thinly sliced
- 3 garlic cloves (2 minced, 1 grated to a paste)
- 1 tablespoon tomato paste
- 2 ½ tablespoons all-purpose flour
- 1 ½ cups dry red wine
- 1 ½ cups beef, mushroom or vegetable broth
- 1 tablespoon tamari or soy sauce, plus more to taste
- 3 large fresh thyme branches or 1/2 teaspoon dried thyme
- 1 bay leaf
- 3 to 4 ounces chanterelle or oyster mushrooms, thinly sliced (about 1 cup)
- Smoked paprika, for serving
- Polenta, egg noodles or mashed potatoes, for serving
- Chopped flat-leaf parsley, for serving

PREPARATION

1. Add 2 tablespoons butter or oil to a large Dutch oven or pot and set it over medium heat. When the fat is hot, stir in half the mushrooms and half the pearl onions. (If it doesn't all fit in the pot in one layer, you might have to do this in three batches, rather than two.) Without moving them around too much, cook the mushrooms until they are brown on one side, about 3 minutes. Stir and let them brown on the other side, 2 to 3 minutes more. Use a slotted spoon to transfer mushrooms and onions to a large bowl or plate and sprinkle with salt and pepper. Repeat with another 2 tablespoons butter and the remaining mushrooms and pearl onions, seasoning them as you go.

2. Reduce heat to medium-low. Add another 1 tablespoon butter or oil to pan. Add leeks and carrot and sauté until the leeks turn lightly golden and start to soften, 5 minutes. Add the 2 minced garlic cloves and sauté for 1 minute longer. Stir in tomato paste and cook for 1 minute. Stir in flour and cook, stirring, for 1 minute, then add wine, broth, 1 tablespoon tamari, thyme and bay leaf, scraping up the brown bits at bottom of pot.

3. Add reserved cooked mushrooms and pearl onions back to the pot and bring to a simmer. Partly cover the pot and simmer on low heat until carrots and onions are tender and sauce is thick, 30 to 40 minutes. Taste and add more salt and tamari if needed. Stir in the grated garlic clove.

281

4. Just before serving, heat a small skillet over high heat and add 1/2 tablespoon butter or oil. Add half of the sliced chanterelles or oyster mushrooms and let cook without moving until they are crisp and brown on one side, 1 to 2 minutes. Flip and cook on the other side. Transfer to a plate and sprinkle with salt and smoked paprika. Repeat with remaining butter and mushrooms. Serve mushroom Bourguignon over polenta, noodles or mashed potatoes, topped with fried mushrooms and parsley.

From *The Meatlovers Guide to Eating Less Meat* by Melissa Clark for the New York Times

Aggi's Rustic Heirloom Tomato Tart with Thyme Crust

Aggi likes to serve this with cashew cream but Labneh is also nice. You can also add tofu or ricotta to your version!

INGREDIENTS

Thyme Pastry Dough (If you want to make this super fast, just substitute store bought crust like Immaculate)

- 1–1/2 cups flour – all purpose or whole wheat pastry
- 1/2 teaspoon sea salt
- 1 tablespoon fresh thyme leaves
- 7 tablespoons shortening
- 2 tablespoons extra virgin olive oil
- ice water

Rustic Heirloom Tomato Tart

- thyme pastry dough
- 2–3 cups mixed heirloom tomatoes sliced to 1/4″ thick
- handful of fresh basil leaves
- 2 tablespoons extra virgin olive oil
- 1 teaspoon of sea salt
- 1/2 teaspoon fresh ground black pepper

INSTRUCTIONS

Prepare Dough:

1. Stir together flour salt and thyme leaves with fork in a mixing bowl. Cut shortening and oil into flour mixture using your fingertips or a pastry cutter until it resembles coarse breadcrumbs with some pea sized bits.

2. Add ice water 1 tablespoon at a time and stir with a fork after each addition until dough comes together into a ball. The total amount of water needed will change depending on the humidity of that day. (It's been very humid here this summer and I only needed 3 tablespoons of ice water at the time I made this recipe.)

3. Form dough into a disc and wrap in plastic wrap or a waxed food wrap. Store dough in refrigerator if not using right away. Dough will keep refrigerated for several days or freeze for longer storage. Bring to room temperature before rolling out.

Prepare Tart:

- Preheat oven to 425°F.

- Roll out pastry dough on floured parchment paper to a 1/4" thick round, flipping and reflouring as needed if dough becomes sticky. Slide dough still on parchment onto a baking sheet.

- In a mixing bowl gently fold tomatoes with olive oil, salt and pepper using a rubber spatula just until they are evenly coated.

- Place several basil leaves onto rolled out dough. Layer tomatoes over basil leaving about a 2″ border of dough. Trim rough edges of dough with a knife if you want a cleaner look. Fold and tuck dough over tomatoes.

- Bake galette at 425°F for 25-30 minutes until tomatoes are bubbling and crust is golden brown.

- Cool to room temperature before slicing. Enjoy!

NOTES

Best eaten the day it's made but leftovers will keep covered and refrigerated for a couple of days.

Courtesy of @fairisle

Glossary of Fundraising Terms

accountability The responsibility of the donee organization to keep a donor informed about the use that is made of the donor's gift as well as the cost of raising it.

acknowledgment Written expression of gratitude for gift or service.

acknowledgment letter A letter sent by a donee, or on behalf of a donee, to the donor, expressing appreciation for a gift and identifying the use that will be make of the gift. An acknowledgment letter may be a form letter, but it is usually personalized.

acquisition mailing (or prospect mailing) A mailing to prospects to acquire new members or donors.

advance gifts Gifts given or pledged in advance of a public announcement of a campaign. Advance gifts are solicited before a campaign is announced because the success or failure of a campaign may depend on the size of the advance gifts.

advisory board A group of influential and prominent individuals whose association with a development program is calculated to lend luster and implied endorsement of the program's goals and objectives.

analysis That section of a study that deals with the factors essential to success in a fundraising program; principally the case for support, leadership potential, and fields of support.

annual giving Annually repeating gift programs; seeking funds on annual or recurring basis from the same constituency; income is generally used for operating budget support.

annual report A yearly report of financial and organizational conditions prepared by the management of an organization.

anonymous gift A gift whose announcement, by specific wish of the donor, can include only the amount; the name of the donor is withheld.

appreciated real property and securities gift Gifts of real estate or securities, which when held long term are deductible for federal income tax purposes at the full fair market value with no capital gain on the appreciation. However, the appreciation is a tax preference item, and proper counsel should be obtained to evaluate whether this would have alternative minimum tax consequences.

associates A term used variously to describe a group of individuals who may be supporting an institution through contributions at a prescribed level, serving in a special advisory capacity, or serving as a sponsoring body for special insti- tutional events.

audit An internal evaluation of development procedures as practiced by a nonprofit institution or agency; normally conducted by professional fundraising counsel.

bargain sale The sale of property at less than its fair market value. Frequently, a person will sell property to a 501(c)(3) organization or institution at a "bargain" price (for example, the individual's cost as opposed to its market value). The transaction is partly a gift and partly a sale.

benefactor One who makes a major gift to an institution or agency; also, an arbitrary classification of contributors whose gifts are above a certain level, which is calculated to single them out as a group and to stimulate similar giving by others.

benefit event A form of fundraising that involves the organization and staging of a special event for charitable purposes; all proceeds above expenses are desig- nated as a contribution to the charitable institution concerned.

benevolence A disposition to do good; an act of kindness; a generous gift.

bequest A transfer, by will, of personal property such as cash, securities, or other tangible property.

big gifts A general term used to signify gifts in upper ranges, the precise limits varying from institution to institution. Their importance is emphasized in all fundraising campaigns.

board of directors Individuals selected (for example, by other directors or members) in accordance with law (usually reflected in bylaws) to establish policy and oversee the management of an organization or institution.

book value The amount of an asset stated in a company's records, not necessarily the amount it could bring on the open market.

bricks and mortar Common manner of alluding to the physical plant needs of an institution and to the campaigns designed to secure the neces- sary funds. A "bricks and mortar campaign" is a campaign to raise building funds.

budget A detailed breakdown of estimated income and expenses for a develop- ment program, prepared in advance. Budgets show various cost categories, including personnel, printed materials, purchase and rental of equipment, office expense, headquarters, mailing charges, costs of events, and so on.

campaign An organized effort to raise funds for a nonprofit organization.

campaign costs Expenditures that are deemed essential to the planning and operation of a campaign and that are directly related to campaign budget projections.

campaign leadership Top volunteers who are an essential ingredient of any campaign organization and one of the three major pedestals on which fundraising success must rest, the others being the case and sources of support. Campaign leaders provide and maintain the momentum and enthusiasm essential to the motivation of the entire organization of volunteers.

campaign materials General term used to denote campaign forms of all kinds; materials required for campaign workers, fact sheets, prospect lists, and numerous other items essential to the effective functioning of a campaign; printed materials such as brochures used to advance a campaign.

capital campaign A carefully organized, highly structured fundraising program using volunteers supported by staff and consultants to raise funds for specific needs, to be met in a specific time frame, with a specific dollar goal. Allows donors to pledge gifts to be paid over a period of years.

case Carefully prepared reasons why a charitable institution merits support (in the context of the "case bigger than the institution"), including its resources, its potential for greater service, its needs, and its future plans.

cash flow Predictable cash income to sustain operations; in capital campaigns or whenever pledges are secured, anticipation of annual cash receipts resulting from payments on pledges.

cash gift The simple transfer of cash, check, or currency (other than special collections) to a gift-supported organization or institution.

cause related marketing An arrangement that links a product or service with a social cause to provide the cause with a portion of the profits received by the corporation.

certified fundraising executive (CFRE) A credential granted to a fundraiser by the Association of Fundraising Professionals, which is based on performance as a fundraising executive, knowledge of the fundraising field, tenure as a fundraiser (minimum of five years), education, and service to the profession.

challenge gift A substantial gift made on condition that other gifts must be secured, either on a matching basis or some other prescribed formula, usually within a specified period, with the objective of stimulating fundraising activity generally.

charitable contribution A donation of something of value to a gift-supported charitable organization, usually tax-deductible.

charitable deduction The value of money or property transferred to a 501(c)(3) organization, deductible for income, gift, and estate tax purposes. In most cases, the term *charitable deduction* refers to the portion of a gift that can be deducted from the donor's income subject to federal income tax. A donor's charitable deduction should not be confused or equated with the value of a gift; that is, gifts for the purpose of life income agreements are not federally deduct- ible at their full value.

charitable deferred gifts A gift made using any one of the following methods:

> 1. Wills: A charity may be named as beneficiary under a will in many ways.
>
> These include (a) gifts of specific property, whether it is real property or personal property; (b) a gift of a stated amount of money; and (c) a percentage of the remaining estate after specific gifts are made.

2. Revocable Trusts: A revocable trust allows the grantor to withdraw any or all assets during his or her lifetime, as well as having full enjoyment of the property during his or her life. At death the assets can flow efficiently to the beneficiaries, saving probate and administrative costs. A charity can be named as one of the beneficiaries.

3. Irrevocable Trusts: Charitable Remainder Unitrusts and Charitable Remainder

Annuity Trusts. Although the principal of these trusts cannot be withdrawn, there are additional benefits to the donor through immediate income tax deductions and fund management. The donor will receive yearly income from the trust as well as an immediate partial federal income tax deduction for the interest that ultimately passes to the charity.

4. Charitable Gift Annuities: Involves a transfer of cash or other property to the organization. In return, payment of a specified amount determined by age is made to the donor during his or her lifetime. The rates paid are the most recent ones adopted by the Committee on Gift Annuities as agreed to by most major charities. There is an immediate income deduction for the present value of the amount ultimately to pass to the charity; part of the income received by the donor is also tax free.

5. Gift of Home or Farm Retaining a Life Estate: Through this gift the donor retains use of the property for his or her

lifetime. The federal income tax deduction will be based on the present value, figured on the prospective years of using the property before it goes to the charity.

6. Totten Trusts or Accounts P.O.D. (payable on death): The charity can be named beneficiary of a bank account, bond, or other security, provided state laws allow.

community foundation A philanthropic foundation that is specifically committed to the support of institutions in its own community, often receiving bequests from persons whose legacy is modest.

company-sponsored foundation A private foundation whose corpus is derived from a profit-making corporation or company and whose primary purpose is the making of grants. The company-sponsored foundation may maintain close ties with the donor company, but it is an independent organization, most often with its own rules and regulations (like those of other private foundations). Companies form foundations to enable them to invest in philanthropy with funds that otherwise would be subject to capital gains tax or income tax, and to make maximum use of the corporate charitable deduction.

constituency All people who have in some fashion been involved with the institution seeking support; consists of members, contributors, participants (past or present), clients, and relatives of clients.

consultant A specialist in one or more areas of fundraising who is hired by an organization for the purpose of recommending solutions to problems and generally providing advice and guidance related to fundraising efforts.

corporate foundation The philanthropic arm created by a corporation to deal with requests for contributions from various agencies——locally, regionally, or nationally.

corporate giving program A grantmaking program established and controlled by a profit-making corporation or company. The program does not necessarily include a separate endowment, and the annual grant total may be directly related to the previous year's profits. Giving directly from corporate profits is not subject to the same reporting restrictions as giving from private foundations. Some companies may make charitable contributions from corporate profits, operating budgets, or company-sponsored foundations.

corporate philanthropy Support through gifts, equipment, supplies, or other contributions by business firms to charitable institutions, sometimes through organized programs that may include corporate foundations.

cultivation The process of promoting or encouraging interest and/or involvement on the part of a potential donor or volunteer leader; an educative process to inform about an institution and the reasons why it merits support.

deferred gift See *planned gift*.

designated gift A restricted or commemorative gift made for a specific purpose and designated for a specific use.

development Refers to all dynamics of a continuing fundraising program (annual giving, special gifts, planned gifts, public relations).

direct mail Solicitation of gifts or volunteer services and distribution of information pieces by mass mailing.

director of development The individual who heads an organization's development program, with either this title or another, such as vice president for development or vice president for external affairs and development.

donor The individual, organization, or institution that makes a gift.

donor acquisition The process of identifying and obtaining donors.

donor-directed gift A gift or bequest to a foundation, organization, or institution whose donor specifies to whom the money should be distributed.

donor list A list of contributors prepared for a particular purpose or in conjunction with list building.

donor recognition The policy and practice of recognizing gifts, first through immediate acknowledgment by card or letter and subsequently through personalized notes, personal expressions of appreciation directly to donors, published lists of contributors, and other appropriate ways.

donor relations Planned program of maintaining donor interest through acknowledgments, information, personal involvement, and the like.

drop date Date on which direct mail letters must be delivered to a post office for mailing.

electronic funds transfer (EFT) A method whereby donors instruct their banks to make monthly deductions from their accounts, designated for the charitable organization of their choice.

employee matching gift A contribution made by an employee to a 501(c)(3) organization, matched by a similar contribution from the employer.

endowment (pure) Principal or corpus maintained in a permanent fund to provide income for general or restricted use of an agency, institution, or program.

endowment (quasi) A fund, the principal of which can be and often is invaded by a board in order to meet its operating costs. Such endowments include gifts for which donors specify their use; they may also include gifts that are given for no specific purpose, which a board treats as an endowment.

enlistment Involvement and agreement by an individual to serve an agency, organization, or institution in some voluntary capacity.

estate The total assets of a deceased person; also, the legal status or position of an owner with respect to property and other assets.

ethics The moral considerations of the activities of a philanthropic organization. Also, standards of conduct and methods of doing business by organizations of fundraising counsel that provide assurances of professionalism in client relationships.

face-to-face solicitation Soliciting a prospective contributor at the prospect's home or office or other location.

family foundation A foundation whose funds are derived from members of a single family. Generally, family members serve as officers or board members of the foundation and play an influential role in grantmaking decisions.

feasibility study An in-depth examination and assessment of the fundraising potential of an institution or agency, conducted by fundraising counsel and presented in the form of a written report setting forth various conclusions, recommendations, and proposed plans.

foundation See *philanthropic foundation*.

fundraiser One who makes his or her living from working as a member of an organization's or institution's development department, as an independent fundraising consultant or as a member of a fundraising counseling firm; a volunteer who raises funds for a cause is also referred to as a fundraiser; a fundraising event has come to be called a fundraiser.

fundraising counsel An individual operating as an independent, or a firm organized specifically for the purpose of counseling charitable institutions in all aspects of fundraising.

fundraising executive An individual employed by an institution or organization to provide direction, counsel, and management of its fundraising operations.

fundraising plan All of those elements comprised by an organization's procedure for attaining a campaign goal: a fundraising program, including objectives, case, leadership requirements, timetable, personnel requirements, and budget; and the overall strategy or grand design for successful implementation of a campaign.

fundraising program An organization's or institution's strategy, tactics, objectives, case, and needs in their entirety; a campaign that is loosely defined in terms of time frame and specific funding opportunities; a campaign; a timetable for a campaign.

GAAP An acronym for "generally accepted accounting principles."

gift A voluntary, irrevocable transfer of something of value without consideration at the time of transfer or any time in the future. If the individual making the gift entertains any ideas of reclaiming it, the transfer is not a gift.

gift annuity A contract between the donor and the charity wherein the donor transfers property to the charity in exchange for the charity's promise to pay the donor a fixed annual income for life or some other mutually agreed-upon period. The donor's right to income may be deferred for a period of years. The annuity may be in joint and survivor form.

gift-in-kind A contribution of equipment or other property on which the donor may place a monetary value and claim a deduction for income tax purposes.

gift range chart A chart of gifts that enables campaign leaders to know, in advance of a campaign, the size and number of gifts likely to be needed at each level of giving in order to achieve the campaign goal. The chart focuses the attention of campaign leaders on the sequence of gifts that will be needed.

gift receipt A form that is send to donors (with copies to appropriate officials of the campaign and organization or institution), either separately or as an enclosure with acknowledgement, officially recognizing their contributions.

gifts Any of the following types of charitable donations:

1. Advance: Strategically important gifts solicited in advance of the formal public beginning of an intensive campaign to ensure a level of giving equal to the requirements of the campaign dollar objective.

2. Big, leadership, key, strategic gift: Terms used interchangeably to indicate substantial or largest gifts——generally of six or seven figures——required to provide the stimulus for a major campaign.

3. Major gifts: In an intensive campaign, *major* refers to gifts below the level of *big* or *leadership* gifts and above the level of *general* gifts.

4. General gifts: Final 5 to 20 percent of funds raised through a multitude of gifts from constituencies or through a wrap-up mail campaign.

giving clubs Categories of donors who are grouped and recognized by the recipient organization or institution on the basis of similar gift level.

goal A concerted focus for an effort supported by specific objectives that an organization determines to achieve; the amount of money to be achieved by a fundraising campaign——that is, the dollar objective.

governance Oversight by those persons who constitute the governing authority of an organization or institution.

grant Generally an allocation from a foundation, corporation, or government agency.

grassroots fundraising Raising modest amounts of money from individuals or groups from the local community on a broad basis. Usually done within a specific constituency or among people who live in the neighborhood served or who are clients. Common grassroots fundraising activities include membership drives, raffles, bake sales, auctions, benefits, and dances.

house file The names and addresses of active and recently lapsed donors and members of an organization.

identification The process of ascertaining, through investigation, research, and analysis, which of various candidates appear to be most promising as prospective leaders, workers, and donors.

independent sector A term used to describe all nonprofit organizations, as distinct from government and corporations formed to make a profit, also called the *third sector*; not to be confused with the organization Independent Sector.

indicia Mark on an envelope indicating a nonprofit mailing permit for reduced rate bulk mailing; used in place of stamps or meters.

involvement The calculated effort, perennially undertaken by development offices, to stimulate interest and enthusiasm on the part of prospective donors and candidates for volunteer leadership through active participation in institutional affairs; an extension of cultivation.

intestate Without a will.

LAI principle The fundraising axiom of qualifying prospects on the basis of Linkages, Ability, and Interest.

leadership The force within an institution, agency, program, or fundraising campaign that stimulates others to act or give.

leadership gift Normally, the second tier of gifts to a campaign that will inspire extraordinary giving by subsequent donors.

legacy A disposition in a will of personal property. A *demonstrative legacy* is a legacy payable primarily out of a specific fund. A *specific legacy* is a legacy of a particular article or specified part of the estate.

letter of inquiry A letter sent by an organization to a foundation or corporation presenting a project for which funding is being sought and asking the foundation or corporation if they will consider funding the project or receiving a full proposal.

letter of intent A pledge form stated in less formal, nonlegalistic terms for use by potential donors who view the pledge card as a contract and refuse to commit themselves to multiple-year gift payments because of this contractual aspect.

LIA principle The fundraising axiom of separating advocates and askers from donors on the basis of Linkage, Involvement, and Advocacy.

life income gift An irrevocable gift of cash, securities, or real estate to a gift-supported organization, with the donor receiving income from the donated assets for a period of time through an annuity or trust arrangement for him- or herself or other beneficiaries.

life income pooled trusts A charitable remainder trust that holds the com- mingled irrevocable gifts of donors who receive income annually based on the earnings of the trust and their individual entitlement as participants. On termination of an income interest, the underlying property is transferred to a charitable organization or institution.

life insurance gifts The irrevocable assignment of a life insurance policy for charitable disposition for which the present value is fully tax-deductible, as are the premiums paid by the donor.

life interest An interest or claim that does not amount to ownership and that is held only for the duration of the life of the person to whom the interest is given or for the duration of the life of another person; an interest in property for life.

LYBUNTS Acronym for donors who gave "last year but not this" year.

major gifts A gift of significant amount (size of gift may vary according to organization's needs and goals); may be repeated periodically. Also a program designation.

market Potential source of funds, members, or clients (individuals and organizations).

matching gift A gift that is made on condition that it be matched within a certain period, either on a one-to-one basis or in accordance with some other formula; also a gift by a corporation matching a gift by one of its employees.

memorial Gift made to perpetuate the memory of an individual. *Memorial* should not be confused with a gift to honor a living person.

mission A philosophical or value statement that seeks to respond to the "why" of the organization's existence, its basic reason for being. Mission statement is not defined in expressions of goals or objectives.

needs In fundraising terms, refers specifically to the institution's dollar requirements that can constitute objectives for an intensive campaign or for a continuing fund development program, as follows:

1. Capital: Building or property needs, in the form of new construction, additions, expansion, or remodeling or acquisition of property. Sometimes related to equipment purchase or to raising funds for an addition to endowment capital.

2. Endowment: Funds required to add to the invested principal or corpus with only income used for sustaining funds, special project support, and so on.

3. Program: Annual support for the operational budget; funds required to supplement income through revenues to sustain operation of the agency or institution.

4. Project: Refers to program activity or small equipment acquisition.

5. Validated: Needs that have been identified, analyzed, and approved by management and by the governing body and other volunteers as being valid and appropriate to the functioning of the institution.

nonprofit (or not-for-profit) organization Organizations of members or volunteers, classified by the Internal Revenue Service as providing a public benefit without purpose of profit for members of the corporation.

NSFRE (now AFP) National Society of Fund Raising Executives (formerly; now Association of Fundraising Professionals).

operating foundation A fund or endowment designated by the Internal Revenue Service as a private foundation, yet which differs from a typical private foundation in that its primary purpose is to conduct research, promote social welfare, or engage in other programs determined by its governing body or establishment charter. It may make some grants, but the sum is generally small relative to the funds used for the foundation's own programs.

outright gift The simple transfer of gift property to the donee without any conditions or terms of trust.

philanthropic foundation A corporation or trust that has been created through contributed funds, whether by an individual, family, corporation, or community, for support of nonprofit organizations, and to which such organizations may appeal for grants in support of their programs and projects.

philanthropist Broadly speaking, anyone who makes a gift, but usually used to describe a wealthy individual known for his or her exceptional generosity in support of charitable causes.

philanthropy As used at the Center on Philanthropy, voluntary action for the public good, including voluntary service, voluntary association, and voluntary giving.

planned gift A gift provided for legally during the donor's lifetime, but whose principal benefits do not accrue to the institution until some future time, usually at the death of the donor or his or her income beneficiary.

planned giving The application of sound personal, financial, and estate plan- ning concepts to the individual donor's plans for lifetime and testamentary giving.

pledge A signed and dated commitment to make a gift over a specified period, generally two or more years, payable according to terms set by the donor, with scheduled monthly, quarterly, semi-annual, or annual payments.

private foundation Although there is a technical definition of *private foundation* in the federal income tax law, the generic definition of the term is as follows: A private foundation is a 501(c)(3) organization that is originally funded from one source, that derives revenue from earnings on its investments, and that makes grants to other charitable organizations as opposed to administering its own programs. Gifts to private foundations are not normally as advantageous to the donors as gifts to a public charity.

proposal A written request or application for a gift or grant that includes why the project or program is needed, who will carry it out, and how much it will cost.

prospective donor Any logical source of support, whether individual, corporation, organization, government at all levels, or foundation; emphasis is on the logic of support.

public charity A 501(c)(3) organization that is not a private foundation, because it either is "publicly supported" (that is, it normally derives at least one-third of its support from gifts and other qualified sources) or functions as a "supporting organization" to other public charities. Some public charities engage in grantmaking activities, but most engage in direct service activities. Public charities are eligible for maximum tax-deductible contributions from the public and are not subject to the same rules and regulations as private foundations. They are also referred to as *public foundations*.

rating An evaluation or "guesstimate" of a prospective contributor's ability to contribute. The rating becomes an asking figure for the solicitor to suggest in requesting a contribution or pledge.

real estate gifts The transfer of property to a 501 (c)(3) organization or institution, the value of which is determined by the fair market value of the property.

recognition Formal or informal acknowledgment of a gift or contributed services; an event, communication, or significant item honoring a gift or a service.

renewal mailing A mailing to donors or members requesting renewed support.

restricted fund A fund in which the principal and earnings are bound by donor guidelines as they relate to investment or expenditure or both.

restricted gift A gift for a specified purpose clearly stated by the donor.

screening The process of assigning prospects to broad categories of potential giving ranges, preliminary to conducting more refined evaluations through the process of prospect rating.

seed money A substantial gift, generally by a foundation or an affluent individual, to launch a program or project.

sequential giving A cardinal principle of fundraising counsel: gifts in a campaign should be sought "from the top down"; that is, the largest gifts in a gift range chart should be sought at the outset of a campaign, followed sequentially by the search for lesser gifts.

social media The widely available electronic tools that generate interaction, participation, and collaboration, including blogs, videos, podcasts, photo sharing, and the use of social networks.

solicitor(s) Volunteers and institutional staff who ask for contributions to a campaign or development program; professional solicitors are paid to solicit for programs or causes.

special event A fundraising function designed to attract and involve large numbers of people for the purpose of raising money or cultivating donors.

special gifts Gifts that fall within the fourth tier of giving to a campaign; gifts that require special attention by the recipient organization in order to attract donor participation.

standard of giving Arbitrary but generally realistic assignment of giving potential to groups or categories of prospects, based on past performances and other criteria.

stewardship The guiding principle in philanthropic fundraising. Stewardship is defined as the philosophy and means by which an institution exercises ethical accountability in the use of contributed resources and the philosophy and means by which a donor exercises responsibility in the voluntary use of resources.

strategic plan A program incorporating a strategy for achieving organizational goals and objectives within a specific time frame and with substantive support in the form of methods, priorities, and resources.

support services Full range of activity required to support a fundraising effort: office management; word processing; gift receiving, posting, and acknowledging; budget management and control; and so on.

tax benefits Savings in income, gift, and estate taxes brought about by giving to charitable institutions.

telemarketing Raising funds or selling products or services by telephone.

telephone-mail campaign A fundraising technique, often referred to as *phone mail*, that combines mail and telephone solicitation in a sophisticated manner through the use of paid solicitors and management of the program; a tele- phone solicitation supported by a mail component for confirmation of verbal pledges.

third sector Used to describe all nonprofit organizations and institutions. Also known as the *independent sector*, not to be confused with the organization called Independent Sector.

timing Determination of the most favorable times to complete certain fund- raising objectives in order to achieve maximum results.

trust A fiduciary relationship with respect to property, subjecting the person who holds the title to property to equitable duties to deal with the property for the benefit of another person. For example: A gives property in trust, with A as trustee, to pay income to B for life and then to give property over to C, free and clear.

trust funds Money, securities, property held in trust by an agent of wealth (bank, estate manager, attorney) or managed by an institution under trust agreement to produce income for the beneficiary.

trustee A person or agent of a trust, such as a bank, holding legal title to property in order to administer it for a beneficiary; a member of a governing board; in a corporate trust, the "directors."

unrestricted gift A gift to an institution or agency for whatever purposes officers or trustees choose.

vehicle The particular form in which a fundraising program is organized and executed; for example, annual giving, capital campaign, or direct mail.

volunteerism The willingness of private citizens to serve voluntarily a great variety of programs and causes, both in fundraising programs and in other capacities.

wills Normally a legally executed written instrument by which a person makes disposition of his or her property to take effect after death. *Holographic will*: A will entirely written and signed by the testator or maker in his or her own hand. *Nuncupative will*: An oral will made by a person in his or her last illness or extremity before a witness, often not honored in a court of law. *Pour-over will*:

A will whereby assets controlled by the will are directed to be poured over into a trust. *Reciprocal wills*: Wills made by two persons in which each leaves everything to the other.

Made in United States
North Haven, CT
29 July 2023